PACHUNGA

JOHN A. MACDONALD

iUNIVERSE, INC.
NEW YORK BLOOMINGTON

Pachunga

iUniverse books may be ordered through booksellers or by contacting:

iUniverse
1663 Liberty Drive
Bloomington, IN 47403
www.iuniverse.com
1-800-Authors (1-800-288-4677)

Because of the dynamic nature of the Internet, any Web addresses or links contained in this book may have changed since publication and may no longer be valid. The views expressed in this work are solely those of the author and do not necessarily reflect the views of the publisher, and the publisher hereby disclaims any responsibility for them.

ISBN: 978-1-4502-1821-4 (sc)
ISBN: 978-1-4502-1823-8 (dj)
ISBN: 978-1-4502-1822-1 (ebk)

Printed in the United States of America

iUniverse rev. date: 3/16/2010

For the Sixth Grade Class of
St. John's School
1981-1982
Puerto Cortés, Honduras

Pachunga *was written for you.*

ACKNOWLEDGMENTS

I first would like to thank the Sixth Grade class of 1981-1982 of St. John's School, Puerto Cortés, Honduras, for being the reason *Pachunga* was written in the first place. There was a shortage of fiction in English available at the time, and the only solution was to write the story myself. *Pachunga* began as an oral narrative that quickly turned into a written chapter that was read aloud to the class once every ten days to two weeks. By the end of their Sixth Grade year, all but the final two chapters had been presented, so when we returned to school the following fall, they heard the end of the story.

Out of that class I would like to especially recognize Salvador Martínez who fell in love with *Pachunga* from the beginning and was my most ardent cheerleader to finish the task. I would also like to thank Peggy Noll, who read an earlier version of the story to some of her children—when they were children—and encouraged me to continue with the project. Clare Johns has done a brilliant job with the cover, for which I am grateful. And obviously, I would like to thank Beth Priest whose eagle eye and discernment as an editor has significantly improved my efforts. I am grateful to my daughter, Parry, who caught some things that the rest of us missed and offered good insight. And finally, I would like to thank my wife, Gail, who kept telling me that *Pachunga* was worth all the work. Her belief helped sustain it.

CONTENTS

A Short Pronunciation Guide

Several of the names and words might be hard for some to pronounce, but most should be simple enough to pronounce as written. In the case of Kjaz-Barbaroi, the name is intentionally almost unpronounceable. He does get frustrated when people and animals do not pronounce his name correctly—but that is good. It's nice to frustrate him. He deserves it.

Olugbala: Oh-LOO-bah-lah (the "g" is silent)
Kiritiri: Kee-ree-tee-ree
Kjaz-Barbaroi: Kuh-JAZZ Bar-bar-oy
Kasuku: Kah-soo-koo
Matoke: Mah-TOE-kay
Mosi-oa-tunya: Mo-see oh-ah toon-yah
Mwailu: Mah-why-loo
Mzungu: Mah-zun-goo
Bazungu (plural of Mzungu): Bah-zun-goo
Ngaba: N(almost silent)-gah-bah
Waragi: Wah-rah-jee

THE VILLAGE

The small grey parrot with a bright red tail flew across the sky, flapping his stubby wings furiously. There was no time left. He had to get to the Jungle as quickly as possible and the Village of the Kiritiri people. There was much at stake—too much at stake, and he felt as though his wings could not carry him fast enough. The journey there from Olugbala's Mountain was a long one. He had lost track of the number of days he had been flying. He was tired, thirsty and hungry—all in that order, and while he could have satisfied his thirst and his hunger with the many sources of food and drink far beneath him, he did not want to take the time to do so. He could not be late.

The Great Grassland below stretched all around him from horizon to horizon to the right and the left. Antelope, zebras, and elephants had stopped grazing and stood like statues on the grass or near the scrubby trees that dotted the flat terrain, watching and waiting. Far ahead of him were the High Falls sending clouds of water vapor billowing up from huge rocks at the bottom. And finally, beyond the falls was the Jungle itself. From his perspective it was only a thin band of dark green partially obscured by the heat and dust which arose from the sun-baked ground beneath him. Cutting through that thin band of green was a brown stripe which was interrupted by the falls and then continued on through the Great Grassland. This was the Great River: the best and most efficient way to travel through the region—if you had to stay on the ground.

But he could not think too much of such things now. He had to keep his mind on getting to the Village in time.

* * * *

The old man squatted in his hut, a loose and frayed robe hanging over his shoulders. Wrapped around his torso, it hung down to about his knees. His hair was white—none of it was black anymore—and it was patchy and thin. Aging skin hung loosely on his bony frame. In places it was dry and flaky—coarse to the touch. The old man was not eating well. It was difficult to swallow the food he was given—but he had no appetite for it anyway. Gone were the hunger pains he used to feel around mealtime. And what he was given and tried to swallow didn't have any taste. It was like eating grass or dust. Once he had been given a small bowl of his beloved cooked termite paste to eat—a bowl of food that mysteriously appeared inside his door in the middle of the night—but he could not eat it. It would have strengthened him, but he left it where it was, not even touching it. The next morning the bowl was gone, and he hadn't seen another one.

The hut had become his prison—a prison he felt he deserved because of the terrible thing he had done. All he felt anymore was remorse and sadness.

He had betrayed his people in a moment of weakness, thinking that the invitation he had extended to the Bazungu to come in and mine the diamonds that were below his lands would result in prosperity for his people. They would have schools. They would have medical clinics. They would have jobs that would allow them to buy the latest fashions in clothes, vehicles and other symbols of wealth. That was what the Bazungu promised to him at least. And Pachunga would die as a respected elder, the Chief of the Kiritiris who had positively transformed their lives for the good.

But that was not the case. As he squatted in the dark corner of his hut, brushing away the flies and feeling old and tired, he realized that he had been tricked—tricked not only by the Bazungu, but tricked by his own greed and selfishness. His desire to change his lifestyle and change from the customs and ways he had known since childhood had cost him dearly. His current state of affairs, the death of his beloved Kijana and the disappearance of his daughters–he had not had any sons—were all because of his stupidity and his greed. He had no idea what to do. He could not go anywhere. He was too heavily guarded. But, even if he could escape, who would receive him? How would he get there? He deserved to suffer for the wrongdoing he had done. It was just punishment. He could not be forgiven. He could not be pardoned. He had betrayed Olugbala and he had betrayed his people. The voice in his head accused him of this crime over and over again. It was impossible for him to be released from the prison of his own doing.

So he stayed in his hut not moving, his eyes staring straight ahead at nothing because there was nothing more to see.

* * * *

Boom! Boom! Boom! The sound of the Drum carried across the Great Grassland to the edge of the Jungle. In the hearts of all people and animals was a sense of despair. Mothers immediately gathered up their children and hid them out of sight. Those working in the fields stopped what they were doing and rushed back to their homes. Boys fishing in the river grabbed their nets and ran for the safety of their families, leaving the fish they had already caught lying on the bank to spoil in the hot sun. The birds stopped calling to one another and sat silently in the trees and brush, not daring to move—as if an eagle or a kite were patrolling overhead looking for someone to devour. Monkeys stopped their chatter and were still. Baboons hid deeper in the brush and sheltered with their young clinging fearfully to their mothers' backs. Even the jackals were still: peering through the khaki-colored grass, watching and waiting to see what was going to happen.

Boom! Boom! Boom! Kjaz-Barbaroi was on the move once again. And that meant more trouble for everyone. What was going to happen? Would it be war? Would it be further enslavement? It would certainly mean more suffering and pain for some. And if so, where would it happen? When? And who would be the poor victims this time around? What children would become orphans? What families would be ripped apart never to enjoy time with one another again? One thing was certain: the period of relative calm—though not without its difficulties—was ending.

While the Drum beat steadily, echoing across the land and pounding in his ears, the parrot finally passed the High Falls and followed the

Great River upstream. Here the jungle started. The river would lead him directly to his destination: the Village of the Kiritiri peoples and Chief Pachunga, who had ruled them until three rainy seasons before. Pachunga had invited in the Bazungu, but it had not produced the desired result. They had inspired his people to rebel against him, blaming him for all their troubles and forcing him from the High Seat: the symbol of his rule and authority. He was now their prisoner, of course, still alive only because Olugbala still needed him, in spite of his age and his failure.

* * * *

"I have to get there," the parrot said to himself. "I have to get there." He was more tired than he had been in a long time and had stopped only once under the cover of darkness to hide, rest, and take a quick sip of water. He did not take the time to eat anything. The journey was too important. He had to get to Pachunga before their enemy, Kjaz-Barbaroi, did. If Kjaz-Barbaroi got there first, it would be too late for them all.

The parrot was now flying below tree level above the middle channel of the Great River. With a downward thrust of his wings and an upward tilt of his head toward the blue sky above him, he flew high into the air to see how much further he had to go. It was just a little bit more. Off in the distance, he could see the Village on the left bank of the river. It was the largest village of its type containing over four hundred huts made of adobe and roofed with thatch. Pachunga, who was now ninety-four rainy seasons old, would be in one of those huts. All was quiet. There was no sign that Kjaz-Barbaroi had arrived.

"Good," thought the parrot to himself. "I will arrive in time. Olugbala be praised!"

He dropped down again to his original height and felt much less tired now that he had seen his destination. Reports had reached the Mountain saying that Kjaz-Barbaroi was to reach the Kiritiris that afternoon just before sunset. The tyrant was traveling along a new, wide path through the jungle. It was the longer, slower way to get there, but it gave him the opportunity to be seen by more people and animals: a sad reminder of his rule and authority over them. "That is another good thing," thought the parrot. Had he chosen to go by boat, he would have been there by now.

It was the middle of the afternoon, and the parrot moved from above the river to the left bank. He knew that he could now be seen by the animals and birds that were on Kjaz-Barbaroi's side, but it didn't matter anymore. In one part of the Village throngs of people gathered in the central area—the place where they had community meetings. But they were distracted and not noticing what was going on around them. They would certainly not notice a small parrot—especially if he did nothing to call attention to himself.

He had been told that Pachunga was inside a small hut that was close to the edge of the river. A guard, usually with a spear and a small round shield, was supposed to be standing at the front entrance. It would make it easier to find out which hut the Chief was in. The parrot flew on, thinking only of getting there in time.

* * * *

Chief Pachunga noticed a change—and it disturbed him out of his thoughts. Something wasn't normal. In fact, as he thought about it, nothing had gone normally that day. In the three rainy seasons that he had been kept under guard, his life had settled into a routine. He had been allowed to leave his hut only under the watchful eye of his guard and only for a very short period of time. It was ridiculous that the guard had to accompany him when he did this. Where would he have gone? He had no plans for escape. And his people—as much as he had harmed them—were there, and he could not leave them. Besides, Olugbala's last instructions had been for him to remain in the Village. As disobedient as he had been, this was one order that he was going to obey.

Everything was different. For one, this entire day the guard had not allowed him to leave his hut. He was required to stay right where he was. And for another, the Kiritiris were not working in the diamond mine as usual. They were all outside. From what Pachunga could see, it looked as though they were preparing for some important event. Men and women were fixing up the huts and animals were roasting on the cooking fires. The smell of cooking meat reached Pachunga's hut and normally it would have reminded him that he hadn't eaten anything that day, but his appetite was still gone.

What was going on was odd, because he had been told that festivals were against the new law. The Bazungu—the people who came from the North and whose skin was not dark and whose hair was not curly and black—had forbidden feasts and any kind of celebration. All the old customs had been abolished—especially those related to Olugbala— and the Bazungu had come with new ideas and new laws. At first they were considered to be very strange in their behavior, their dress, their language, their customs, and their overall appearance. Bazungu did not look like real people, but more like people who had never been in the sun and therefore must live underground. In the minds of Pachunga's people, they looked like some kind of mistake. Now, though, while different, most people accepted their presence as something inevitable— something that could not be avoided.

However, that did not take away from their ability to control the people and to use their machines and weapons from the North to get what they wanted. They were the bosses of the mine and said that festivals took away from productivity.

So why would they now allow one holiday? Pachunga asked himself that question—and then called out to the guard, who came and looked through the window to see what his prisoner wanted. He looked menacingly at Pachunga and only grunted a few words that did not make any sense. Then he smiled cruelly as if he knew something that Pachunga did not know. Pachunga decided to leave him alone and not press the matter.

As Pachunga squatted in the dark corner of his hut, his eyes started to focus on something in the far corner that he had not seen there previously. This was even stranger. He gathered his energy together to go and see what it was, standing up painfully and trying to focus on the objects on the earthen floor in front of him. They were his knife and his bow and arrows, as if he personally had left them in that spot earlier in the day. How did they get there? Where had they come from? And there was more: there were two spears and a shield. He didn't think they had been there just before he talked to the guard. He was certain that he would have noticed them. Was this a gift, or was it a trap?

Did he now have an ally in the Village? The same ally who had brought him food? Or was this some way to trick him into trying to escape so that they could kill him? Once again, he did not have any answers, and he continued to brood. The only good thing that was coming out of this was that he was not quite as despondent as he had been. Now he had something else to ponder instead of just thinking about himself. It was possible for Olugbala to be behind some of these strange occurrences. He hoped he was, but at the moment Pachunga was not sure. He did know that he would have to be especially alert and watchful—ready for anything.

It was not too much longer before he began to get some answers. As he squatted in the corner of his hut, he began to feel a rhythmic vibration that came up through the soles of his feet. It was a steady beat—something that began to get stronger and stronger until he began to hear it with his ears as well. It tingled his toes. It was steady. It was persistent—ever increasing in volume.

It was a sound that he had hoped he would never hear again. Instead of being perplexed or even worried now, he became afraid. The sound was the sound of the Drum.

Pachunga knew exactly what it meant: it meant that Kjaz-Barbaroi was starting something once again after having been quiet for a long time. Nothing good ever happened when the Drum beat with its ominous sound crossing the savannah and the jungle filling most creatures with fear. Even Kjaz-Barbaroi's allies were afraid.

And then, to worsen matters, there was another sound: the sound of a Dark Creature growling in his usual hyena and monkey-like manner. When did it arrive? And why had it arrived? The noise it made was not pleasant—it was hard on the ears and even harder on the nerves. Pachunga shuddered to think that there was now one of those creatures in his Village. It would be even worse if there were more—and there usually were more—but he heard only the sound of one. They had left his people alone for a long time, even though they were known to be working with the Bazungu and not just Kjaz-Barbaroi. Why was it here? The fear that he felt in the tightness of his throat moved down to his stomach and made him feel like throwing up. Through his window, the sky that had once been bright blue now was darkening and turning grey.

Pachunga stood up again and walked quickly—but cautiously—on broad, flat feet to his front window. He could not see the guard anywhere. But where was that Dark Creature? He kept well to the side

7

so that he would not be noticed and peered out. His fear mixed with even greater worry and concern. There was not just one Dark Creature. There were fifteen of them standing about twenty meters away.

He decided that trick or no trick, he would at least get his knife and belt, which he quickly attached around his middle. He brought the bow and arrows closer to him to be within easy reach, but left the shield and spears where they were. He could get them if and when it was necessary. He would not go down without a fight.

The Dark Creatures were the private army of Kjaz-Barbaroi. They were almost two meters tall when they chose to stand erect. They had large, monkey heads covered with short, bristly black hairs. Their eyes were also black and readily flashed in anger and hate. The more pain they could inflict on someone else, the happier they were. They would torture someone cruelly just for the joy and pleasure of hearing them scream in pain. They would kill for the thrill and the excitement of seeing a life snuffed out—and then rip apart the carcass and consume it—bones and all—because they were forever hungry. They loved no one and tolerated no one. They were, after all, mean, evil creatures.

Behind thin, grey lips they had pointed yellow teeth that could gnaw and tear the flesh of any human or animal that tried to oppose them. Their monkey heads rested on top of the spotted bodies of hyenas, which meant that they could run and cover a lot of distance very quickly, though their forelegs were flexible and limber and their paws could grasp a spear, club or a knife. To cover themselves—which they did not do very well—they wore black vests made of leather collected as a tax from the Cattle People. Intricate, geometric patterns—usually diamond shaped—decorated the vests.

Pachunga noticed something new about some of them. Around the necks of some were collars studded with white stones. Those stones could have come from only one place: the mine where Pachunga's people had been sweating and even dying for the past three rainy seasons. Somehow, the Dark Creatures were getting them—perhaps as a reward or some kind of recognition for serving Kjaz-Barbaroi well.

But why were the Dark Creatures in his Village right now? The last time he had seen them had been when he was thirteen. He and his people, along with Prince Baree and his Cattle People Warriors—and not to mention Kasuku the Parrot—had overpowered the Dark Creatures during the Battle of a Thousand Cries eighty or so rainy seasons before. Now they were back again in *his* Village. They were walking around freely while Pachunga was a prisoner. What was happening? He decided that the beating of the Drum and the reappearance of the Dark Creatures were tied together—they meant something, but what? And with the other changes he had noted that day from the usual routine of the Village, he was beginning to suspect that whatever was going to happen was going to happen here.

One of the Dark Creatures suddenly turned around and pointed at Pachunga's hut with his paw. With a few yips and yaps and hoots and howls, he spoke to the rest. Pachunga crouched just out of sight below the window's edge as they approached him. After stopping about six meters from the hut, they mockingly bowed in Pachunga's direction. "Hail, O great Chief Pachunga! Hail, O great Chief Pachunga!" Their voices dripped with false respect.

One of them called out, "Come here so that we can bow down to you properly, mighty warrior!"

"We wish to see your old face!" called another.

Pachunga had no intention of leaving his hut. They would have to come in and get him—especially since he now had some weapons with which to defend himself. He took out the knife from the hiding place and firmly gripped the smooth, wooden handle. It felt good in his grasp. In spite of his age, he still had some fight in him. "Let them come! Just let them come!"

The Dark Creatures outside thought that they were being riotously funny. They shrieked and laughed lustily. "How will you fight us now that Kjaz-Barbaroi —may he live for eternity!—is coming to take your place on the High Seat? Not that you've been sitting on it recently!" This was followed by yips and yowls and their hyena laughter.

"Oh, no!" thought Pachunga. "That couldn't be true!" Was he merely going to march right into his Village and declare himself the Chief of Pachunga's people? Of course he could—what could Pachunga do about it? Not much. Not much at all. Pachunga did not have any warriors who were loyal to him anymore. They were loyal only to the mine. It would be a fitting end to the betrayal that he had done to his people.

But how could Kjaz-Barbaroi still be around? Why was he still alive? He had been an old creature at the Battle of a Thousand Cries, when Pachunga had last seen him. Pachunga's own grandfather had even fought him over one hundred rainy seasons before that. There was no reason for him to be able to live that long: he was a creature like everyone else. It didn't make any sense. Then again, very little was making any sense at all. Things were not normal.

Yet, what had Olugbala said after the Battle? He had said that Kjaz-Barbaroi drew on powers that were available only to him. They were evil powers that had nothing to do with Olugbala. They were black and sinister. They were the kinds of powers that kept ghosts floating around burial grounds and witch doctors doing dances at night under the fullness of their moon. That evil, Pachunga now realized, could certainly keep Kjaz-Barbaroi alive—as long as he kept nourishing himself with it and strengthening himself with it.

If Pachunga were being honest with himself—even before the Drum had started to beat that afternoon—he would have realized that Kjaz-Barbaroi was still around even though he had lost the Battle of a Thousand Cries in the end. Hadn't Pachunga still heard the Drum from time to time in his heart, soul, and mind as it had gripped him, confusing his ability to think and do right? Was it not the Drum that was causing the evil now taking place in his Village? Oh yes, he had known that very well. And the source of the Drum could have come from none other than Kjaz-Barbaroi.

As if to answer the questions that Pachunga had been asking himself, the Dark Creatures outside the hut said: "Yes, Pachunga. Kjaz-Barbaroi—may he live for eternity!—is returning with powers far stronger than he has ever had before. He is coming to defeat Olugbala once and for all. He is not merely going to challenge him and see who wins. He *will* defeat him. He *will* vanquish him and eliminate him from this place where he won't even be a memory. Let's see if that despicable rogue of yours—whom you worship—can save you before our all-powerful leader comes and personally does you in!"

This was followed by their usual shrieks and howls and hoots and barks. Some were so excited about the misfortune that they believed was about to happen to Pachunga that they leapt high into the air. They turned in circles and snapped the air with their teeth the way a dog does when it is jumping for a stick.

It was the way they had said, "personally does you in," that seemed bad for Pachunga. In their excitement, the Dark Creatures had given away an important piece of information—information that most likely should have been kept secret. Kjaz-Barbaroi must have decided that he could not possibly keep Pachunga alive, even though he was a feeble old man. Besides himself, Kjaz-Barbaroi was the only creature living who had seen Olugbala in the flesh—as far as he knew. It was possible that some of the animals—especially the elephants—might still be alive, but he didn't know where they were or what they would remember.

Pachunga symbolized the old way of doing things. The mere fact that he was still living was enough of a threat to Kjaz-Barbaroi that he would have to be eliminated if Kjaz-Barbaroi were to have full control over all people and animals. And Pachunga was still a follower of Olugbala. As long as Pachunga lived with Olugbala's power to support him, he would be a tough opponent. Yes, the only thing for Kjaz-Barbaroi to do would be to have Pachunga destroyed.

But what could Pachunga do?

Once again, he found himself quietly squatting in the corner of his hut trying to hide from all the problems that were outside, feeling again remorse and regret for what he had done. He was so distracted by his own thoughts that he almost didn't hear the sudden rustling and fluttering of wings to his left—coming from a window at the back of the hut on the opposite side of the Dark Creatures.

At the noise, he turned his head quickly and saw that he was not alone in the hut. A parrot had joined him and was perched on the sill.

The parrot looked tired and dazed. His eyes were not as clear and as bright as they normally would have been. His little chest went up and down as he gasped for breath. His grey wing and body feathers were ruffled, his red tail feathers ragged. They looked dull and flimsy, having lost their usual crispness. He turned his head so that his face was in profile. The eye that Pachunga could see had a white ring around it—a feature unique to this particular bird. After taking a few moments to recover, the parrot spoke.

"Well, Pachunga!" greeted the parrot in his best man-speech. He was tired enough that he wished he could speak in his own parrot language, for it would have been a lot easier. "Don't worry! You are not seeing a ghost! I am not one, and I can assure you of this by Olugbala. So, it is perfectly all right for you to give an old friend a proper hello. But you'd better be quick about it because of the Dark Creatures outside."

Nowhere in that entire world at that moment was there anyone with more joy in his heart than Pachunga. Slowly, the ends of his mouth turned into an enormous smile. Water filled the corners of his eyes. All he could say for the first few seconds of disbelief—and this he didn't do very well—was: "Kasuku! Kasuku!"

"Ah, so you still recognize me. Yes, I am here in the flesh."

"But—? I don't—?"

"Shhh. For the moment we don't have any time for explanations. We've got to get rid of those Dark Creatures outside so that we can talk and make plans for your escape."

"Escape? I—" Pachunga was confused.

"You must leave here as soon as you can. Kjaz-Barbaroi is—"

"I know." Pachunga felt sad again. "He is on the way to the Village. He's going to place himself on the High Seat after he personally does me in."

From their yips and yaps, it was apparent that the Dark Creatures were getting bored with their game. Getting bored with each other or with whatever they were doing was something that happened frequently. They had short attention spans and needed new entertainment on a regular basis. However, instead of boredom meaning that they would go away, it usually meant that they would try something more vicious and mean. With so many, they would taunt each other into doing something foolish—something they thought was courageous and brave.

"Pachunga!" growled one of them again. "We want you to come out!"

"We want to see you as you now are: old and wrinkled and weak—helpless to do anything. Perhaps once you were a great warrior, but a tiny child could easily defeat you now. We want to see you now, you old geezer!"

"Come out, now!" one of them repeated.

"Yes, come out now if you are even strong enough to walk!" said another. He thought this was terribly funny and original. He hooted at his own sense of humor.

"We—we—" The Dark Creature was struggling to think of something to say, but couldn't quite get it out. After a great deal of mental effort, he said, "We—we—want to *play* with you."

Play with him? *Play* with him? Yuck. Pachunga wondered what they meant by that. He knew that it certainly would not be any fun.

"We want to see you before Kjaz-Barbaroi—may he live for eternity!—arrives!"

"Before he personally does you in!"

Their laughter sounded even more terrible and horrible. They began to get more and more worked up. One picked up a stone and threw it at the hut. Another did the same. A third threw a stick. Soon, all fifteen Dark Creatures had spread out and were throwing anything they could get their paws on. They had found a new game.

A few of the stones and sticks came through the window and door, but they did not reach Pachunga. One large stone thudded heavily against the outside, causing cracks to appear on the inside and fragments of dried mud to fall to the ground.

"Why don't they just come in?" Pachunga stood up and moved towards the door, fingering the handle of his knife again, wanting to do as much damage to as many Dark Creatures as possible—even if it meant dying in the process. He looked in the direction of his bow and arrows and wondered whether it would be better to start with them first.

"They are still afraid of you," said Kasuku. "You do have the reputation for being a mighty warrior—in spite of what they are saying about you. They'll stand out there and tease you where they think they are safe—but they won't dare come in."

"Afraid of me?" Pachunga couldn't believe it.

"You are on the side of Olugbala. They know his power."

"What can I do then?"

"That's for you to decide. But I would say that you don't have much time."

More rocks and stones came down on top of the hut. By now, though Pachunga could not see them, the Dark Creatures' behavior had aroused the curiosity of many Kiritiris who looked on from about sixty meters away. They didn't dare get any closer.

Pachunga puzzled over what to do. He wished he weren't so old. If he were younger, he knew that his mind would think faster. He knew that he would be able to fight better. Dark Creatures might be strong and tough—but they were generally stupid. Had he not once been a famous warrior? Had he not been a great leader? Had he not been able to think clearly and quickly and to make decisions in just a moment or two of rapid thought? Why was it so hard when he was now old and without the strength and abilities that he used to have? He was a prisoner of his own people, his enemies—and of his age.

"All right," thought Pachunga fiercely. "Just let them come in and get me. I may only take care of one or two, but at least they will have finished me off before Kjaz-Barbaroi comes. I would rather die in battle than be coldly executed." Even though his words were brave, he felt very much afraid—afraid to the point of not wanting to die—of not wanting everything to end in this way. Was there another way to go that would give him a better chance of surviving? As this thought grew, so did something else. Way, way down in the back of his thoughts was the sound of a drum. It was a deep-sounding drum and it beat in time with the Drum that was traveling across the jungle. It was *the* Drum all right. And it was beginning to give Pachunga all kinds of thoughts that he should not have had. Maybe he could make an arrangement with Kjaz-Barbaroi in some way—make some kind of a deal.

Kasuku knew Pachunga well enough to know that he was hearing the Drum. The face of the old Chief had lost its warmth, its peace, its—purpose. It had become hard and his eyes were dull. If Pachunga continued to listen to it, he could end up making a very grave mistake—a mistake that could put the entire plan into danger.

"Pachunga," said Kasuku very softly and slowly. "You're not listening to the Drum, are you?"

"Of course not!" snapped Pachunga angrily. "I wouldn't do any such thing!" He turned and looked at Kasuku fiercely, clenching his free hand into a fist and tightening his grip on his knife even more.

The Drum beat louder. Pachunga began to think that Kjaz-Barbaroi was not such a bad creature. He was certain that he could be reasoned with.

But the name of the Drum had been mentioned, and Pachunga realized that he had been under its spell. He looked at Kasuku and saw that the parrot had a hurt expression on his face. The bird had been right. Once again, remorse and shame filled him. Couldn't he ever do things right?

"I'm sorry," said Pachunga quietly.

The Drum stopped inside Pachunga's head.

"It's okay," said Kasuku.

"I should be counting on Olugbala to help us out."

Another heavy stone hit the side of the hut with enough force to create even more cracks. Smaller stones continued to come through the open window. The Dark Creatures were getting wilder and wilder. Some ran closer to the hut, and then backed away very quickly. They yipped and yapped and hooted and howled. Others began to screech like monkeys in a frenzy.

"Come out!" screeched one.

"Come out!" screeched another.

"Come out, old man! Come out!" they chanted together. "Come out and bow down to your new masters! Come out, old man! Come out!"

One of them had grabbed a burning branch from a cooking fire that was not too far away. He waved it frantically around and started to get closer and closer to the hut. If he burned the thatch roof, Pachunga could either stay in the hut and die—or escape into the midst of the Dark Creatures. The noise they made with their jeers, cries and calls increased in volume and pitch. They lost all self-control and were capable of doing anything. What could Pachunga and Kasuku do?

"Olugbala help us both!" murmured Pachunga.

THE ESCAPE

"**N**ow you're on the right track," said Kasuku. "This should be a simple problem with a simple solution for Olugbala."

Pachunga felt new hope as he remembered that Olugbala was there to help him. He felt a charge running through his body and he was becoming stronger. He felt younger, and he had more energy than he had ever had in his adult life.

"Come out, old man! Come out!"

"We want to see your white hair!"

"We want to see your wrinkles!"

"We want to see your bony arms and legs!"

"Don't you think that you should give them what they want?" asked Kasuku.

"Do you mean go outside?" Pachunga could not believe what he was hearing. How could Kasuku suggest that he go outside? He was no match for so many Dark Creatures.

"Yes."

"Why?" asked Pachunga to himself.

Because I am with you. Go.

Those words did not come from Kasuku. They did not come from the thoughts of Pachunga. He knew who was telling him to step outside.

"Go ahead," said Kasuku. "You'll stop them. You'll see."

Still feeling confused—and wanting to do what the voice told him to do—he left the hut. There was something different about the way he was walking—and his vision was so much better than it had been:

everything was in focus down to the smallest detail. For a second, he was distracted by a little weaver bird flitting around its nest in a bush some distance away. What was going on? He looked at the Dark Creatures in front of him.

They stopped throwing stones and jumping up and down. As soon as they had seen movement by the door, they had backed up a few meters. They looked at Pachunga now with wary eyes. Some were already frightened and made little, scared puppy noises. Their leader was the first to speak.

"And where is Pachunga?" he asked. "We want to see him—not some boy he has sent in his place."

"I am—" Pachunga stopped. Instead of his deep, quiet voice that he had had for many rainy seasons, his voice was high and clear. He looked at his hands and saw that they were small and smooth. His arms were forming the muscles of the early teenage years, and his legs were straight and slender. Pachunga felt as though he could run for thousands of meters on them. He probably could have.

"Where's the old man?" demanded another Dark Creature.

"We want to see him!"

"I am he," said Pachunga simply. He had decided that he still was he, even though he was different from the way he had been. He would ask questions about his new youth after he took care of the Dark Creatures.

The Dark Creatures looked at him in disbelief.

"Yeah, sure you are," said one of them. And he bowed lowly, but in an obviously mocking manner.

The rest of the Dark Creatures laughed raucously. This was good entertainment for them.

Pachunga was not amused by their behavior. He looked straight at them and said in as chiefly a voice as he could: "And by the power of Olugbala, Chief of chiefs, Lord of all, and Son of the Father the Creator, I command you to leave this place at once!"

The words took on a power all of their own, and Pachunga was just about as surprised as the Dark Creatures as he spoke them. He hadn't done anything like it in a long time. He had sort of given up saying things like that—especially since his failure—but now he said the words with conviction and strength.

That was all it took to get rid of the Dark Creatures. As soon as Pachunga spoke in Olugbala's name, all fifteen of them turned and ran, yipping and yelping like a pack of wild dogs. They passed the crowd of Kiritiris who were looking on and went out through the gate of the Village. Some of the Dark Creatures at the gate tried to stop them but they were running too fast and too hard.

They didn't stop running until they reached Kjaz-Barbaroi, who was by now only an hour away from the Village. He demanded to know what was going on—and all they could do was babble, "Pachunga... Pachunga...Pachunga..." That was too much for him to hear, so he killed them all for their cowardice and left their bodies for anyone who was hungry. Kjaz-Barbaroi was proud of himself for being a good provider, but only to those who obeyed his every wish, of course.

Back in the Village, Pachunga turned around and entered his hut. The Kiritiris who had gathered to watch the Dark Creatures now watched Pachunga disappear inside.

"Is this our old Chief?" asked one of them.

"Impossible!" exclaimed two or three.

"But didn't you see him?" asked one old man. "That boy had Pachunga's face."

"Did you hear the way he called on Olugbala?

"And the way those Imperial Guardsmen (this is the name Kjaz-Barbaroi gave to the Dark Creatures in his service) ran away?"

"Goodness!"

"I can't believe it!"

"It must be someone else!"

And so the conversation continued until someone reminded them that they had a festival to prepare for. So they all returned to what they had been doing.

Now that those fifteen Dark Creatures were taken care of, Pachunga could address the matter of having a young body again.

"Kasuku," he began with a very quiet voice. "How many rainy seasons do I have?"

"Ninety-four, old one."

"And a rainy season lasts for three moons and starts again nine moons after the end of the last rainy season, right?"

"Right."

"So a rainy season is a long time. Right?"

"So it is for some." Kasuku then asked, "What is troubling you?"

"It is not troubling, parrot. It is only marvelous. My hands, my legs and my body are as though I only have thirteen rainy seasons or so. And on my face, there is no beard."

Kasuku was enjoying every moment of this. It gave him pleasure to see someone become young in Olugbala again.

"And my hair??" asked Pachunga. "Is it still as white as the feathers of an egret?"

"No, it is as black as a piece of charred wood."

Pachunga squatted in Kiritiri fashion. It felt wonderful to be able to do that simple motion without making his joints ache.

"I don't understand," he finally said. He shook his head.

Kasuku perched on Pachunga's shoulder so that he could speak to the Chief more easily. "Don't you understand? He needs you now so he has changed you so that you can better serve him. You came to Olugbala as a child many rainy seasons ago. As a child, you shall return to him."

"Then may Kjaz-Barbaroi come! I am ready for anything that he can throw against me!"

"In the name of Olugbala, that's the way to talk, man! Er, boy." He laughed as only grey parrots do.

Pachunga laughed with him, and then became serious. "But Kasuku, one thing only. How did you come to be here? When I last saw you it was at the—"

"Yes," said Kasuku. He flew over to the window at the back of the hut and rested on the sill. "It was at the Battle of a Thousand Cries. Prince Baree, my master, as you remember, was put in charge of the left flank of defenders. During the first attack, one of the Dark Creatures spotted the Prince and realized that he was a general—though Baree, like you, only had thirteen rainy seasons. He immediately threw his spear. Out of the corner of my eye, I saw it coming toward my master. In a flash, I placed myself between the spear and Baree, hoping that I could stop it with my body. The spear was thrown too hard and fast. Its point passed through me and went into the Prince. It was not one of our better moments."

"But we believed the spear to have killed you both."

"So it was believed by you and the rest of the Kiritiris. After the Battle was won, our bodies were brought back to the camp of the Cattle People for burial since Baree was a prince, according to our customs. Most people would just be taken away from the village and left on the ground. We were placed side by side at the bottom of a deep hole and they were just about to fill it in with earth.

"Then Olugbala appeared and was said to have wept when he saw us. Without wasting a moment, he stood by the edge of the hole and asked his Father that we be revived. The next thing we knew, we were standing up in the bottom and some men lifted Prince Baree out. I was able to fly out, of course.

"So it happened. The Cattle People rejoiced because they thought they had their leader back, but Olugbala told them that Prince Baree and I could not stay with them. He needed us on his Mountain in the East where we have been ever since."

Pachunga shook his head in amazement. "And Baree, will I ever be able to see him again?"

"Of course," said Kasuku. "But all in good time. He should show up in a very unlikely place." Kasuku moved over to the side of the hut and clung to the wall with his claws. "We have some important things to talk about. There is a lot to do before Kjaz-Barbaroi arrives."

Pachunga rose to his feet and looked out the window at the Great River. East was the direction that it flowed. East it continued until it reached Olugbala's Mountain as some had once said. "When you first arrived here, you mentioned escape. But I don't want to now. I can't leave my people. I have to pay them back by serving them because of what I did to them—if they will have me. If I'd wanted to escape, I would have done it three rainy seasons ago. I think my people and those two Bazungu would have preferred that I did. Then I wouldn't have been a nuisance to them. Of course, they could have just killed me. It would have been simpler."

Kasuku was on Pachunga's shoulder. "You cannot help your people by remaining with them right now. Kjaz-Barbaroi is too strong here, and you do not have an army. That army needs to be called together. My trip here is to call you into service once again. Olugbala needs you. He needs you to form an army."

Pachunga continued to stare out the window. He clicked his tongue quietly in his mouth. "I am going to have to give it some thought," he said after a minute of silence. He knew that the decision had already been made, for he had known Olugbala long enough to know that when his Master gave a command, it was far better to obey. Pachunga only wanted time to think about leaving all that he knew behind. Only once had he left the Village to go off into battle for Olugbala, yet he always had known that he would be coming back. Now, he was not so sure if he ever would come back. This was his land. This was his family's land. They had had it for longer than anyone could remember—long enough that the songs about his people's arrival there were vague and mystical with Olugbala always in the center of all that they did. How could he leave? But he knew he would. In a few minutes, he would tell Kasuku that he was ready to make the necessary plans and go.

* * * *

The sun began to set over the Village of the Kiritiri peoples. Darkness was coming such as no one had ever seen. But the people were excited about it. Shouts and cheers filled the air. They beat numerous drums and sang chants that praised Kjaz-Barbaroi. Vicious Dark Creatures in ceremonial uniforms walked on their hind legs with their heads held high. Their diamond collars glistened in the light of a thousand torches, though the night was now as black as the mines where the diamonds had come from. Bonfires were lit in places around the central part of the Village. A row of torches led to the main gate, and a throng of men, women and children gathered along the triumphal route. Tension and excitement grew as a rumor spread through the crowd that Kjaz-Barbaroi was coming. "The Liberator," some were recalling him. "The Rescuer," he was called by others—the "Protector" of all the Kiritiri peoples. Gone were the ways of Pachunga and Olugbala. This was now the new way of prosperity and wealth. This was their future. For three rainy seasons—years, the Bazungu called them—they had worked in the mines. Now they were going to be set free. They were convinced of this.

The Master of All was coming to their Village. What an honor for them! For certain he was just outside the gates, for they were now being pulled open, and all Dark Creatures were lowering themselves to the ground. He was here! Kjaz-Barbaroi, who claimed to be the Emperor of the Land Where No One Dares to Live, King of the Cattle People and Owner of All Cattle, High Chief of the Cave People and soon to be enthroned on the High Seat as Chief of the Kiritiris and Ruler of all Domains as far as the eye could see and the foot could walk, was here.

"On your knees!" barked a Dark Creature to the Kiritiris. They immediately fell to the ground and sank so low it looked almost as if they were trying to bury themselves in the dust beneath them.

"Long live Kjaz-Barbaroi!" they shouted.

"May he live for eternity!"

"Liberator!"

"Protector!"

"Rescuer!"

"Guardian of us all!"

And their cries and cheers and chants increased more and more as the ruler of all evil in their world came into sight. The Kiritiris clapped their hands and danced in the Kiritiri fashion on work weary legs. This was a night worth remembering. This was a night they would tell their grandchildren about—if they lived long enough to know them.

Yet how little did they know of the real Kjaz-Barbaroi! And how much had they fallen from Olugbala since the Bazungu had first arrived in the Village.

Kjaz-Barbaroi stood just inside the gate of the Village and rejoiced inwardly that he was at last here in the heartland of the people who had once been his worst enemies. Outwardly, he had never looked more terrible. Although he was of the same species as the Dark Creatures, he never walked on four legs. His black leather vest was decorated in orange, brown and white triangles and diamond shapes. In his right hand was a large Drumstick, now decorated with diamonds from the mine. It was symbolized his power—the power that he had to keep the Drum beating.

Around him stood ten Dark Creatures who stayed with him at all times. They guarded their master. Even though these creatures were smaller than most (so that Kjaz-Barbaroi would look bigger), they were the best of his troops. They were always fighting with each other to see who could receive the most recognition from their leader. Kjaz-

Barbaroi didn't mind their fighting, of course. It kept them fit, fierce and sharp.

The Emperor of All lifted the Drumstick high into the air.

"The Drum!" he called in a cruel, strong voice.

"The Drum!" responded all the Kiritiris and Dark Creatures.

"Remember the Drum at all times! Remember the one who beats it!" he declared.

And there were more screams and chants as the Kiritiris worked themselves into a frenzy. Kjaz-Barbaroi began to walk through the middle of the Village. As he did, there were deep groans and wails from the people. The groans sounded not so much as if they came from pleasure, but from pain. Their faces reflected agony and suffering in the light from the torches and bonfires. In spite of their suffering, though, they continued to pay homage to Kjaz-Barbaroi. Wave after wave of people threw themselves down onto the ground and moaned at his sight. Some were trampled in the confusion and perished in their moment of greatest ecstasy. In them all, the Drum beat and beat, making them jerk and move to its rhythm.

It was terrible. It was horrible. It was awful. It was Hell.

* * * *

The noise of Kjaz-Barbaroi's procession through the Village felt deafening to the ears of Pachunga and Kasuku. But it made them work harder as they prepared to escape under the cover of darkness. Kasuku had found a dugout canoe about forty meters down river from Pachunga's hut. It was old and not in good repair, but it would have to do. Pachunga remembered that Mbinda, one of the men in the Village, had used it to go fishing in until he had to start working in the mine. Mbinda had died one rainy season earlier from exhaustion.

"Do you have everything?" asked Kasuku.

"Yes."

"He is coming now."

Pachunga said nothing to that. Instead, he thought of the things that he was bringing with him: the curved knife, the bow and twelve arrows, and the two spears and shield. He also had a fishing line with a hook carved from bone, and a large piece of cattle skin given to him by Prince Baree. Although it had been tanned well, it was not in good shape. But Pachunga could not leave it behind. Inside the skin were some tinder and a piece of steel and a stone to start fires with. The steel had come from one of the Bazungu who had thrown it away.

The noise from the Kiritiris in the Village increased more and more as Kjaz-Barbaroi and his entourage made his way through the center and headed towards Pachunga's hut. That was his obvious destination. Pachunga gathered his things together more quickly as Kasuku flitted nervously from one perch to the next.

Pachunga was thinking thoughts and feeling emotions that he hadn't experienced since the days of battle. His breathing shortened, every muscle in his body tightened, and his heart beat faster and faster. He was ready for action.

"We have to go now!" hissed Kasuku.

"I know, but first—" Pachunga went to the window and peered out. The spectacle in front of him made him numb as he gazed at his people writhing and jerking to the beat of the Drum. He stood like a statue, looking at the Dark Creatures. Kjaz-Barbaroi came into view and immediately a combination of fear and loathing surged up inside Pachunga, making him almost nauseous. He had a sudden, intense desire to strike out and to do as much harm to Kjaz-Barbaroi as he could—even if he died in the process.

His adversary approached the hut.

"Now!" hissed Kasuku.

Pachunga turned quickly and climbed out the back window.

"Pachunga!" a cold voice called. "Come out and greet your old enemy. Now is the time to make peace, or are you still at war with me? I am not at war with you. And do you know why? It is because I have already won. The victory is mine."

The boy heard Kjaz-Barbaroi's voice, but he didn't pay any attention to it. He had to concentrate on fleeing. He stepped carefully down the path that led to the dugout. All his provisions were wrapped tightly in Baree's leather. When he and Kasuku reached the dugout, he threw his cargo on board. Then he lifted up one end and pushed the canoe into the river. A wooden paddle, half-rotted, was under one of the thwarts. "Thank Olugbala for that," thought Pachunga. He started to paddle quickly, but quietly, away from the riverbank.

"I think we're making it," said Kasuku when they were a good distance out into the river. The current had already moved them downstream.

Kjaz-Barbaroi and his Dark Creatures had now discovered that Pachunga's hut was empty. The tyrant strode quickly down the path to the river's edge, his pack of guards yipping and yowling at his feet. He was in a screaming rage.

"Come back, Pachunga! You coward!" Kjaz-Barbaroi shrieked. He cursed. He stomped on the ground, causing several explosions that with loud bangs killed a few of his Dark Creatures who happened to be in the wrong place. Or maybe they were in the right place at the right time because Kjaz-Barbaroi liked nothing better than to kill someone when he was angry. He found it a calming and soothing activity. Several other Dark Creatures immediately pounced on the corpses and began tearing them apart, fighting each other over the meat.

One of his guards, Ngaba, went to him and whined, "Shouldn't we go after him?"

And one of the Bazungu, a short, fat man named Snippet said, "We can get him in a moment if I send out the launch."

"No," said Kjaz-Barbaroi. He had stopped his yelling and cursing. He was now calm and thoughtful. "No, that will not be necessary. Everything is working out according to my plan. I have other ways of dealing with Pachunga when the time comes. He thinks that Olugbala will protect him. But he won't. I am stronger than he. I will win!"

"Oh, come now," said Snippet. He listened to Kjaz-Barbaroi with amusement. "Don't tell me you believe in all that hype about Olugbala and the Father the Creator? You of all people—er, creatures—at least, would have more sense than that." Snippet shook his head. "Imagine! Believing in all that myth!"

Kjaz-Barbaroi was not pleased when he heard what Snippet was saying. Though they came from the North and had a lot of wonderful gadgets and mechanical devices, and although they thought they knew a lot, they actually knew nothing. Nothing! They knew nothing of magic. They did not know how the world really worked. They knew nothing of the power that he had. If Snippet had known what was best for him, he would not have said anything at all. Kjaz-Barbaroi's large monkey nostrils became even larger and short bursts of smoky air came out of them. His eyebrows lowered causing his eyes to narrow into slits, and his lips tightened. Slowly—and oh, how slowly it was—he turned his head and gave Snippet such a look that if the Mzungu had had a heart condition, he would have immediately dropped dead.

"Believe in all that myth, eh?" He spat the words out between his thin grey lips. His teeth flashed yellow behind them. Little drops of foam in the corners of his mouth glistened in the white light that came from that world's moon. "I am part of that *myth*, as you call it!" Since he was a Dark Creature, a few yelps and yaps and hoots and howls mixed in with his speech.

Snippet, behaving exactly like the weak-spined Mzungu that he was, instantly believed in the existence of Olugbala. That did not mean that he had joined Olugbala's side. It just meant that he understood Olugbala to be real.

"Oh, yes. It's true all right," he said. "Never doubted it for minute, I didn't. Oh, yes! I believe it all." He nodded his head up and down so vigorously to demonstrate that he was in agreement with Kjaz-Barbaroi that he pulled a muscle in his neck and had to have warm towels put on it for a week.

Kjaz-Barbaroi ignored Snippet. He was thinking instead of Pachunga—thinking very much about him, in fact. Pachunga was behaving as predicted, but Kjaz-Barbaroi could not shake his growing sense of doubt. There was something about the old Chief that was different, as if he were stronger and more dangerous—younger even. This was alarming, although he would never mention these thoughts and forebodings to anyone. Though he didn't see Pachunga as he escaped, he knew that Olugbala had been at work. The whole thing smelled of Olugbala. Pachunga was no longer old and feeble. And if he were young and strong, he would have a body joined together with an old man's wisdom, which would make him a greater adversary. And Pachunga could—and just might—ruin everything.

THE RIVER

Kasuku breathed a sigh of relief that was full of thanksgiving to Olugbala. They were now out of the way of the Dark Creatures and Kjaz-Barbaroi—for the moment. The current of the river was strong, and it had carried them well below the Village. They had only heard the words that Kjaz-Barbaroi had yelped directly. Pachunga had felt strangely satisfied when he had heard them, though Kasuku felt more suspicious. He knew—and so Pachunga would have known, too, had he thought about it—that they were not getting away for free. Kjaz-Barbaroi had the means to pull them back to the shore on his own by using some magic that he had learned since his last defeat at the Battle of a Thousand Cries. Yes, thought Kasuku with certainty, there were many dangers ahead.

"Well, Kasuku," said Pachunga from the stern of the dugout. "We made it." He had stopped paddling once the canoe was in the middle of the river.

"We're not out of it yet," said Kasuku, "though I feel that we may be safe for a while. I think Kjaz-Barbaroi has something more important on his mind."

"Yes. He is going to take my place on the High Seat." The Chief stared at Kasuku, who was perched on the boat's prow and silhouetted against a star-lit sky that stretched ahead of them and met the river at the horizon. "What are we going to do about this?" He felt sad and grieved for his people.

"There is not much that we can do right now except keep traveling toward Olugbala's Mountain. That is the direction that we are to take, though I doubt that we will end up going all the way there. The time is too short for a journey so long. There is also too much expectation of battle. All the creatures sense it. Everyone is fearful of what could happen. We will have to meet the enemy wherever he happens to find himself—and that means we must be as prepared as we possibly can be as quickly as possible."

"But where am I going to get this army?" asked Pachunga. He had no idea how that was to be accomplished. At the moment, the army was just himself and Kasuku—floating down a river in a rotting canoe with a broken paddle and few weapons.

"There are more supporters of Olugbala than you would think," said Kasuku. All they need is to be rallied by a leader—and Olugbala has chosen you for that task."

"I just don't know…" said Pachunga more to himself than to Kasuku.

Kasuku changed the subject. "Tell me, Pachunga. What happened to you after the Battle of a Thousand Cries?"

"It is a sad story. Are you sure you want to hear it?" Pachunga was not sure he wanted to tell it—even to Kasuku. It was very painful and he would rather just bury it in his memory and leave it there. But he knew from experience that burying it completely was not possible.

"It may be sad now, but it will have a happy ending sometime."

"I really hope so," said Pachunga doubtfully.

And he began to tell his story. It lasted for several hours, and by the time Pachunga finished, Kasuku had fallen fast asleep. However, the parrot did hear the most important parts.

"You may have heard that after the Battle was over, I and the rest of the Kiritiris returned to our lands and villages in the Jungle and began to live in a way we had not known since the First Peace. We called them the "Happy Times," for happy times they were. Olugbala blessed us by making the Jungle cool and comfortable. It was not hot, humid and sticky like other jungles, nor was it full of mosquitoes and tsetse flies. Thousands of different types of flowers grew, with beautiful colors of every shade. Oh, Kasuku! Never were our lands more beautiful!

"And Kasuku! The foods that we had to eat! We had jackfruit and honeyed mangoes roasted in banana leaves. There were rice cakes that melted in your mouth. There were roasted bananas and boiled *matoke* covered in ground nut sauce—and chickens and guinea fowl basted in their rich juices..." Pachunga stopped himself. "Er, Kasuku, I hope you don't mind..."

"It's no different than you eating monkey," Kasuku responded. "But I wouldn't go near 'em, myself—or any meat for that matter. I'm a vegetarian, of course." He made a few clucking noises to show his displeasure about eating meat in general. "But this is not important. Go on with your story."

Pachunga took a deep breath and continued. "Everything was going well. I was placed on the High Seat and ruled with Olugbala continually at my side. Peace and stability were maintained rainy season after rainy season. We prospered.

"Soon, the surrounding lands came under our influence and the people began to call me Chief Pachunga the Good. Festivals were celebrated regularly as we remembered Olugbala and all that he was doing for us. We had much singing, dancing, feasting and drank the most delicious fruit juices ever. These celebrations would last until the rising of the sun and no Kiritiri ever tired of them.

"And so it continued until my ninetieth rainy season and the festival that the people gave in my honor. I had been feeling very old and knew that I could no longer rule as well as a younger man. A successor needed to be chosen, though I didn't know who it should be. I was troubled about this, and who should come to me in secret during the night, but Olugbala.

"Olugbala!" I cried. "What are you doing here?"

"I am here to put your mind at rest," he told me. "You shall continue to rule your people."

"But I am an old man," I protested. "How can an old man rule with the strength of someone younger?"

"And Olugbala, who at one moment seems like the oldest and wisest of men, yet at another time is as strong, limber, and agile as a young man, looked steadily into my eyes and said, 'Am I not Olugbala the Chief of Chiefs? Is my Father not the Creator Himself? Have I not taught you much over these years?' And to demonstrate his greatness,

29

he became as tall as the tallest of giants, while I felt very, very small. Or, maybe he kept his size while he made me small.

"Yet, in spite of Olugbala's words and his visit, I could not stop feeling old. I am sure that the Drum had something to do with it, for it was about that time that the trouble began. Within a few weeks, a small problem arose that quickly turned into a very big one."

Pachunga's throat felt dry. He scooped up some river water and drank it. It tasted warm and muddy and had an earthy smell.

"At first, there was only one of them. He appeared in the earliest hours of the morning during the heavy rains. We still don't know how he got there. He just showed up. He didn't say a single word, but erected a hut out of cloth on the edge of the Village and by the river. He didn't make a hut out of wattle like we normally do. His cloth house was quite different from our own, just as he was quite different from us. He lived there for many weeks. The few times that we tried to speak to him in our own language failed. We tried speaking to him in the Common Speech, and he knew some, but we didn't learn anything about him then. He would just greet us politely, smile a little smile, and go on with his business. He wouldn't hunt for food—he ate it out of metal containers and boxes. It must have been spoiled, but he ate it anyway. He would go for long walks outside of the Village, looking at rocks and soil—sometimes putting the rocks in a bag that he would take back to this hut. It was all odd behavior, and since he seemed harmless, we just ignored him.

"This man—whom we called Mzungu—was short and very fat. His skin was nearly the color of the inside of a banana, though when he got hot, it would become very pink—like a flower. His hair was not curly and black like the rest of us have. It was the color of bad earth. And there really wasn't much of it. His teeth were square because he had never filed them, and on his body he wore far more clothes than we do. His feet were covered in the skin of cows.

"After a time, he finally spoke to us. He introduced himself as Doctor Snippet, and he told us about many new and exciting things that my people could have: machetes with blades of sharp, shiny steel, metal plows to farm the land, and axes to chop down trees to build better huts with—houses he called them. The most important tools of all, he said, were the shovels and picks that my people could use to find the white rocks that sparkled like the stars at night, only more so. They were found deep in the ground and they were quite valuable. Many Bazungu would pay us a lot of money—whatever that is—for these white stones.

"With big and complicated words, and with much shouting and arm waving, Snippet said that his treasure of diamonds was the treasure of a new and better Kiritiri people. We were now in a new age and with the money we earned, we could buy more machetes, more plows, more axes, and most importantly, more shovels and picks. With much work, the young people could harvest this new treasure and the Kiritiri people would become rich, which is something my people suddenly wanted to become."

Pachunga was quiet. "But we were already rich in other, better ways."

"True," said Kasuku.

Pachunga breathed deeply to get on with his story. "This Mzungu said that they would prosper like they had never dreamed until he, the good, gracious, and benevolent Doctor Snippet had arrived."

"Hah!" interrupted Kasuku. "He certainly was not very good."

"No, he wasn't. And to make matters worse, that Mzungu was not happy when he learned about Olugbala and his teachings.

"Tribal religion," he said. "Superstitious gobbledygook! That is only for children and old ladies. He sniffed and spat on the ground saying that science was a better way."

Pachunga looked frustrated. "What could I do about it, Kasuku? Nothing. They would not listen to me. They would not hear what I had to tell them. I was the only one living who had seen Olugbala in the Flesh. And I am—was—an old man. Why should they listen to me? They wanted power and wealth. They asked, 'What good are the teachings of Olugbala today? Will they put food on the table for my family? This is a new age, the age of possessions and money. This is the age of a new life that is not primitive.'

"And the truth is I was beginning to think like they were. I thought that if I went along with what they wanted, they would continue to respect me as their leader—and maybe it was time to make changes in how we did things. The Mzungu made sense. He told me that as the Chief, I would receive more than anyone else and that I would then become a stronger leader. I was stupid! I listened to him, not knowing that behind his voice was Kjaz-Barbaroi's Drum, beating through every word that was spoken—beating through every thought that went through my head until I embraced and accepted these changes gladly and enthusiastically—not knowing that I was actually condemning my people to a slow and painful death.

"So the men started digging and digging and digging. Another Mzungu came named Snipe, and he began to carry a small whip to make the young men—then the older men, then the young women and children—work in the mine. He was a lot harder and meaner than Dr. Snippet. His cruelty knew no limit. The children, Kasuku! They were forcing the children to work in that pit—children who never saw the sunshine! Children, because they were small, could go into places that grown men could not—places that were dangerous and foul. What he did to the children!

"My people rejected Olugbala. As they did, the Jungle became hot and humid once again. Mosquitoes and tsetse flies returned and brought disease. All the good luscious fruit and food disappeared. All they have to eat now are boiled potatoes and mashed beans. And the men, when they were not working, began to make *waragi* and drink it until they passed out. In their frustration and anger, they would beat their wives and beat their children.

"At first, they kept the festivals, but they changed the names. One became the Festival of the Day the First Mzungu Arrived. Another celebrated the Day the First Shovel of Dirt was Dug. And then there was the Day of a Thousand Diamonds. These were not like the earlier festivals we used to have. When they drank more *waragi*, the men would lose their self control. There was a lot of fighting and sometimes someone would be killed. The women changed, too. They started to drink *waragi* to forget their troubles. They laughed and shrieked and forgot exactly who their husbands were. They gave no consideration to their children, who became just as bad as their parents—because that was all that they were seeing. They argued and fought and called each other nasty names."

Tears began to flow freely from Pachunga's eyes. His voice became thick and hoarse. His lower lip trembled as he fought to control himself, but he could not. And somehow he knew that Olugbala was feeling the same sadness he was—perhaps even feeling it worse than he was, if that were possible.

"The rest you know. I want my people to forgive me, but they do not even know enough now to forgive me. All they feel is hate. Snipe placed me under arrest and under guard so that he could have more influence over the people, and they cheered his decision. I am old—was old—and forgotten and even Olugbala became distant to me."

"He was always there," replied Kasuku. "But because of the Drum and because of the decisions you made, you stopped hearing him. But he will not let you or your people down. They have rejected him now, but he will not reject them forever."

The night became cooler and their moon was getting lower and lower in the sky.

Kasuku smiled. "Tell me something of your life as a prisoner. It could not have been all bad."

Pachunga continued talking late into the night. He noticed at one point that Kasuku had finally fallen asleep, but the little bird would wake up now and again and say something. Usually his commands were whistled or tweeted in his own parrot language. This didn't bother Pachunga at all. He was happy to have a friendly audience before sleep finally overtook him and he dozed off.

* * * *

The river was wider now, but the current remained just as strong, if not stronger. Dark, impenetrable jungle grew on each side. Since it was late, there were no sounds other than the infrequent growl of a leopard or a panther on the hunt. But that didn't mean that the Jungle was asleep.

Many, many pairs of eyes quietly watched the dugout as it passed by. Most of them were not friendly. They watched, then turned and reported to another pair of eyes. These new eyes reported to another, until the exact location of the canoe reached the ears of Kjaz-Barbaroi and his lieutenant, Ngaba. Ngaba would receive the information. If Pachunga and Kasuku had done anything different than expected, he would share it with his master. For now, they were letting things run their course.

* * * *

When Pachunga awoke the next morning, he momentarily forgot where he was and almost climbed out of his boat into the river. He would have gotten very wet had he done so. What prevented him from making this silly move were two things. The first was the sun. It was beating down on his face, something that it didn't do when he was in his hut because the roof blocked it. The second thing was that he had been sleeping on something hard and uncomfortable. His mat at home had been softer than what he was sleeping on now. The sound of water splashing against the side of the dugout would have been a third clue, but by that time, he had awakened sufficiently to remember where he was and what he was doing.

"Good morning, Pachunga," said Kasuku from his perch on the bow.

"Ah, good morning to you Kasuku Broka (tweep!) Kngaka (squawk! whistle!)." That was Kasuku's full name in parrot language.

"Did you sleep well?"

"I must have. I fell asleep in the middle of my own story."

Pachunga looked at the Jungle on either side of them. He hoped to see something new and exciting. He didn't. The Jungle looked very much like it had every morning from the back window of his hut in the Village. While dark and mysterious, many of the animals and birds who lived in it were now visible. Along the riverbank, water birds with bright white or pink feathers and long yellow legs waded in the shallows between the reeds of the inlets. Dozens of hippopotami clustered in groups, grazing along the bottom of the river's shallows. They watched the canoe warily as it went by. Several times, the sight of the canoe caused crocodiles to slip into the river with a small splash. And once, they distracted a water buck from its drinking so that it looked up just in time not only to see the canoe, but also to see a crocodile that was swimming slowly towards it. With a snort, the water buck turned and ran from the edge of the water to safety.

In the Jungle itself, birds of every shape and color made a terrific noise as they screamed about their territorial rights and who had the privilege of eating which berries from what tree—or which worms and insects. Most of the birds were on Olugbala's side, so there wasn't much to worry about there. However, the monkeys had the potential for causing the most trouble, for the majority had sold themselves to Kjaz-

Barbaroi. Because of this, they frequently caused problems for the other animals and no one trusted them. They would be the ones reporting to Ngaba the location of the canoe for they could travel quickly from branch to branch across the tops of the trees.

Since most of the birds were allies of Olugbala, Kasuku hoped that they would try to confuse the monkeys with their message sending. He didn't know how good they would be, however. They were not smart like he was and were even more excitable than the monkeys, so would get easily confused.

"Are you hungry?" asked Kasuku.

"I sure am," said Pachunga. "Are you offering something?"

"You just wait here and—"

"I'm not going anywhere!"

"Yes, but I am." Kasuku was already in the air. "I'll be back soon." And he was off.

The breakfast of fresh pawpaw was just the thing to eat. It was a small one, though it was ripe, wet and refreshing. Pachunga felt full and satisfied when he finished it. With the sun shining on the surface of the water, the pawpaw filling his belly, the activity in the Jungle and Kasuku's companionship, Pachunga was beginning to feel more optimistic than he had in the middle of the night as he had recounted his story.

Perhaps things would work out well after all.

THE FIRST ATTACK

They traveled peacefully down the Great River for many, many days. The current took them quickly, but they had a great distance to go. While it was restful, it was also boring. Pachunga felt stiff from sitting in the canoe for so long, and they only had the briefest of visits to land—usually only if there were an island or some rocks in the middle of the river that would be in less danger—but except for those quick stops, they stayed in the canoe.

Pachunga was becoming more and more impatient. He could not see how sitting in a canoe and floating and paddling down a river was getting them any closer to forming an army that could defeat Kjaz-Barbaroi. In his mind, he was already reviewing battle strategies and plans—even though he did not know what kind of army he would be commanding. Mentally, he felt more than prepared. From his perspective, he was ready to meet Kjaz-Barbaroi and his army in battle and be done with the whole thing—even though his army consisted of one parrot, a handful of old weapons and a leaky canoe. Every day on the Great River seemed to be a day wasted, though Kasuku did remind him of something important.

"You may think that you are doing nothing right now. But remember that Olugbala is going to use you in a specific way. Trust him that this is where you ought to be right now. We are not the only warriors. There are countless others who are fighting a battle greater than you have ever seen—right now."

"I know," said Pachunga. "I would have thought that after all this time I would know something about patience. Even your master, Baree, had a lot more patience than I did at the age of thirteen. And he was a much better leader than I will ever be."

"Don't compare yourself to Prince Baree," instructed Kasuku sternly. "What Olugbala has appointed for him is different from what you are to have."

Pachunga let the air in his lungs come out in a long, slow whoosh. He was frustrated with his own shortcomings. "There is too much to learn."

"Patience, boy. Have patience and enjoy your surroundings. Have you ever seen a more beautiful Jungle since we left your Village?"

The scent of many flowers and the richness and lushness of the Jungle reached him, even out in the middle of the river. The birds saluted them both, and many of the monkeys screamed and ran in fright. They feared the power of Olugbala that was with Pachunga and Kasuku. But none of this made Pachunga any happier. He had waited too long since the last battle, and the Jungle was only reminding him of his people and the Village.

"I want to be with my people," he said. "As they used to be, not they way they are right now. I want to walk in my garden—my old one—with Olugbala at my side teaching me."

"I know how you feel. But remember that Olugbala is with you now—even as we speak. "

Pachunga knew that what Kasuku said was right, but he found little comfort in the words. Underneath everything, he doubted his ability to do what Olugbala wanted, and his grumpiness was actually more with himself and what he felt were his shortcomings. He desperately wanted to believe that everything would work out for the best and that he was adequate for the task, but he just was not sure. There was too much that had to happen—too much that had to fall into place. He had felt Kjaz-Barbaroi's power when he had come into the Village—and it was a lot greater and fearsome than it had ever been before. He knew in his mind that Olugbala was stronger than Kjaz-Barbaroi—far stronger—but still he had doubts about whether or not he was going to be able to do what he was being asked to do. The canoe ride was getting far too long—and it was allowing far too many negative thoughts to run through his head.

Would everything work out for the best? All he could do was hope. What else could he do? He was stuck on this stupid canoe and couldn't go anywhere else. He thought he would have been better off back in his hut in the Village. At least he could be keeping an eye on his people.

* * * *

"We're moving faster," observed Kasuku on the morning of the eleventh day. The river raced so smoothly and quickly that if it weren't for the boat's slow turning in the current and the moving shoreline, they would not have felt as if they were moving at all. The surface was drawn tight by gravity, and the bottom was deep beneath them. There were no waves but only small ripples from the wind. "It is because of the *Mosi-oa-Tunya*—the 'Smoke that Thunders.'"

"The High Falls?"

"Yes. We shall be there in a few days. It will be a very tricky part of the trip. It will mean having to say farewell to this old boat. It will go over the Falls, but we will have jumped out beforehand."

"I am glad that Olugbala has sent you," said Pachunga. "I have heard of the Falls in legend only. If you weren't with me, I could have gone right over in the middle of the night!"

Downstream, just over the horizon, a cloud was forming. From their distance, it looked like a brilliant white cotton ball against a deep blue sky. Pachunga remarked that it was unusual to see a cloud like that in just one place—there were no other clouds around.

"That is no cloud," explained Kasuku. "That is the mist created by the Falls. That is why they call it the 'Smoke that Thunders.' When the water passes over the edge, it falls hundreds of meters until it crashes on boulders larger than the size of your old, great hut. The river itself is four kilometers wide there. If you were to stand on the edge of the Falls and look down, the boulders would appear to be the size of pebbles. On either side of the top of the Falls are high, sheer cliffs made of smooth, water-polished stone. There is a ledge at the bottom of the cliff on the left. We will abandon the boat there and jump for it. Well, you will jump. I will fly."

Pachunga didn't like the idea at all. "Couldn't we go ashore earlier—before the cliffs—and go through the Jungle?"

"Impossible. Well, not impossible, but it would take too many days traveling over land through thick jungle and in dangerous territory. If you were a monkey, I could see it. You could travel from tree to tree. But being a boy, you're stuck on the ground. No man has ever been through that section. It is too thick. We need to take advantage of the speed of the river while we can."

* * * *

Another night passed, but when Pachunga woke up, he could see that Kasuku was concerned. Something was up.

"We must be careful," said Kasuku. "During my flight over the Jungle in search of food today, I was warned many times about a coming danger. Even the trees were talking about it. You know how little they like to speak. The monkeys—never trust them with a secret—have been blabbing about an attack on us."

This got Pachunga's attention. It looked like something was going to happen after all—something interesting. He just hoped that with the peace and stillness of their trip, his defenses had not weakened. The river felt almost hypnotic—and because nothing had happened up to that point, he was beginning to think that Kjaz-Barbaroi had lost interest in them.

"Where do you think the attack is going to take place?"

"At the High Falls, I am almost certain. We will be our most vulnerable there, for they suspect that we mean to jump on to the rock ledge. If we are engaged in battle and distracted fighting them, we won't have the chance and the current will take us right over the edge of the waterfall."

Kasuku did not think it appropriate to say that only Pachunga would go over the edge. But they would try and get him, too. He would not be allowed to escape.

"How will they attack?"

"I don't know. It could be from anywhere—from the cliffs, from under the river, or from the air. Kjaz-Barbaroi is now master of the Falls. He will use all the resources that he has. We have to keep our guard up at all times.

"I—" Pachunga stopped and listened. "I hear the Drum again. Kjaz-Barbaroi is continuing to call his armies together."

"Yes," said Kasuku. "The Drum will beat and beat. It will become even easier to come under its spell. Kjaz-Barbaroi has the power to draw all creatures to him if they do not ask for the protection of Olugbala. It is the only defense against it."

"Kasuku, swear to me as a brother that you will strike me down dead if I ever come permanently under the spell of the Drum. It would be far better to be dead than to be a slave of Kjaz-Barbaroi."

Kasuku clucked loudly. "I can do no such thing, and you know it! Trust only that Olugbala will see you through any temptation. You have heard the Drum many times before. Olugbala helped you then. There is no reason why he won't help you now."

On the morning of the day that they were to reach the Falls, a fine mist settled on them both. And they could hear the steady roar as the water plunged hundreds of meters down to the bottom. The current flowed even faster, and to their left and right, high cliffs now rose up as the river dropped lower and lower. In the sides of the cliffs were many black openings. Kasuku said that they were holes so that the Cave People living inside could get air. "The Cave People used to be our allies—but they are our enemies now. Their ancestors known as the Tall Men helped Kalopa and his lions during the First Rebellion. Now they, like so many, have followed the sound of the Drum."

The Falls now roared louder than anything Pachunga had ever heard. He could understand why they were called the "Smoke that Thunders." They had to shout at each other when they had anything to say.

"Have your weapons ready!" ordered Kasuku. "The attack will come soon! And try to point the canoe over to the left so we can make it to the ledge!"

Pachunga arranged the arrows carefully in the quiver so that he could grab them as he needed them. He put the two spears within easy reach and adjusted and tightened the belt around his middle. The knife he had would be useful only in hand-to-hand or hand-to-claw combat. Kasuku had not been able to learn what kind of enemy they would be meeting in battle.

"More towards the left! More towards the left! Paddle on the diagonal!" bellowed Kasuku. "We won't make it to the ledge if you don't!"

Pachunga could not hear what Kasuku said, but he understood the message from the bird's gestures. He continued to paddle vigorously and in silence. There was no point in doing any talking, because the noise of the Falls had grown even louder. And they were still a kilometer away. The canoe raced along at a faster and faster speed. At times, it would surge up and then down as the water became shallower and shallower as they approached the edge. Kasuku was tempted to fly ahead and do some scouting, but he did not want to be separated from Pachunga. He was under orders to take good care of him.

The sun set behind them. The last traces of day disappeared with it. Their moon was almost full, but the mist blocked out a lot of its light. Little did they know, but Kjaz-Barbaroi was trying hard to blot out the light by sending dark clouds from the West. But Olugbala had sent a wind from the East to keep them away so the two travelers could see what they were doing.

Pachunga struggled with his paddle. Perspiration mixed with the droplets of mist and spray that settled on his skin. He looked skyward for a moment and saw some movement along the top edge of the high cliff above them. Silhouettes of spears and tall, narrow shields were outlined against the dark sky.

"Cattle People! Hundreds of them!"

It was scary indeed. During their trip down the river, Kasuku had explained to him that a group of Cattle People, under the leadership of Prince Baree's great-grand nephew, Prince Mwailu, had switched over to the side of Kjaz-Barbaroi. Their grazing lands in the Great Grassland were closer to the Land Where No One Dares to Live, so they had quickly succumbed to the sound of the Drum. Because of their numbers and their skill with a spear, they represented a major threat to Kasuku and Pachunga.

Pachunga watched the Cattle People above him and felt the same sadness for them that he felt for the Kiritiris. They had been his beloved allies in the Battle of a Thousand Cries—the people of his best friend, Prince Baree, and he hated to think that they had turned to the side of Kjaz-Barbaroi. He hardly dared to breathe, because he knew he would start crying again if he did. He was a warrior preparing for battle and there was no time for tears. He was also on edge because he knew that the attack was about to happen—although just keeping the canoe upright and moving towards the left side of the river was taking most of his energy and concentration. They were in the middle of it now and there was no turning back.

Pachunga fought the strong current with his paddle. They were getting closer to the ledge, but they weren't doing it fast enough. So intent was he on achieving the side of the river—and so preoccupied was Kasuku with the Cattle People—that they were not paying any attention to their backs.

The first strike was almost successful.

Kasuku smelled the cold stench of enemy behind him before Pachunga did. A long, black, sleek and slippery snake had swum underwater and now slid over the back of the dugout, preparing to grasp Pachunga in its jaws and pull him over the side of the canoe where he certainly would have drowned. The head was over twenty centimeters wide and the teeth were long, sharp and yellowed from the muck the snake lived in and the types of creatures that he ate to sustain himself.

"Pachunga!" warned Kasuku as he flew into the air in the shadowy dusk behind the Chief. He could not be heard. However, the boy did sense that Kasuku was alarmed about something, and he could feel the canoe tipping from something heavy in the stern. He whirled around, his hand instinctively grasping his knife. In a second, the head of the snake lay on the floor of the boat and its body slid backwards into the water and disappeared from sight leaving a trail of blood that quickly dissolved in the soaking mist. Kasuku swooped down and picked up the head with his claws and dropped it over the side.

They didn't have a moment to comment. Hundreds of tawny eagles and black kites fell from the sky like stones and tore at them both with specially sharpened claws. They were under Kjaz-Barbaroi's orders to destroy Pachunga and Kasuku. Their claws and their bills were as sharp as knives and could easily tear the flesh of any creature that they attacked. They were the raptors of the Great Grassland and they descended without mercy on Pachunga and his friend.

Pachunga managed to get two of them with his knife before he could reach his bow. Only there were too many of them to use it effectively. He switched to a spear, but one heavy tawny eagle broke the first spear, and he could not get to the second one in time. Their claws burned as they dug into his flesh. Their beaks ripped away pieces of his skin. He remained on his feet, though the boat rocked wildly back and forth. The barrage would not stop. Many times he almost fell into the river, only just saving himself each time. Once or twice, due to the number of birds attacking him and the pain he endured from their beaks and claws, he almost felt that just giving up and falling into the river would be the better thing to do—just to get away from the pain. The river would end the agony of those terrible claws.

Kasuku, smaller and more maneuverable, used his own sharp claws to blind the eagles and kites. Unable to see, they would crash into the cliff walls or plunge into the river and drown.

Pachunga used his knife again as the attack continued. He was successful every time he made contact. His hand was sticky with their blood and bits of feathers and bird flesh clung to it. But there were too many eagles. There were too many claws. His arm felt heavy. He could not slash anymore with his knife. If only he could reach the shield!

And they were getting closer and closer to the edge of the Falls. Through eyes that were partially blinded by his own blood and the mist and spray that never went away, Pachunga tried to find the paddle. Perhaps he could ignore the tawny eagles and reach the rock ledge. It wasn't there. The paddle was gone. It had fallen over the side in the fighting. The boat began to move up and down in the water even more as the river became choppier and rougher. Here and there, rocky islands emerged that threatened to shatter the canoe before it even reached the High Falls.

Kasuku flew close to Pachunga, attacking the tawny eagles around the Chief. There was no way they were going to make the ledge. In fact, Kasuku saw it go by out of his left eye, and he knew that that option was gone forever. If Pachunga stayed in the canoe, he would certainly be torn to bits by the eagles and kites. After a few precious seconds, he was able to get the boy's ear and scream: "Jump!" He only had time to say it once.

It was all that Pachunga needed. He was confused and disoriented. He didn't know why he was being told to jump, but he knew he had to. The pain was so great. His skin burned. He was too tired. Every muscle in his body throbbed from wounds and fatigue. After thrusting his knife into his belt, he didn't so much as jump, but collapse over the edge of the canoe and fall into the water. He hadn't the strength to do anything more.

The moment he hit the river, the tawny eagles unexpectedly stopped their attack and flew away screeching victoriously. They had done their job. They knew the boy was a goner.

Pachunga was now alone, caught in a current that was going to carry him right over the edge. He lost track of Kasuku and hoped that he was safe.

What Pachunga did see was Olugbala standing on a ledge high up on the cliff to his left. His form was illuminated by the moon, and the mist created a glowing circle of light around him. Pachunga was certain he was looking at Olugbala. His heart was warmed and he relaxed. The fighting was over for good. "I will be with you soon," he thought, meaning that he expected to die.

With that, he closed his eyes and was carried by the river over the cascading edge of the Smoke that Thunders.

THE CAVES

The bright, warm sun shone directly on Pachunga's face. It felt comforting and soothing, and as Pachunga began to wake up, he just wanted to lie there and enjoy it. Several sensations and thoughts happened at once. At first, he assumed that he was still on the boat because that was where he had been for so long. But there was a difference. He was not moving. That is, he was not rocking slightly from side to side as he would have done in the canoe. And there were not the usual morning sounds that he heard day after day on the river. There was a loud roaring in his ears that could only come from one thing: the Falls.

Instantly alert, he opened his eyes see where he was. His warrior training kicked in and he assessed immediately his state and his situation. He was on his back on some kind of rock shelf. Without standing up or even moving, he looked up at the sky above him as the memory of the attack by the tawny eagles and black kites came flooding back. He could see that the shelf he lay on was just about four meters from the top of the Falls on the one side, just out of reach of the pounding torrent of water that cascaded hundreds of meters to the bottom. The current must have taken him over to the very edge of the river (at an angle? It didn't seem possible) out of the main stream, then dropped him neatly on the ledge.

He then felt his face and his body with his hands. No, he was not dead yet. He remembered that he had been severely wounded, but he had no pain and there was no sign of any wounds. He was perfectly healed. Or, maybe he was actually dead and this was the body he was to have in the next life. But, wouldn't he be on Olugbala's Mountain? He wouldn't still be here by the Falls, would he? He couldn't remember seeing anything after he had seen Olugbala. The thought occurred to him that he might have been lying there for several days, which would have explained why his wounds were no longer there. He felt amazingly dry and not drenched from the Falls' spray. Most of the mist that rose up from the base of the Falls was being blown South away from him.

Now that he had discovered where he was and that he was still alive, he stood up carefully. A moment of dizziness made him start to fall. He threw himself backwards against the cliff wall to keep from plunging over the side of the ledge. He got his balance back after leaning against the wall for a few seconds and taking a couple of deep breaths. When he recovered his balance, he stepped timidly to the precipice to see what was ahead of him and beneath him.

Facing East, away from the Falls, he could see that the dark green Jungle continued on either side of the river, but at its edge on either side, the Great Grassland began, stretching like a khaki-colored carpet almost to the horizon. Here and there were spots of green, black and brown from the various trees that dotted the landscape. Nearer to him and below to the left, he saw a strip of grey and green terrain, only he couldn't tell what it was. It was too far away. He could see a thin band of something tan and white on the horizon, but it was hard to tell what it was because of the dusty haze in the air there. Perhaps it was the Great Desert that Kasuku had told him about. It was supposed to be further away than the Great Grassland.

The river did not continue East beyond the Falls. It turned South and went as far as the horizon, although it would eventually turn East again. He peered toward the eastern horizon trying to see any sign of Olugbala's Mountain but there was nothing but small white clouds. If he were to go all the way to the Mountain, there would be a great distance to travel. It would have to be overland too. With the dugout gone and the river turning to the South, the faster way—it seemed to him—would be to cut through the remaining Jungle, cross the Great Grassland and the Great Desert, and try to avoid the Land Where No One Dares to Live. He did not want to meet Kjaz-Barbaroi in his home territory. He estimated that it would be another two full moons or more before he would reach his destination—if he were supposed to go that far.

To Pachunga's left a drop equal to that in front of him fell far down to the boulders below. All this thinking of how long it would take him to reach the Mountain was pointless if he could not find a way to get down. He looked behind him and studied the rock wall that rose four meters from the back of the ledge to another ledge that was level with the top of the Falls, but then the cliff soared a couple of hundred meters beyond it. At least that was what it looked like from his perspective. The rock face was smooth and vertical. There wasn't even a single crack to stick in a finger or a toe.

The Falls to his right were a cascading force that plunged down without interruption until they exploded into clouds of water-smoke on the boulders beneath. It was all very beautiful. But Pachunga was not in a position to admire its beauty. The ledge on which he was standing disappeared into the waterfall to his right. From all that he could see—unless he could miraculously fly—he was stuck on that rock shelf.

Pachunga wondered where Kasuku was. He wasn't sure how the bird could help. Perhaps he could find a tough vine to drop down to him. Yet that was ridiculous. The parrot was too small to carry a large enough vine to do that. And where and how would he attach it? Also, what would be the point of climbing up to the next ledge even if it did provide a means to get to the top? He suspected that the Cattle People were still around with their spears and shields ready. But facing them was preferable to starving to death where he was or plunging hundreds of meters to the plain below.

Where was that parrot? Could he have gone back to Olugbala to leave Pachunga to travel on alone? Of course not. Did that mean he had been killed by the raptors? Pachunga didn't think so. Wherever he was, he was probably doing something important. Or maybe he had been taken prisoner. Perhaps he was in some kind of horrible danger. If so, Pachunga would have to find him to help him.

But how?

Pachunga! The voice that called his name was soft. It was sweet. It could mysteriously be heard above the crashing of millions of tons of water. It was frightening, but not in a terrifying sort of way. It was a command.

It was the voice of Olugbala.

Pachunga! Come to me, here!

Pachunga could not see him, but he did hear him. Where was the voice coming from? It sounded like it was coming from behind the waterfall. How could that be? And how could he go where Olugbala was? The waterfall was a wall of water plunging hundreds of meters to boulders the size of houses below. Surely if he tried to pass through it, he would be washed down the Falls and smashed to pieces on the rocks below. The water moved too fast and too strong.

"Is that y-you, Olugbala?" He knew that it was, though he found that he had to ask anyway. The Drum beat faintly, filling Pachunga's head with doubts as to whether the voice really came from Olugbala or whether he should obey what it was telling him to do.

Pachunga took a step. All his reasoning told him not to do it. The Drum beat louder. Perhaps it wasn't Olugbala at all. Perhaps it was Kjaz-Barbaroi leading him to his death.

Boom! went the Drum.

He was afraid of dying.

Boom! Boom! It wasn't time yet. He had just been made young again.

Boom! Boom! Boom!

But he couldn't stay on the ledge forever. And Olugbala would never lead him to his death in this way. The Drum began to weaken. He had to make a move. Right now Olugbala was calling him. He had to obey. The Drum stopped.

"By your blessed name!" he exclaimed, taking a step forward right into the falling water. It splashed over him lightly, drenching him.

To his amazement, he wasn't swept to his death. Instead, he discovered that he was standing in the mouth of a cave behind the falling water. Olugbala was not to be seen. But that didn't matter very much. He had come to where Olugbala wanted him to be.

Pachunga noticed the quietness immediately. At first, he thought he had lost his hearing. But he realized that he could still hear the Falls; they were not as loud as they had sounded when he was outside them. The water behind him acted as a shield and blocked their thunder. In front of him, the walls of the cave itself glittered and danced in golden patterns as the morning sun shone through the Falls and became broken up into bits of moving lights. The floor of the cave was smooth and grey. In the direct center of the rear wall was an opening that was lower than the top of Pachunga's head. The remarkable thing about the opening was that it was perfectly rectangular. It was not a natural opening but a doorway carved into the stone.

But that wasn't the strange part about it. Normally one would expect any kind of an opening in a cave to be an entrance into a deep, black pit or tunnel. This was not so. A faint glow came from it that slowly went from a cold, clear blue to a cold, clear green—and then back to blue again. Looking at it made Pachunga shiver, though the temperature of the cave was very pleasant. There is just something about certain shades of green and blue—especially blue—that makes you feel chilled. The Chief had no clue how this light was being manufactured. He had never seen anything like it. For him, light in dark places came from torches or fires or from the special electric lamps of the Bazungu.

Pachunga was still dripping with water when he took a step toward the doorway. Since he was so wet and the floor of the cave was so smooth, there was not much friction to keep him from standing up straight. Before he knew it, he was falling backside first onto the hard cave bottom.

"Ahhh!" he exclaimed in too loud a voice. "What a—"

Then, he abruptly stopped himself from saying anything more. He remembered that he was in Cave People territory and Kasuku had said that they were enemies.

"That was silly," he thought to himself. Kasuku would have gotten a good laugh if he had seen it.

His bottom felt sore as he stood up, but after a step or two it stopped bothering him. He carefully walked toward the door, firmly planting each foot on the floor and taking smaller steps. Ducking down, he passed through the opening and immediately heard the sound of voices, nothing more than mutterings, coming up a long tunnel that stretched several meters ahead of him. The tunnel then turned abruptly to the right. The voices were obviously in conference.

Pachunga's guard went up. He took the knife out of his sheath. He would sneak down the tunnel and get as close to the voices as he dared. A lot could be learned from the conversation. Were these the voices of friends or enemies? The light that kept changing from blue to green to blue again looked brighter in the tunnel. The Chief could see with this light that the walls on one side were all carved with the patterns of the Ancient Empire, which had been destroyed during the First Rebellion. This empire had been vast, and its subjects had worshiped the image of Kozak-Baros, a Dark Creature and supposed ancestor of Kjaz-Barbaroi.

Pachunga had thought that all traces of the Ancient Empire had been destroyed after Kalopa the Lion and his army had been victorious over the Empire's warriors. He studied the carvings more closely. There were beasts with the heads of hawks and jackals that were on the bodies of men. There were tall, thin black men with rings around their necks marching in a line. They wore war masks and carried shields with the likeness of Kozak-Baros on them. Fighting for the Empire also was a race of olive-skinned men who were tall, fierce and rode on camels and horses. There was Kozak-Baros himself, riding a camel in the center of the warriors. The camel had an elaborate saddle and bridle decorated with what appeared to be gold and jewels. A patterned blanket hung down from the camel's hump. Kozak-Baros rode proudly and high, surveying the vast army marching with him.

Pachunga thought that he looked just like Kjaz-Barbaroi—and in a moment of understanding, Pachunga wondered if Kozak-Baros and Kjaz-Barbaroi were not one and the same. They had to be. Why didn't anyone know that?

The boy was entranced by the carvings. It had been a long time since he had been in a real battle. The thought of going off to war like that in a marching line appealed to him. He could imagine them walking in rhythm to the sound of the Drum. The designs captivated him with their images of creatures and beasts and races of men who had long since disappeared. The Drum beat louder and louder as he looked at the men and creatures marching to it. The carvings attracted him more. The men with the rings around their necks appeared to be marching. Their mouths opened to sing chants in preparation for battle. Their feet trod upon the dusty ground. The Drum grew louder still. Pachunga began to wish that he were right in the middle of everything that was happening. The scenes in front of him were becoming more and more alive. His eyes followed the marchers to the battle itself.

Then suddenly Kalopa and his lions appeared—just like in the old story. But wait, Mamosa and all his bull elephants were there, too. And so were Prince Baree and Kasuku with hundreds of Cattle People behind them to support their Prince! They were there! They were all there! What battle was this? How could they all be at the same battle at the same time? Pachunga was mystified, but he wanted to be there, too.

The Drum beat stronger and faster. The armies of Kozak-Baros attacked, thrusting their spears into the flesh of the lions and elephants and Cattle People. Mamosa was being encircled by Dark Creatures and the tall warriors. They began to poke at the elephant, jabbing him viciously and wounding him severely. Kalopa, too, was being trapped by the enemies of Olugbala. Prince Baree and Kasuku were facing twenty Dark Creatures and there was no help in sight. Corpses of Cattle People, elephants and lions now covered the ground, which was turning dark with their blood. Some raised arms or legs or trunks or heads briefly before collapsing, never to move again.

Baree lost his weapons. Kasuku refused to leave his side. The battlefield continued to fill with the corpses. And, wait! No! There were Kiritiri people now fighting and they were being slaughtered by the dozens. They were horribly outnumbered and the battle had turned into a complete rout.

Where was Pachunga? He couldn't see himself in the battle. More importantly, where was Olugbala? Why wasn't he there?

"Olugbala," groaned Pachunga aloud. "Help!"

The Drum stopped.

The carvings became just as they had been a few moments earlier: figures carved in stone. Pachunga's head cleared, and he vaguely remembered being alarmed about something, only he couldn't remember what it had been.

"There is magic in this place," he thought. "I had better be careful."

He walked away from the carvings and reached the point where the passageway turned sharply to the right. The voices grew louder. From time to time, someone laughed merrily, a high, shrill soprano laugh. He stopped and listened. He could now understand what was being said.

"So I said to him, 'Marvin (this was the high voice that must have belonged to a girl), that is no way for a gentleman of your position and means to act.' And he said, 'Madam, when I am confronted by such beauty and grace—' He really had a way with words—'I cannot help myself.' What a line! He had a look in his eyes that reminded me of a puppy that needed to be fed or let outside. Poor guy. And to think that he almost became my second husband!" More of that high-pitched laughter echoed down the passageway.

"So who was it that you finally married?" the second voice asked.

Pachunga gasped with joy. The second voice belonged to Kasuku! He was alive! And he sounded all right. There wasn't the slightest hint of danger.

Without hesitating, though his knife was still out of its sheath, Pachunga turned to the right and entered a small, circular room lit by the blue and green light as in the passageway. In the center of the room stood a very low wooden table. Around it were several wooden stools. Seated at one of the stools was a Mzungu. She was about eleven or twelve, Pachunga guessed. Bright orange hair stuck out from underneath a pith helmet that was several times too big for her. She was wore a well-worn khaki safari shirt that was also too large for her. Her khaki shorts were cinched around her waist with a piece of coarse rope, and they reached well past her knees. Her face was bright red and dripped with perspiration. Pachunga thought that she was the strangest and most baffling girl he had ever seen.

Kasuku was there, too. He was walking back and forth like a general on top of the table. He was absorbed in conversation with the Mzungu and appeared to be enjoying himself very much.

Pachunga couldn't understand what was going on. Bazungu were the enemy.

"Kasuku!" he cried, waving his knife in the air.

"Oh, hi, Pachunga," said Kasuku, as if the Chief had only been away long enough for a breath of fresh air.

"I—uh—"

"By all means, put that knife away. This Mzungu is a friend."

"She is?"

"Yes," said Kasuku patiently and tolerantly. "She is."

"Oh." Pachunga felt blood rising to his face.

"How do you do," said the girl politely. "My name is Muriel Sniggins."

He didn't feel very articulate and suddenly felt shy. "M-M-M-Mine is P-Pachunga."

"I figured that was you. Kasuku was expecting you to show up eventually. I'm glad that you were able to find your way here."

Was Muriel Sniggins being sarcastic? Pachunga couldn't tell.

"Kasuku, I'm happy to see that you're safe. How long have you been here?"

"Since last night."

"Last night? Was it only then? I thought I had been lying on the ledge for days—weeks, maybe. The wounds from the eagles were healed." He looked at the parts of his body that he could see. "And there aren't even any scars!"

Kasuku sighed. "Pachunga, old man. After all that Olugbala has done for you—and you still don't understand?"

"Uhhh…" Why was he having trouble getting his words out? He was about to say, "Of course," but then he realized that that would be lying. He wasn't remembering Olugbala very well. Pachunga fell silent.

"Well," said Muriel. "You must be absolutely starving. Would you like something to eat?"

Before Pachunga could answer, she stood up swiftly and left the room. She had to walk carefully so that she would not trip on her over-sized clothes. She disappeared through a door opposite the one Pachunga had entered by.

"Is everything all right?" asked Pachunga in a whisper. He sat down on one of the stools.

"Shhh," warned Kasuku. "It will be okay if we mind our p's and q's. All that is said has a way of eventually being reported to the enemy. Just keep your guard up at all times. We should be safe enough here for the moment, but once we descend to the lower levels of the cave system, it will become more and more dangerous."

"And Muriel Sniggins? She's okay?"

"She's fine. She has a fascinating story about how she got here. Maybe she will share it with you, if there's time."

Muriel came back into the room carrying a thick wooden tray full of steaming food. "I'm afraid that all we have are leftovers: some reheated gazelle stew, beans and boiled peanuts. Would you like some warm goat's milk?"

"Thank you," said Pachunga. He was feeling a lot more relaxed and more himself.

"This isn't what they serve in the best restaurants, but it should fill you up."

"Anything that I put in my mouth right now will be the most delicious food ever. I don't know that much about gazelle meat. We are too far from the Great Grassland for it. I am sure that it is very good. I haven't had a hot meal since leaving the Village."

Pachunga picked up a piece of meat and gnawed on it. Even though it had been stewed for hours, it was still tough—but not so tough he couldn't chew it. The flavor was incredible. He was instantly a fan. With his mouth full of meat, he asked, "Kasuku, how did you get here?"

"After I told you to jump, I knew that there was nothing more that I could do. I flew over the Falls and entered these caves by a small hole beneath the ledge where Olugbala put you."

"So you saw him too!"

"Yes. It was he who gave the original command to jump."

"I see," said Pachunga doubtfully. He just remembered hearing Kasuku.

"Then once I was inside the caverns—you wouldn't believe how vast they are—I found Muriel here. Some Cave People, Mwema and Mwenda, warned me to be careful. They're okay, too. They are on our side. You see, Olugbala has more to support him than you would think. Now that you have arrived, they will take us to the bottom so that we can continue with the trip."

Pachunga glanced at Muriel and continued to be puzzled about her. She looked young, but she had said some things that didn't fit her age at all. "Muriel," he said. "I heard you mention having had a husband. Is that a custom of Bazungu—to marry so very young?"

"No, we don't get married when we're children. In fact, we probably get married at an age much older than your people do. I've been married—twice. I even have some children up in the North. I really don't understand what happened to me, but maybe if I tell you my story it will make sense to you. It doesn't make sense to me—and it certainly wouldn't make sense to anyone back home!"

She leaned against the table, took a deep breath, and started to speak.

Muriel's Story

"I still don't know whether I'm just in the middle of a long dream," she began, "or if this is really happening. I am forty years old, though you wouldn't think it to look at me. You see these clothes? They are for a very large woman. I weighed over eighty kilograms and was only 160 centimeters tall. Now I look exactly the way I did when I was eleven or so. The change happened last night while I was sleeping—after Kasuku told me about Olugbala."

"I had the same thing happen to me!" said Pachunga. "Would you believe that I am actually ninety-four rainy seasons old?"

"Ninety-four rainy seasons!" exclaimed Muriel. "That's years, right? Wow! I guess I'll have to think of you in a different way."

"And I, you," said Pachunga. He smiled. "But not too differently. Olugbala obviously wants us this way."

"I guess so," said Muriel. It was still all too new for her to process properly.

"I'm keeping you from your story," said Pachunga. "Go on."

She stopped and reflected for a moment. "I was starting at the end of the story. That won't do. I should start in the middle."

"My second husband—his name was Elmer—and I were sitting at home one day watching some sporting event on TV. I think it was Killer Hockey or something like that. All of a sudden, Elmer slumped over dead in his chair from a heart attack. I had become a widow for the second time in my life.

"I discovered that I was left alone to take care of balance sheets, checks, a portfolio the size of most small banks, ledgers, fiscal reports, securities, bonds and stocks—we were very rich—and after a year, I couldn't take it anymore. 'This is all useless,' I thought, 'Why am I wasting all my time keeping track of my poor dead husband's factories and stores and lands and gold and silver and cash—" She stopped and took a deep breath. "'—and other investments, when there has to be something more important in life?'

"So I left everything in trust for my children—bless them—kissed them all good-bye forever—they had almost grown up and are perfectly capable of taking care of themselves—and set off in search of Meaning and Truth.

"I traveled all over the North to our best cities and universities and couldn't find it there. I traveled all over the West and couldn't find it there, either. And in the far East, I climbed mountains and talked with funny little men in white robes who told me things like:

"'Truth and Meaning are found in yourself. Say this word over and over again. Descend into yourself. You will find the happiness and contentment that you are seeking.'

"I tried it for a few months. Ate nothing but vegetables, shaved my head and put on white robes. I looked inside myself and discovered only a lot of dirt and garbage and skeletons and ghosts and—nothingness. No speaking of some idiotic word would get rid of it all. So I left the little men on their mountain.

"Then I went to this island in the middle of the ocean and tried to go native. Er, excuse me, Chief Pachunga, I didn't mean—"

"That's all right," he replied. "I know what you mean. The Bazungu refer to us as natives all the time. It's a better word than "savage," which is what we also are called. Going native must have been something you were not meant to do."

"It certainly wasn't! I lived on an atoll—that's a small island made from a volcano and ringed by a coral reef, if you get what I mean, for almost a year. I tried to imitate the people who lived down there. Yet I soon learned that I was always an outsider and too used to all the conveniences of a developed country. And look where I am now! It doesn't follow, does it? Anyway, I went to the North for a few months, recovered from my island experience, and decided that heading South was the only place left in the world to look for Meaning and Truth. I'd always wanted to go on a safari."

Pachunga winced, though Muriel didn't notice. He didn't like safaris—at least the ones that were made up of Bazungu who were after animal trophies. They seemed pointless to him since the meat was not going to be eaten and the skins were not going to be used.

"I somehow ended up in the Land Where No One Dares to Live. I can see why it is called that. There, I met a lot of funny looking people. Well, they weren't people, I guess. They were large, strange monkey-like creatures that talked. They were pleasant enough at first. But after a while, they began to turn nasty. They frequently fought, were horribly greedy, and continually craved all the things I wanted to leave behind. For a few weeks they played up to me because they thought I would give them all sorts of gold and money and perfume and TVs and mobile phones and laptop computers. All those things. And they didn't even have electricity! I suppose it didn't matter to them. I told them I didn't have anything anymore. So they got really mad and threatened me with all sorts of consequences if I didn't give them what they wanted. I sneaked out in the middle of the night with a few hired porters and ended up in the Great Desert.

"We traveled over the desert taking the trade route and just managed to survive. I must have lost twenty kilos in weight. We were almost across the desert, when off in the distance, I saw those creatures I was talking about. They were walking like an army across the sand. My porters saw them and fled in fright, leaving me all alone in the middle of an open desert with no place to hide. There wasn't even a large rock to go behind. I was in the part that was all sand dunes. Those creatures were moving faster than I ever could have. I was in a real bind. I didn't want to have anything to do with their leader anymore."

"Kjaz-Barbaroi is his name," interrupted Kasuku.

"Yes, that was it. Thought he was pretty important. Called himself 'Emperor' and 'King' and 'High Chief'. I didn't believe any of it."

"He is those things to some," said Pachunga. "But not to us."

"I should hope not! He once gave me a long, hard look that made me feel all creepy-crawly inside. This was when I was back in the Land Where No One Dares to Live. He told me: 'One day, Muriel Sniggins, you will meet me again. You will hear my Drum. You will come to me.'

"Ohhhh, did that make me feel awful. I felt like I had been listening to Death himself. Go to him? Never! With that, he left me standing there in his stone palace—er, whatever it was. I knew that I was no longer his guest. But this hasn't much to do with my story. Where was I?"

"Where?" asked Pachunga. "In the Great Desert, I think. Your porters had all run away, and you had no place to hide."

"Yes, that was it. There I was with nowhere to go, and I thought, 'Well, if I were an ostrich I could hide my head in the sand and maybe they wouldn't see me.' Ostriches don't do that, of course. The thought just gave me an idea. Using my helmet, I dug a big hole in the sand. Was that hard work! I nearly died from the heat. I mean, it was really that close. I kept thinking how stupid it was for all my searching to end this way. I would have disappeared without a trace. Those funny creatures would probably have had my body for their supper!

"Once the hole was dug, I lay down and tried to push all the sand over me. Only it didn't work. Did you know that it is impossible to bury yourself in the sand? I always had one arm that stuck out. And anyway, all that work had taken a lot of time. They knew that it was me out there, and they could see the boxes and crates the porters had dropped. So I had to be nearby. I kept the one arm that stuck out very still and had my helmet over my face to keep the sand out of my nose and mouth. I still swallowed a lot. Ugh.

"An advance group started yipping and yelping when they saw my arm sticking out. I kept it as still as I could.

"'Is she dead?' one of them asked excitedly.

"'No, I don't think so,' said another. He sounded disappointed. I could feel his hot breath on my arm as he sniffed it.

"They dug me up and left me sitting there until the rest of the army came along. In the meantime, the ones that found me began to fight each other over who would get credit for capturing me. They all thought that I was an escaped prisoner—which I really wasn't. Yuck! What a mess! Two of them were killed in the process and when, uh, what's-his-name arrived, he couldn't have cared less. He strolled over to me and very pompously stood in front of me. Giving me that death look again, he said, 'So, Muriel Sniggins, you want to find Meaning and Truth? Understand this. I am the only meaning and truth!' With that, he turned and left again—he and his army with him.

"I was left all alone in the desert. His band of rogues took all my things with them, too. All that was left was a bottle of water I had hidden away in the sand that somehow had escaped their notice. I thought to myself that he, of all things, could not be Meaning and Truth. If he was, then there was no point in living anymore. He seemed black with dirt—like he needed a bath or something. And he definitely needed to brush his teeth. Imagine that! Giving Truth a bath and brushing Meaning's teeth! Well, I suppose if you could actually hold them in your hands. I once had to…"

And Muriel was off for several minutes talking about things that were neither here nor there—nor anywhere in between. Pachunga and Kasuku continued to listen patiently. The more Muriel talked, the more fascinating she became.

Muriel finally got back to her story. "Back in the desert, it had become night, and it was very cold. My jacket and blankets had been taken by those vagabond animals. I collapsed in a heap and cried and cried. I am glad that my children weren't there to see me. They would have been embarrassed if they had. I would have been a disappointment to them. I must have gone crazy. I kept repeating over and over again: 'All that is love, all that is Meaning and Truth, all that is Good and Perfect come and help me…help me!'

"The next thing I knew, it was morning. And the strangest thing happened. An old man—er, a young one, I couldn't really tell—came up to me from over a sand dune and asked me for a drink of water. He was dressed in a simple robe and carried a staff. Around his neck were some beautiful necklaces of different colors carved from pieces of wood. He had a number of similar bracelets on both arms, too. But the most distinctive thing he was wearing was an ebony pendant–like a medallion– that was intricately carved in a beautiful and complicated pattern. It was something to see. My eye was drawn to it immediately."

She took a breath and remembered what she was really talking about. "Well, can you imagine that he asked me for a drink of water? There I was, out in the middle of the Great Desert with only a liter of water to my name. The sun was already hot. I was very thirsty, and this man comes along and asks me for a drink! The nerve! Didn't he think that I might have needed it?

"But you know, when he spoke, I was suddenly filled with fear and respect and reverence and love and peace. I thought, 'Muriel Sniggins, this man is bigger than any man you have ever known.' So I couldn't help but give him a drink. Any selfish thought I had disappeared. I knew I had to give him my water to drink.

"He took a long and satisfying drink and my heart sank as I saw him finish all that was in the bottle. My last hope for survival had disappeared down his gullet. I began to cry again.

"'Why are you crying?' he asked me.

"I said, 'Now I don't have any more water.'

"He said, 'Be patient. You will have all the water that you will ever need. What you are looking for is quite close to you.'

"'There is an oasis nearby?' My hopes were rising.

"'I am talking about something more important than ordinary water. I am talking about Meaning and Truth, as you call it.'

"'So you know what I am looking for!' He was getting more and more interesting as he went along, I must say.

"'I know what you are seeking and that you don't know quite how to find it. Cross this desert and the Great Grassland after it. You will come to a river. Follow the river to the High Falls—you won't miss them—and wait there. There are some people in the caves next to the Falls who will look after you.'

"'But how—?' I started to ask. Only for some reason I couldn't see him very well anymore. It must have been the glare off the white sand, for he was gone. "'I am really done for now,' I thought to myself. I was almost tempted to give up right then and there without moving from the spot where he left me. But he had been so hopeful and reassuring when he had talked to me—and he had acted so certain that I would make it to the High Falls. I began to walk in the direction that he wanted me to go. I struggled wearily to the top of the high hill of sand and couldn't believe what I saw.

"There, at the bottom of the dune was a camel, complete with saddle, blankets, and other provisions. It was drinking from a water hole in an oasis. I thought at first I was seeing things. That's supposed to happen in the desert, you know. But when I got down to the bottom of the hill,

I realized that the camel and the oasis were real, all right. I knew that the camel wasn't what's-his-name's. It must have belonged to the other fellow who had spoken with me. He wasn't in sight. And somehow, I knew that the camel was for me. You know, I've often wondered what would have happened if I had not given that man a drink..."

She stopped talking and thought to herself for a few moments. A small smile came to her lips and her eyes became distant. Then she finished her story.

"I filled some animal skins with fresh water, loaded them on the camel's back, and set off across the desert and then the Great Grassland. I traveled for many, many days. Didn't see a soul. I did sometimes see the places where what's-his-name and his army had camped. In the Great Grassland there were a lot of vultures picking over piles of bones and rotting meat. Bones from what, I don't know. I made sure I didn't get close enough to find out."

Pachunga shivered at the thought of what the vultures might have been eating.

"All the while, I kept wondering if that man was crazy. But there was something that rang true about him. You know what I mean? So I went on and on, going through more and more dangerous country. There were lions, jackals, and plenty of vultures. Once I saw a great herd of elephants and another of wildebeests. And a rhinoceros gave me a pretty good scare once. But I made it. Who would have thought it possible?

"I found the Falls. At the base there was this big cave. The Cave People took me in. They're kind of quiet and gave me funny, whispering looks. They still do, but they're good hosts—Mwenda and Mwema especially. Most of them didn't seem to say anything one way or the other. I asked some of them about this man I met in the desert, and they didn't know much. Some of them thought that it might have been O-something-or-other. I didn't know the name at the time. Mwema and Mwenda were the only two who were certain of it. Several of the Cave People began to argue with those who said that he was O-something-or-other—saying that he was dead. Another group said that he never existed at all. Anyway, I left them, and Mwenda and Mwema guided me up here and told me that the man who had helped me was named Olugbala. They've been taking care of me ever since. Between them and

62

Kasuku I've learned a lot about Olugbala. And then I discovered this morning that I was back to being a young girl again—like thirty years younger. It's very odd—but very nice. I have my whole life in front of me again!"

"That is a wonderful story!" exclaimed Pachunga. "But you have been through a lot!"

"It seems like nothing now—like a dream from the past. I'm a girl now, so I'd better start acting like one. There is a lot I have to learn."

Kasuku walked across the table and stopped in front of Muriel. "We—Pachunga and I—are on our way to meet Olugbala and to raise an army to fight against Kjaz-Barbaroi. It may be a long, hard journey, for it is possible that we will have to go all the way to his Mountain. You have met him once already because he must need you to help us out. There can be no other explanation. What we will be doing is important, and I know that Olugbala would want you to join us."

"I would love to," she said. Her eyes were bright with excitement. "That is, if it's okay with Chief Pachunga."

"It's fine," he said. "And you don't have to call me Chief." Pachunga was a little surprised at himself for saying that, because he would have considered it the respectful thing for this Mzungu to say. But somehow it didn't seem that important right now.

"Why, thank you," said Muriel. She was pleased and acted as if a king had just told her she could call him by his first name, which actually was true.

"It's time for us to go," said Kasuku in a whisper. "But do not mention anything aloud about our leaving this room to escape. We don't want anyone to know it."

"Perhaps I shouldn't have talked so long," said Muriel.

"No, that was all right. But change quickly into the new clothes that Mwema brought you earlier. Your old clothes won't do."

Muriel laughed. "You're right about that. I should have changed an hour ago." She picked up a beautiful piece of red and white cloth that was made by the Cave People and went through the same door the food came from.

"I'm getting worried," said Kasuku. "It's been too quiet. Something is up."

"Then we really must go," said Pachunga. He rose from the table.

Muriel appeared with the cloth wrapped around her in native fashion. Although it fit snugly, the folds of cloth were loose enough to make the garment cool, even in the hot sun. She was pensive as she looked at Kasuku. "Don't you think we should wait for Mwenda and Mwema?"

"I really think—" Kasuku started to say, but he was interrupted when a Cave Person burst through the door with a wild look of alarm in her eyes and on her face.

"Mwema! What is it?" asked Muriel.

"They're coming for you all! Dark Creatures! The word is out that there is a high reward on Pachunga's head. Chief Mkumbo is having a meeting of all the inhabitants of the caves to offer our allegiance to Kjaz-Barbaroi. As a show of loyalty, he has instructed the Palace Guard to assist the Dark Creatures in finding Pachunga. But this is taking too much time to explain! You must get out of here while there is still a chance!"

Pachunga was so flabbergasted that he couldn't move.

"Who—? What—? I don't understand," he babbled.

"Come, Pachunga!" Kasuku's voice was stern. "We must do everything Mwema says."

"I'll get my things," said Muriel.

"No time for that now," said Mwema in her bravest sounding whisper. She was really afraid. "Mwenda is waiting for us at the entrance of the Old Tunnel. He's knocking down the stone wall that is blocking it. It is the only way to get you safely away. Let's go—please!"

They were out the door in an instant. Mwema was in the lead. Muriel and Pachunga followed. Kasuku came last and looked behind him from time to time as he flew. He used his sensitive parrot ears to listen to the sounds of an approaching enemy.

Tunnel followed tunnel. Passageway followed passageway.

They passed cave after cave. Each was lit by that strange green-blue light. Pachunga could not wait to see the brightness of their sun instead of this strange light. It wasn't natural. He wanted very much, too, to breathe air that was fresh and pure—and to feel a light breeze on his cheek. He did not like caves.

There was no one to be seen. They were all at the meeting. There had to be Palace Guards and Dark Creatures behind them, though.

"What's the Old Tunnel?" asked Pachunga as they hurried along.

"It's the tunnel that is believed to be haunted by the spirits and ghosts of the Tall Men. They are destined to stay trapped until the Drum beats no more. We must remember one thing. We cannot be afraid of them if we encounter them. If we show any fear, they will have us in their power."

Mwema's face was serious and steady, yet her eyes did not appear as strong as the words she was speaking. She knew this. But she also knew that the courage she needed would come at the right time from Olugbala.

"Who is this Chief Mkumbo?" asked Pachunga.

"He is Chief of all the people living in these caves. And he is declaring war right now against the enemies of Kjaz-Barbaroi and all evil destroyers of freedom—"

"Us? Evil destroyers of freedom?" protested Pachunga. "How can they think that we—"

"Pachunga," said Kasuku from the rear, "people who are corrupt and see only Kjaz-Barbaroi do not see the Truth as we do. In their eyes, we are the evil destroyers of their freedom."

"Well they really have that backwards," said Muriel.

"Yes, they do," replied Kasuku.

Mwema went on. "They will gather at sunset. Even though we live in caves, we do know when the sun is shining outside. There is talk of all the young warriors joining with Kjaz-Barbaroi and fighting with him. The Drum, I'm afraid, has been beating long and loud in the hearts of my people."

Since Mwema was in front, no one was able to see the tears slowly dribbling down her cheeks. She dared not brush them away for fear of being noticed.

The group went on silently for over an hour. Muriel was traveling through parts of the cave system that she had not seen in her ascent to the circular room that had been her residence for the past few days. She had been told by Mwema's husband, Mwenda, that the Cave People had been allied with Olugbala—at least in name—until recently. In fact, the greatest desertion had taken place in the past couple of weeks when the Drum had started to beat and the Dark Creatures had come and told them of the diamonds that were in the Kiritiri mines. "They will all be yours," the Dark Creatures had promised. However, Mwenda, being a lower government official, had learned accidentally that the Dark Creatures and the Bazungu were more interested in having Cave People work in the mines once the Kiritiris died off.

They were short and squat and thrived underground. While they were descendants of the Tall Men, each generation had become progressively smaller and smaller as they adapted to living in caves. They talked in whispers most of the time. And they could run up and down the passageways in between rooms on little legs like two-legged gophers. Because they rarely saw the sun, their dark skin had paled considerably to the color of milky coffee. Even their hair was no longer a pure black due to the foods they ate. Their eyes were good in the dark and in the blue-green light that came from special, domesticated glowworms. The only time that they would emerge from the caves—except in an emergency—would be between sunset and sunrise. When the first morning light crept over the horizon, those who were outside would quickly scamper back into the security of their caves.

Mwema was trying to go as fast as she could—and she was doing very well—but Pachunga wanted to go faster. His legs were longer. Every second wasted in the passageways out of the Old Tunnel seemed to bring them closer and closer to discovery and capture. Surely the guards and the Dark Creatures would have found the circular room empty by now and were following the same path after them. One hope that they had was that the Palace Guards would not think that they would be trying to escape down the Old Tunnel. To their simple minds, it would mean escaping to their deaths. They would be looking for them along the routes that led to the main entrance to the caves at the bottom of the cliff.

"We're almost there," said Mwema. "It's just ahead. It won't be long."

These were the words everyone wanted to hear.

"Too soon is not soon enough," said Muriel. "I was never one for much walking—except when I have to, of course."

"That's the old Muriel talking," said Kasuku. "You're young now."

"I know, but—"

"Shh!" whispered the parrot. He had just heard the sound of someone who was probably not a friend. He zoomed ahead to Mwema. "Stop!"

She stopped.
Pachunga and Muriel stopped.
"Listen!"
Mwema heard them. Pachunga and Muriel did, too.
"Bazungu!"
"Yes," said Kasuku. "And they're coming this way!"
What were they going to do?

The Bazungu

"Yes," said Muriel. "What are we going to do?"

Pachunga turned to Mwema for advice. "Is there a way around them?"

"No, there's not."

"They might hear us if we turn and run. We cannot go back the way we have come," said Kasuku. "And who knows where the Dark Creatures are now."

"The Bazungu are almost here—just around the bend," said Pachunga. "Somebody's got to do something!"

An idea was forming in Muriel's head. It was not a complete one, but she figured that she would make things up as they went along. "You wait right here and don't make a sound."

Before anyone could do anything, she was walking down the passageway toward the Bazungu. When she rounded the bend she discovered there were two of them. One was short and squat. The other was tall and thin. She didn't know it, but the first one was Dr. Snippet, and the second one was Snipe.

"Oh, hello!" said Muriel with a note of surprise in her voice. She was acting, of course. "Real people at last." It was a terrible thing to say, but Muriel knew that in the case of the two Bazungu it was the best way to keep them from becoming suspicious.

"Why, hello," said Snippet. "How do you do?" His voice sounded weak and gave Muriel the impression that he did not have authority over anyone. This was true. Snippet did everything that Snipe and Kjaz-Barbaroi told him to do.

"What are you doing here?" demanded Snipe. He was not polite. He was also naturally suspicious of anyone whom he met. It was how he stayed alive. "It's not often that we find a little girl in these parts." He glared menacingly at Muriel. This kind of behavior usually caused people to give him the answers he sought.

Muriel was caught off guard. This man was very dangerous. She wasn't used to thinking of herself as eleven and she was not prepared to be interrogated so aggressively. "I'm, uh, here with my-my p-parents," said Muriel thinking quickly. It was the first thing that came out of her mouth and she immediately regretted it. She didn't want to lie, but the words were coming out anyway. And she immediately knew that she was not convincing. The entire plan was crumbling around her and she could not think of a way to pull herself out of the hole she was digging.

"Th-They've been sent down here by the University." She had another thought. "They have to study the anthropological and sociological differences between the Cave People and the Cattle People. You know, to, uh, study how they have been modified to fit their environments because of the various stimuli they have been receiving and the conditions to which they—"

"Oh, yes," interrupted Snippet, nodding his head up and down.

His neck had recovered from the strain he had put it through back at the Village when Pachunga had escaped. "I know all about that sort of thing. A fascinating study. It's not geology—which is my specialty, of course—but—"

"That's enough of that," said Snipe. He had to remain in control. He stared at Muriel intently. "How do you come to know so much? You're only a little girl."

"Uh, I'm older than I look?" It was the first truthful thing she had said. She really was not good at lying. She needed to get the conversation away from herself. "What are you two doing here?" She asked the question as sweetly and innocently as she could.

"We work for the Company," said Snippet proudly.

"You do? That must be very important work." She made herself sound much more enthusiastic than she felt. Her second husband had once owned a large part of it and had been on its board of directors.

"It is," said Snippet. "We were sent over here to see how good a work force these Cave People will make in the mines over in the Kiritiri lands."

In the meantime, Pachunga, Mwema, and Kasuku were all listening to the conversation very carefully. When Pachunga heard what Snippet had said, his entire body stiffened and he reached for his knife. He was very angry. Angry enough to kill. It was bad enough that they had stumbled across Snippet and Snipe, but what did it mean that the Cave People would start working in the mine? It meant that the Kiritiris would be replaced once they died off or maybe were even exterminated because they were no longer useful. That was the way of the Company. The Drum by this time beat in the recesses of his being. He crouched down low, ready to turn the corner and pounce on his adversaries. He despised these foreigners—these Bazungu—and more than anything else, he wanted to end their lives then and there.

Kasuku could tell what was going through Pachunga's mind. "No!" Kasuku said firmly but quietly into Pachunga's ear. "That is the way of the Drum. Wait and see what Muriel can do."

Kasuku's voice broke through the cloud of hate that encircled Pachunga. The Drum was silent in his head. But he still was convinced that what he wanted to do was better. These Bazungu were evil and could do a lot of damage.

Muriel was talking. "The Cave People should be right at home in the mine."

"Ideally suited," said Snippet.

"Like moles they are," said Snipe. A thought came to him—which was unusual. "We've been looking for that outlaw Pachunga, he's—"

"Pachunga!?!" exclaimed Muriel too loudly. "Darn! That was foolish," she thought to herself when she realized what she'd said.

"So you've heard about him?" questioned Snipe. He suspected this girl of hiding or knowing something even more.

Muriel was scared. She could blow it all for them. "Uh, h-hasn't everybody?"

"Oh, yes! Everybody's heard of him," agreed Snippet. Snipe wasn't being very polite to this girl and he wanted her to know that he, at least, wouldn't ask questions that seemed to be embarrassing her. She was just a little girl, after all. "He has an extremely bad reputation, you know. Was said to have killed thousands of women and children in his earlier days and forced his people into slavery. I'd believe it. I had to deal with the maniac back in his Village. He was definitely the most evil person I have ever met."

"Slander!" said Pachunga under his breath. He had his knife out again.

"Their lies cannot hurt you!" pleaded Kasuku.

Snipe's head jerked up and he stared down the passageway beyond Muriel. "What was that noise? There is someone there!"

Snipe was wearing a holster that held a very powerful pistol. He unfastened the leather flap and fingered the handle of the gun nervously. He gave Muriel a probing look. Only one of Snipe's eyes met hers, because the other turned out like a wall-eyed pike. Muriel no longer felt scared. She was terrified.

"Voices? I-I didn't hear any voices. It's probably just the bats. There are, uh, dozens of them, you know. Uh, vampire bats." She looked right at Snippet when she said that. She thought she could frighten him—or at least worry him—more easily than Snipe.

She was right. His face went white. The blue-green light made his skin look deathly sick. Snippet was afraid of bats. His older brothers used to lock him up in the attic in his house, and bats were the only creatures to keep him company. Their droppings would fall into his hair—when he had had hair. They would fly around him when disturbed, and he was always afraid of being bitten.

"V-Vampire bats?" he stammered. He put his hand to his head to make sure his pith helmet was there to protect him. In his mind, he could imagine the entire passageway filling with bats and attacking him. "M-Maybe w-we'd b-better go b-back to Chief M-Mkumbo's m-m-m-meeting!"

Snipe remained very quiet. He was not going to leave. He knew that there were no bats—especially of the vampire variety. They lived on a continent on the other side of the ocean. Snipe had to learn something about this girl, and a plan came to mind—a plan that involved a Palace Guard with burly, hairy arms whom he had recently met. "Yes," said Snipe very slowly. "Yes, I think we'd better be getting over to that meeting." He continued to stare at Muriel. The corners of his mouth turned down toward his chin. He did not believe any of it.

Snippet sighed with relief.

Whatever hope Muriel had for getting them out of this situation disappeared in an instant. Snipe knew that she was hiding something. She groaned inwardly and did her best to avoid Snipe's one eye that was staring at her. She should not have said anything about vampire bats. The suggestion had worked with Snippet, but Snipe was the one to worry about. He did not look the least afraid of bats, though she was glad that he had said that he was leaving. All she could hope for was that she had bought them all enough time to get away.

"Are you going to the meeting?" Snipe asked Muriel. He made his glare as penetrating as possible.

"No, I don't think so," she said. "I-I have some lessons to prepare for my mother who's tutoring me since there're no schools here."

"Oh, I see," said Snipe dubiously. "I would have thought that your mother would be attending the meeting if she is here in the caves with your father." He continued to stare at her.

"Uh, you know," said Muriel, grasping once again for something to say. "S-S-School comes first."

"Yes, I guess it would." Snipe's one eye continued to probe her face, looking for some kind of reaction that would give her away.

Snippet saved the day once again. "Let's get out of here!" he exclaimed. He had had enough talk about schools and meetings. He didn't want to be around any bats should they show up.

"Yeah, sure," said Snipe. "See you around, kid."

"Yeah, see you around," said Muriel.

The two Bazungu turned around and headed toward a tunnel that would eventually take them to the central part of the caves and Chief Mkumbo's meeting. Yet, when they had disappeared out of sight, Snipe told Snippet to go on.

"What are you going to do?" asked Snippet. He wasn't sure he wanted to walk alone through the caves, even though he was in a more developed area.

"Don't you worry about me. I have something I have to do."

"But what about the vampire bats?" asked Snippet.

"There are no vampire bats here. They don't even live on this continent, you imbecile! Now, go!"

Snippet moved hurriedly along to the meeting muttering to himself. He was more confused than ever. Snipe frequently did illogical things.

Snipe, for his part, remained hidden and waited and watched. But he wouldn't do anything...yet. He knew that he would be rewarded in a few minutes.

* * * *

When the two Bazungu had gone, Muriel returned to her friends. She was crying and trembling with fear. She knew she had given them all away. Snipe might not know exactly what was going on, but his suspicions had definitely been aroused. "I blew it. I said all the wrong things and now Snipe knows that something is up. You should have seen the look the tall one gave me. You heard what he said. He knows I know you, Pachunga. And he probably thinks that you are nearby. I've really made a mess of things. I wish—"

Kasuku cut her off. "There is no point going through all this now. We have to get to the Old Tunnel."

"We must go in all haste," said Mwema. "There will always be dangers no matter where we are. We can't stand around and talk about it!" She brightened. "So, hurry! Mwenda is probably ready and waiting for us!"

* * * *

Snipe heard some noise and some low conversation. Soon, a Cave Person, that strange girl, a parrot and a Kiritiri boy came into sight. There was no old man with them. He fully expected to see Pachunga. Now he was confused. This didn't make any sense. Where was that old geezer? For the moment that did not matter so much. At least he could do something about this group. They were definitely up to something and needed to be eliminated. But first, he had to find the guard with the hairy arms.

* * * *

Mwema, Muriel, Pachunga and Kasuku slowly and quietly passed the entrance to the tunnel which Snipe and Snippet had just gone down. It went ahead to their right and then curved slowly to the left. Ahead of them was a tunnel that was obviously not heavily used. It was dirty, dusty and cluttered with every kind of broken, old, rotting, dried-out junk that you could imagine. The musty odor reminded Muriel of the way her gym locker used to smell at the end of the year when she was in school. Symbols of death had been painted on the walls—skulls and bones and the faces of people in torment and agony. The pictures proved to be effective warnings: they were doing a good job of discouraging the group and increasing their fear. This was definitely a dangerous place, but they knew that they had to go through there.

The last part of a journey always seems the longest, and Pachunga, Kasuku and Muriel felt no differently. It seemed as though they would never get there.

"We're never going to get there," said Pachunga bitterly.

"Can't we stop for a break?" asked Muriel.

"It's only a little bit more," said Mwema.

"Patience!" said Kasuku. It seemed like that was his favorite word.

Pachunga wanted to throw something at him the next time he said it. He was scared and that was making him grumpy because he did not want to admit that he was afraid.

"We will be there and beyond before you know it," added the parrot.

Even Muriel was getting tired of his cheerleading. They went around one more bend, and there, twenty meters in front of them, was Mwenda. The tunnel ended in a wall of stone, and Mwenda was making an opening in it. There were more skulls and bones painted all around the wall—and someone had added a few real skulls stuck on the ends of wooden poles. The blue-green light was dim here. Mwenda had three torches with him so that he could see what he was doing.

"Mwema!" exclaimed Mwenda.

"Mwenda!" exclaimed Mwema.

They embraced and gave each other several affectionate kisses.

"I'm glad you made it," said Mwenda. "You took a long time. I was beginning to worry." He kissed Mwema again—this time on the end of her nose. Mwenda was only a centimeter taller than Mwema and had the same bright smile. As with his wife, there was a sweetness about him that made you want to be his friend. He was known for his cheerfulness and could entertain people for hours with his jokes. His eyes were always sparkling with the joy that comes from being in Olugbala's service. A smile was never far away—even when he was sad. Mwenda always managed to make others smile, too.

He looked at the rest of the group. Kasuku and Muriel he recognized. He did not know who the Kiritiri boy was who was standing there. "I am Mwenda," he said formally.

"I am Pachunga."

"Pachunga? Is your father Chief Pachunga?"

"No, I am he."

Mwenda was confused. "Then you have to be his son, because his valor in the Battle of a Thousand Cries many rainy seasons ago is widely remembered. You could not possibly be that old."

"I am one and the same," said Pachunga.

"Now I understand," he said. "May Olugbala be blessed!" He suddenly felt self-conscious about the famous person who was standing in front of him. "I never expected to meet the great Chief of the Kiritiri peoples. I would welcome you here to our Caves—though I know that you are now anxious to leave them."

"I hope that one day I can return when there is no more war and your people are at peace with each other and with Olugbala."

Pachunga said all of this in his best diplomatic manner. It was one of the things he had had to learn in order to be Chief.

Kasuku was eager to dispense with the formalities. They had their place, but they were now a waste of precious time. "We must work."

Pachunga helped Mwenda. They would take turns using a thick wooden pole to pry the stones loose. They were held together by old, crumbling mortar. To Mwenda's dismay, he had learned that the wall was very thick. There was not just one layer of rocks, but four. He had penetrated all of them, but the opening in layers two to four was only ten centimeters wide. There was a lot to be done if they were to fit through. Mwenda figured that each layer of rock had been built at a different time. He hoped that it was because the older walls had started to fall apart. The oldest layer had been constructed during the time of Mamosa the Elephant.

"I'm glad that I am smaller than I used to be," said Muriel. "So am I," said Mwenda. He didn't want any extra work. There was no time.

"Is there anything I can do to help?" asked Mwema. There was only enough room for two at the wall.

"You'd better go back around the bend and stand guard. But don't go too far. And don't let anyone see you."

"Oh, I won't. Don't worry." She looked at her husband with concern. "You'll be all right here?" He had already been working a long time by himself, and his small body looked tired.

"I'm fine," Mwenda smiled.

Mwema felt better about leaving him. And she was glad to have something to do.

"Pachunga and Muriel can stay and help me here," he went on. "Kasuku, why don't you go through the opening and see what's there. You might want to stand—er, perch—guard. Who knows what's living in there."

"Right," said Kasuku. He disappeared through the small hole that Mwenda had already made.

Mwema went off down the tunnel, feeling confident that they all were going to make it. She began to hum a little song she had written about Olugbala. Pachunga and Mwenda continued to work. But the stones and the mortar seemed indestructible. They pounded at them with hammers made out of ironstone and pried at the rocks with the wooden pole until their hands were red and stinging. After one sharp blow, the handle of the hammer broke, and Pachunga could only use the stone head. Even though it was cool, perspiration covered their foreheads and bare backs. Small drips formed streams that flowed down their bodies and moistened the stone floor beneath their feet. Pachunga was continually reminded of the Kiritiri people. They were working in the mine for the Bazungu and for Kjaz-Barbaroi. He had only been working for a short time. His people had to labor from before sunrise to after sunset. Pachunga ignored his fatigue.

Mwema, at her post, was anxiously walking from one side of the passageway to the other. She listened not only for the sound of an approaching enemy, but also for the signal to come when the opening to the Old Tunnel was made. She was worried—yes. But as she thought of Olugbala and hummed her song to herself, she was also filled with a very comforting peace. She could sense even more how great Olugbala truly was and that he had everything under control. She wished that she were in a position to watch Mwenda work, but she knew that she had to stay at her post. A pebble clattered on the stone floor, and she looked at it quickly. It had not fallen from the ceiling on its own. It was meant to distract her. She started to turn around, but never made it.

A hairy arm—a really hairy and bristly and coarse and dirty one—grabbed her from behind. She was yanked up against her attacker's chest. In a voice that smelled of garlic and beer, this monster—he had to have been a monster to do what he did—snarled quietly: "If you—heh-heh-heh-heh—say one word, then you'll be deader than a...uh...well, you'll be very dead!" The hairy-armed attacker, a soldier from Chief Mkumbo's Palace Guard—couldn't think of something that was very dead, so he just left it at that.

Mwema thought rapidly. Peace came to her. She knew what she had to do. "They're coming!" she cried. "They're—"

She said no more.

There was not even a scream.

"Mwema!" yelled Mwenda. She was in trouble. He clenched the wooden stick in his fists and ran toward her.

"Mwenda!" shouted Pachunga. He lunged after him, but missed, landing in a pile of stones. "Wait! It's too late!" He was familiar with the ways of the Enemy.

"Oh, no!" cried Muriel. It was all too terrible for words.

"Mah-wee-mah!" Mwenda's scream was something they would remember for the rest of their lives.

Kasuku was there. He knew what was happening, though he couldn't do anything about it. Instead, all anyone of them could do was to listen to the last words that Mwenda ever said in this life.

"Run, Pachunga! Run! Flee, all of you! May Olugbala be wi—"

There was a scream.

There was silence.

Then there was that sickening, awful laughter that made them all think of the worst possible evil. It was dark laughter. It was black laughter. It was the laughter of jealousy and hate and disease and murder and death and corpses.

Pachunga knew who it was.

It was Kjaz-Barbaroi.

CHIEF MKUMBO

"Pachunga!"

Pachunga thought quickly. The opening into the Old Tunnel was still small. But maybe he and Muriel could fit through. Kasuku, of course, would have no problem. One thing was certain. He would not be drawn into any conversation with Kjaz-Barbaroi. It was better to ignore him and pretend he wasn't there. Then he remembered his flight from the Village. Doubt filled him about his trip and the task that he had to undertake. Should he be making this journey? Look at what had just happened to Mwema and Mwenda. Perhaps it would be better to give it all up. Feelings of hopelessness, frustration and failure began to grow within him. The trouble and torment never seemed to end. No matter how hard he tried, he could never get away from Kjaz-Barbaroi and his evil work.

"Pachunga!"

The voice came like the crack of an earthquake down the tunnel. So far, Kjaz-Barbaroi had not rounded the bend and met Pachunga face to face. They had not looked upon each other since the Battle of a Thousand Cries.

"I know you're too much of a coward to answer me, so I'll tell you your options directly. You can then make a choice. I'm very fair about these sorts of things." He must have been excited about what he was going to say, for he was panting and growling gleefully between words.

Pachunga felt anger rising up inside of him when he heard Kjaz-Barbaroi calling him a coward. He also became aware of the Drum beating slowly, steadily and quietly. It threatened to beat louder.

"Pachunga," whispered Kasuku in his ear. "Don't listen to him. Do not let him get you angry this way. That is exactly what he wants."

Pachunga agreed. The Drum stopped.

"What are you going to do?" asked Muriel. She was trying to stand as close to Pachunga and Kasuku as she could.

Their adversary continued: "You have two options: You can do nothing else, because you are trapped. The first option is that you can die. You can either be imprisoned here until you starve to death, or I could send in Mkumbo's guards and they could kill you all now. It makes no difference. Either way, you are just as dead."

Pachunga pointed to the small opening that he and Mwenda had made in the stone wall and said, "Go on through. You should fit."

Kjaz-Barbaroi kept talking. "The second option would be for you to give up this silly trip of yours and seek Olugbala no more. You can come and join forces with me. I know that you have no use for wealth and that power does not interest you." Kjaz-Barbaroi was speaking rationally, and Pachunga was surprised at how calm the creature was. His voice did not contain the usual yips and yowls. "You are above that. Power and wealth are only for those who do not see reality as we see it—who know nothing of unseen powers. You are too sensible to fall prey to their little struggles and petty power plays. I will give you something more." He stopped there for the dramatic effect and waited for a count of three.

Without realizing what he was doing, Pachunga began to take small, slow steps towards the sound of the voice. The ruler was making sense for once and was appealing to Pachunga's good reason. Kjaz-Barbaroi made his final offer: "I will give you back your people—the Kiritiris—and you will be allowed to live in peace for the rest of your days. I will bother you no more..."

The Chief tried to ignore those words. He knew he should not listen to them—that they were all a trick—but he could not force them out of his head. When he heard that he could have his people back and that he could live in peace—it was too good to be true. It was what he wanted. Kjaz-Barbaroi would make everything right again, and he would not have the shame of having permitted the Bazungu to come in and change everything. The Drum was beating again. Only it was a pleasant sound. It promised rest and peace. He was getting tired of the entire escapade. There was no way that he or Kasuku would ever succeed in what Olugbala wanted them to do

"Pachunga!" It was Kasuku. "Muriel is through! Come! It's your turn!"

"Muriel?" asked Pachunga. He had been listening to the Drum. "Oh, Muriel. Yes. She's through, you say? Where? Ah, the Old Tunnel. I remember. What's that?" He looked in the direction of Kjaz-Barbaroi's voice. "I was just thinking of something else." The strangest expression came over his face.

Kasuku knew that Pachunga was not himself and that the Drum had a very strong grip on him. Since there was very little time, he did something surprising. It was not very nice, but it helped a lot. Kasuku bit Pachunga's left ear lobe.

"Ow!" Pachunga faced Kasuku and hissed. "Kasuku! Why did you do that?" He touched his ear and felt the wetness of blood. "I'll get you for this!"

Pachunga stepped toward the bird, but Kasuku disappeared through the opening in the wall. Pachunga stuck his head and arms through the hole and grunted. It was very tight. He had to get that parrot. There was something solid in the dark that he was able to grasp, and he used it to pull himself through. The stones around him clung to him and seemed to tighten around him, as if trying to prevent him from entering. With a lot of determination and bad thoughts about Kasuku, he got through.

"There!" he exclaimed triumphantly. "Now, where—?"

"Shhhh!" scolded Muriel. "You're making too much noise!"

Everything was dark and Pachunga could not see a thing but some light that came through the opening he had just passed through. His eyes adjusted quickly and he began to be able to see more.

"Pachunga, I want to apologize for biting you." Kasuku's voice came from somewhere to his right, although he could not yet see his friend in the gloom.

"Why did you do it?" Pachunga asked. It did not make any sense that Kasuku would bite him like that—but then he remembered that he had been listening to Kjaz-Barbaroi and the Drum. "Oh," he said apologetically. "I know why. I was listening too intently to Kjaz-Barbaroi."

"I'm sorry," said Kasuku, "but I had to take your mind away from him or all would have been lost."

Pachunga did not voice what he was feeling, but he was embarrassed about almost causing the mission to fail—again. How would he ever learn? And what would he be able to do if Kasuku weren't there to keep him on the right path?

Though they could not hear him anymore, Kjaz-Barbaroi was still talking. Now, it may be supposed that Kjaz-Barbaroi did not know of the possibility of escape into the Old Tunnel. He had not mentioned it as one of the options that Pachunga and the other two had in front of them. Kjaz-Barbaroi knew that if he had suggested to Pachunga that he escape down the Old Tunnel, he actually would not have done it. He knew humans too well. Pachunga would have tried to escape some other way. By not mentioning the Old Tunnel, Pachunga, Muriel, and Kasuku were going right where he wanted them to go. Kjaz-Barbaroi was smart about a lot of things. It was one of the reasons why he had become so powerful.

On the other hand, Kjaz-Barbaroi was not smart about everything. If he were, then he would have surrendered himself immediately to Olugbala and given up on being so evil. There was more to the Old Tunnel than what even Kjaz-Barbaroi knew about.

However, the intelligent and quick-thinking Chief Mkumbo (at least that was the way he considered himself to be) was another matter. Chief Mkumbo had come scurrying to the entrance of the Old Tunnel with Kjaz-Barbaroi after the meeting. The Chief measured one meter high and one meter around. He mistakenly thought that Kjaz-Barbaroi apparently was unaware of the Old Tunnel and was feeling more and more that he had to share that information with his boss. But Mkumbo was terrified of two things: one, Kjaz-Barbaroi and two, the Old Tunnel. At the moment, Kjaz-Barbaroi was the more terrifying because he was closer.

If he were truly honest with himself (which he never was), he would realize that the need to get nearer the Old Tunnel—let alone enter it—would be more terrible. He was rapidly recalling all the legends told about it. And the paintings of ghosts, spirits, ghouls and demons that covered the passageway were doing an excellent job of reminding him of the horrors that existed there.

Chief Mkumbo really wanted to interrupt Kjaz-Barbaroi and tell him about the Old Tunnel. And each time he had enough courage to get as close as he dared to tap him on the back at waist level (remember that Cave People are not very tall), he would think better of it suddenly. Then he would back away quickly. Then he would approach Kjaz-Barbaroi again—then back away again. If you were a fly on the ceiling looking down on this scene, it would be easy to imagine Mkumbo as a yo-yo going up and down a string held by Kjaz-Barbaroi.

Kjaz-Barbaroi was quite aware of the conflict that was going on in the small head of Chief Mkumbo. Mkumbo, of late, had been wavering in his support. The arrival of that Mzungu, Muriel, and the parrot had caused too many questions about Olugbala to float around the caves. All this angered him. He hated treason and he hated traitors. They were all so tiring and time-consuming—and just eliminating them was downright boring. He always had to think of some creative and new way to get rid of them—and that was getting too boring in itself. But Mkumbo, thought Kjaz-Barbaroi, was truly a lesser being. So it had to be expected of him. A little hocus-pocus would be all that it would take to discipline him. The leader of the Dark Creatures kept on talking until he was sure that Pachunga, Muriel and Kasuku were inside the Old Tunnel. For a moment, he had thought that he actually had Pachunga in his control. But something had happened. And he had sensed the presence of Olugbala.

"There," said Kjaz-Barbaroi. "We will not have to be thinking of them for a while. Some of my servants will do a good job on them."

He turned around to leave. But, as things went, Chief Mkumbo was making one of his cautious advances toward his boss.

Kjaz-Barbaroi was still thinking about Olugbala. He had not anticipated that Mkumbo would be right where he was.

The result was a collision.

And with Mkumbo being so low to the ground, Kjaz-Barbaroi tripped right over him and crashed—nose first—right onto the cave floor.

Now that was not dignified.

It really was most humiliating for all concerned.

Kjaz-Barbaroi's eyes flashed flames, and smoke puffed out of his mouth and nose. The guard with the hairy arms and the breath that smelled like garlic and beer happened to be the first living being that Kjaz-Barbaroi saw from his sprawled out position. With a snarl, a roar and a clap of thunder which loosed rocks from the ceiling, the hairy-armed guard dropped dead and exploded from toe to top.

It is not necessary to describe the mess that he made.

The rocks that fell down hit about fifteen Palace Guards on the head and knocked them silly for the rest of their days. They were so useless that the only thing they could do afterwards was run for public office. They are in government to this day.

Kjaz-Barbaroi was just about to explode Chief Mkumbo when a better idea came to him.

It really was a much, much better idea. He was so pleased with himself and his idea that he smiled.

And then he laughed.

And Chief Mkumbo, of course, was so certain that he was going to burst into tiny bits that he was one mass of quivering, quaking, shivering and shaking rolls of fat. Though he wasn't exactly crying, he was whimpering and babbling. He sounded something like: "Boo-ah, woo-ah, bloo-ah, bubba, glubba, gloo, gloo." His face had also turned white. Now for someone who was normally the color of *café au lait*, this was quite a feat.

Chief Mkumbo was also very confused. Kjaz-Barbaroi was laughing. He seemed to feel that the episode was one big joke. Since Mkumbo couldn't sit there and continue to make little scared noises, he decided it was safer if he laughed, too. "Heh-heh-heh-heh-heh," were the sounds that came in a rapid, high pitch from his throat. It was the best he could do under the circumstances.

It was all really very pathetic.

"Well, well, well," said Kjaz-Barbaroi warmly between chuckles and laughs. These laughs weren't the scary kind. They were designed to make Mkumbo feel relaxed. "That was quite a show, wasn't it?"

"Oh, yes! Oh, yes!" Mkumbo said, finding he could still form words. He nodded his head up and down like Snippet. That happened a lot with Kjaz-Barbaroi. Most people, whenever they met him, were all too eager to nod their heads up and down and repeat, "Oh, yes!"

And that is really even *more* pathetic.

"In fact, it was so funny that it has put me into a very humorous mood. It makes me want to do even funnier things."

"Oh, yes! Oh, yes! What would they be?" Mkumbo was all for Kjaz-Barbaroi thinking of something funnier. Maybe it would make him forget the little mishap.

"Pachunga, that Mzungu and that parrot have escaped into the Old Tunnel. I think it would be very amusing if you were to go in there after them." He turned and looked at Mkumbo. "Don't you?" He laughed again, only this wasn't the kind of laughter that made Mkumbo feel relaxed. It was nasty. Kjaz-Barbaroi stood up to his full height. For Chief Mkumbo, who was still on the floor, the effect was awful. Any hope for a happy outcome was dashed. He saw that he had no choice. Kjaz-Barbaroi was not the sort of creature ever to forgive anyone for anything.

Chief Mkumbo could think of nothing better to do than to start whimpering again. As he began to sit up awkwardly and stand, he began to realize even more what was ahead of him. The ghouls and specters and spirits of the Tall Men in the Tunnel came alive in his mind. He began to feel that being exploded at that instant would have been the better way to go.

Kjaz-Barbaroi had no patience for sniveling fools. "Go!" he ordered. "Go! And bring them back alive!"

Chief Mkumbo gathered what few wits he had left together with his remaining dignity. Behind the fear of Kjaz-Barbaroi that he saw on the faces of the Palace Guards, he saw contempt for himself. He knew that he had lost his honor in front of his people and that he would never be remembered as a great ruler. He no longer felt like the grand and glorious, all-worshipful chief he had been. He started to sob. Great wails of anguish came from between his fat lips.

With Kjaz-Barbaroi's glare prodding him on from behind, Chief Mkumbo walked hesitantly—not to mention slowly—toward the opening of the Old Tunnel.

In the meantime, Pachunga and Muriel were exploring the new cavern which they had just entered. They did not appear to be in a tunnel at all. It was more like a room. The ceiling was too high and the walls disappeared into the darkness on either side of the opening they had just passed through. Everything was wet and moldy smelling. Water dripped in numerous places from above. Some places had mud ankle deep on the floor. In one dry corner—the only spot that was dry–Muriel found some torches.

"Look here, Pachunga. We could sure use these. But I don't have any matches."

"I still have my fire stone," he said.

"Do we have to take the time to light them now?" she asked. All she could think about was Kjaz-Barbaroi and the Palace Guards right behind them.

"We can't go down the Tunnel in the dark," said Kasuku. "Those torches will be a blessing. Who knows what holes and cracks have formed over the years."

"And Mwenda and Mwema? Do you think they could be all right?"

The look on Pachunga's face answered the question for her. There was no hope that they would still be alive. She started to cry. It didn't seem fair that they had been killed. They were such sweet people, and they had done a lot for her.

"Remember them with joy in your heart for their sacrificial service to Olugbala," said Kasuku. "We can mourn them later. There is no time now."

"What about Kjaz-Barbaroi?" asked Pachunga.

"I think he thinks he got rid of us for good. He thinks he has a lot of power still in the Old Tunnel, but we can count on Olugbala to protect us from him—which he is doing right now. Er, at the same time, we should move away from the opening."

They moved a few meters away into a dark corner of the room. Two torches were soon lit. Pachunga and Muriel each held one. Light filled the entire room.

It was then that the clap of thunder from Kjaz-Barbaroi came. It loosed a few rocks above them. The shock threw Muriel and Pachunga onto the floor, and one of the torches went out. A piece of stone just missed Kasuku.

"What—What was that?" gasped Muriel.

"I—I don't know," said Pachunga.

"That was just Kjaz-Barbaroi showing his temper," said Kasuku. "Someone must have done something wrong."

"Let's get out of here, then," said Pachunga. He got to his feet and re-lit Muriel's torch with his own. "All set?"

"Yeah, I guess so," she said. She was still thinking about Mwema and Mwenda. "Which way do we go?" She hadn't seen any exit from the cave they were in. At first, she thought that they would all be trapped there—that the Old Tunnel was nothing but a wild story.

Pachunga moved his torch above his head in a slow circle to see where they would have to go. About ten meters in front of them, opposite the opening they had passed through, was the true beginning of the Old Tunnel. There was a way to get out, after all. What they were standing in was an anteroom which had probably been made to put the real entrance of the Old Tunnel even further apart from the cave system where the people lived. Around the rectangular entrance were some more carvings of the Ancient Empire. They were similar to the ones that Pachunga had seen when he had first entered the caves that morning. Seeing all those images of the Tall Men did not encourage him to want to go any further, but he knew that they had to. They carefully made their way across the room, avoiding any mud puddles they could, but in a few places they had to walk right through them. Muriel didn't like the way the mud squished through her toes.

Kasuku seemed to have had some experience with this Tunnel—or perhaps it was just experience with the way Kjaz-Barbaroi operated. "Now," said Kasuku. "No matter what we see when we get into the Tunnel, we cannot be afraid of it. Nothing can hurt us or touch us as long as we have no fear. Do not think of sad things or unpleasant things—they will fill you with so much despair that your very souls will be in danger. Above all, keep Olugbala's face in front of you. Think of him. Think of the times when you've seen him smile and laugh. Think happy thoughts. It will help you through any difficulty we might face."

Kasuku's words comforted them and filled them both with assurance. Fear. What was fear? At that time, it was an emotion that did not exist. They would get through. They were convinced of it.

"I'll go first if you want me to," said Kasuku.

"That would be—" Muriel started to say.

But just as Kasuku was about to pass through the opening, a noise came from behind them—from the opening they had passed through to get to where they were.

"Oof! Oh!" said someone. "I won't ever..." These words were followed by sounds of someone whimpering and a couple of snorts. Then there was a noise that sounded very much like a heavy duffel bag hitting the stone floor. The three of them turned around quickly. Who had come into the anteroom?

Lying in a heap by the knocked-out hole in the wall was Chief Mkumbo. How someone that wide had been able to get through the little opening remained a mystery for the rest of their lives.

"Chief Mkumbo! What are you doing here?" Muriel crossed to him and held her torch over him.

"Ahhhhhhhhhhhh! Ohhhhhhhhhhhhhh! Ahhhhhhhhhhhhh!" It was all that Mkumbo could say.

"It is only we," said Kasuku. "We won't hurt you."

"Ahhhhhhhhhhh! Ohhhhhhhhhhhhhh! Ahhhhhhhhhhhhh!" he repeated.

"Will you join us?" asked Pachunga.

Chief Mkumbo looked at the boy who was talking to him. Who could this one be? Since he was still so terrified of being in the Old Tunnel, he couldn't form the words to ask the question. He continued as before: "Ahhhhhhhh! Ohhhhhhhhhh!"

"He must have been sent here by Kjaz-Barbaroi," suggested Kasuku.

"What is your purpose here?" demanded Pachunga.

"Come with me! G-Get away! I-I'll g-g-get you all—including Pachunga! G-G-Go away! Kjaz-Barbaroi! Ohhhhhh! Ahhhhhhhh! Ohhhhhhhh! O-O-Olugbala? No? Yes?"

"He seems to be torn between Olugbala and Kjaz-Barbaroi," said Kasuku. "Mkumbo, we are your friends—your allies. We are not your enemies."

"Come with us," said Pachunga. "Be with us on the side of Olugbala."

"He is your only hope," said Muriel.

"N-No! N-Never! Yes! I-I don't know. I—? You—? Olugbala! Yes! Ahhhhh! The Tall Men! Th-Th T-Tall Men! Ahhhh! Noooooo! Nooooo!"

"There are powers at work here," observed Pachunga.

"Can't we do something? He is in such agony!" cried Muriel.

"If only he would join us!" said Pachunga.

"Reasoning with him won't work now," said Kasuku. "Kjaz-Barbaroi has too big a hold on him. It is all up to Olugbala and Mkumbo himself."

"You know what to do, then?" asked Pachunga. He moved near Chief Mkumbo, but was careful to stay out of the way of his flailing arms and legs.

"Yes," said Kasuku. He perched on top of Pachunga's head and spread his wings. In a loud voice he said: "By all the power and by the blessed name of Olugbala, be freed of the spirits of the dead and lost, Mkumbo! Be freed! Be freed through Olugbala!"

"Ahhhh! Ohhhh!" went Mkumbo. His body began to move and shake on the floor. Then, there was the loudest and longest cry that you ever would have heard had you been there.

And then there was quiet.

Mkumbo moaned. Everyone gathered near him.

He slowly opened his eyes and focused on the group staring down at him. "Uhhhhh...." he started to say. Then he swallowed and took a deep breath. A look of understanding and calm came to his face. "Th-Thank you. Thank you," said the Chief wearily. "It is true, isn't it? Olugbala is real. If only I had known sooner. If only I had known..."

"He is real," said Pachunga. "He is so real that we are almost not real in comparison to him."

Chief Mkumbo thought about that and then moaned. "What am I going to do now?" he asked. "I have lost all honor in front of my people. I'm sure they won't even listen to me anymore."

"Those who matter will listen to you, Mkumbo," said Kasuku. "You may have lost your pride. But by accepting Olugbala, you have all the honor you will ever need." He laughed. "Besides, you'll be a hero when they see you came out of the Old Tunnel alive!"

Mkumbo smiled. It was a new thought. But, once again, who was this boy?

"Where's Pachunga? I expected him to be with you," he asked.

Pachunga smiled. Being a boy instead of being an old man was kind of fun because he did not look like the person people expected. "I am he," said Pachunga. "You know how Muriel arrived as a woman in your caves and then woke up the next morning as a girl? Olugbala did the same thing for me just as I was leaving my Village with Kasuku."

"Oh, I understand," said Chief Mkumbo. He didn't really, but there was so much that was new that he really was getting confused. He hoped that Olugbala would not make him young, though. It would make things rather awkward for his wife and family.

"Mkumbo," said Pachunga. "It is only recently that your people have left Olugbala for Kjaz-Barbaroi. There is still hope of getting them back. We are going off to war against Kjaz-Barbaroi, and we are forming an army to oppose him."

Muriel picked up on what Pachunga was saying. "When it is safe, go back to your people. Tell them of Olugbala. Tell them what happened to Mwenda and Mwema. There are those who were their friends. Some will want to fight against you, but others will join you."

"Form an army of your best and most loyal soldiers," said Kasuku. "Someone will tell you what to do with it when the time comes. Kjaz-Barbaroi will not be with you long. If we stay with you, he will stick around. We will always be a danger to you. But he will leave soon, so you will be free to do the things that you have to do."

"Do you understand all this?" asked Pachunga.

"Yes, I do," said Mkumbo. "I understand it all, but I do not know if I can do what you are asking. It will be very difficult."

"With Olugbala all things are possible. We would not be here if that were not the case."

"That is true. Now I have this second chance, I'm willing to try anything!"

"That's the spirit!" said Kasuku.

"You can't do all this yourself," said Muriel. "Olugbala is there to help you at all times now."

"Pachunga!" The voice came through the opening by them. A stone or two fell from the ceiling in a distant corner. The Dark Creature had not left them alone yet.

"Just ignore him!" said Muriel with spunk and defiance.

"Pachunga!" Kjaz-Barbaroi was persistent. "You think you have just succeeded, eh? Well, you are wrong as usual. Mkumbo is a fool. We have no use for him. He will only cost you dearly in the end. Heh-heh. I do have use for you, though. All of you. You are exactly where I want you—trapped in my prison. And now it is too late for you to do anything—anything at all. You should have faced me, Pachunga. You should face me like Olugbala wants. But no. As always, you flee. Coward! Coward!"

Kjaz-Barbaroi's terrible laughter filled all their minds. And doubts about the decisions they had made began to grow in the silence that followed his words.

Muriel broke the silence. "Fiddlesticks!" she exclaimed. "He's just a bag of hot air. A dangerous bag of hot air, but still just a bag of hot air."

"It's time to get down to business," said Kasuku.

The trio faced Mkumbo, who had stood up by this time.

"Until the battle," said Pachunga.

"Until then," said Mkumbo with a sense of destiny and purpose. Already, he was becoming more decisive and sure of himself. "Go with Olugbala."

"And you likewise," said Kasuku.

Muriel, Kasuku and Pachunga left Mkumbo standing in the dark gloom of the anteroom. How long he would have to wait until it was safe for him to go was in the hands of Olugbala. He would watch over the Cave People leader just as he was watching over them.

Now, the three had other, more important things to do. They had to escape from the caves through the Old Tunnel. They did not know what was ahead of them, but they did know that they were not alone.

The Ghosts

Muriel looked at the black door that was in front of them. "This is really creepy."

"We have no choice but to go through," said Pachunga. "Where else would we go? We cannot stay here with Mkumbo. We have to keep moving."

"Buck up, my friends!" exclaimed Kasuku jubilantly. "We'll be through the Old Tunnel before you know it and into fresh air again. Just remember Olugbala."

"Yeah, sure," said Muriel. "I'm trying to think of him as hard as I can."

"Me too," said Pachunga.

"Don't limit him to just your minds," said Kasuku. "They are too small for Olugbala. You have to think of him as being present with you right now—in you and around you."

"Our minds are too small, eh?" asked Muriel. "Thanks a heap!"

Kasuku looked offended. "You know what I mean."

Muriel laughed. "Yeah, I know."

Their mood improved and they began to look optimistically at their situation. However, there was something very perplexing about the door. Pachunga expected the Tunnel beyond to be lit by his torch. It wasn't. The light did not penetrate the opening, though it did light the area around it. The opening was as black as anything they had ever seen. Muriel thought it looked like a window into outer space, only without stars.

"How odd," said Pachunga. "My light does not go into the Tunnel."

"Are we going to be able to get through?" Muriel thought that they actually might be trapped—or that they would have to wait with Chief Mkumbo and take their chances with Kjaz-Barbaroi directly.

"I have never seen anything like this," said Kasuku.

"Let me try something," said Pachunga. He cautiously put the torch forward through the door. It disappeared beyond the wall of blackness. All of it vanished from sight except for the end that Pachunga held in his hand. When he pulled the torch back, it reappeared.

Only it was not burning.

"Oh!" exclaimed Muriel. "Well, I'll be..."

"It's out! Just like that! There isn't even any smoke or glowing coals." Pachunga touched the end that had been burning. There was anxiety in his voice. "And it is cold, not warm."

"Does—Does that mean it's not safe?" asked Muriel.

"What other choice do we have?" Pachunga looked at Kasuku for counsel. "What do you think?"

"I think we should go," he said. "We cannot go back the way we came. Besides it not being the way we should go, it really would make things harder for Chief Mkumbo. There is no exit from the room other than this one—if it really is an exit. I will go first and see what happens."

"No, Kasuku. I should go." Pachunga was insistent.

"Your offer is appreciated. But I was sent by Olugbala to help you and guide you. It is my responsibility to go first."

With that—and before Pachunga could protest—he flew into the blackness and could be seen no longer.

"Kasu—!" Muriel never heard the rest. Pachunga's voice was lost as he plunged through the black hole after the parrot.

"Wait for me!" she cried. She went after them and vanished from sight.

The unusual sensation that now went through all of their bodies was not painful—though it was not pleasant, either. If each of them had had the opportunity to experience it again, they all would have said no—with certainty. The three each felt a gradual tingling that started with the part of their body that first went through the door—like passing through a curtain. This tingling then stopped once they were through. But through into what?

They were suddenly sinking, falling, flying and floating all at the same time. It seemed as though they had left their bodies behind. It was as if their bodies—like some unnecessary part of them—had been flung away and discarded in some forgotten corner. They could see nothing, but that was because it seemed as if their eyes were not working properly. Their lids were heavy—if they actually had lids—and they were prevented from looking up.

From moment to moment—if time still existed—they would get impressions of each other. There was nothing visible, only that Pachunga, for example, would sense that Muriel or Kasuku were both far and near—and never in one place. Pachunga decided that he did not want to look up, even if he could have made himself do it. He only wanted to look down—if there were a down—and away into nothingness. Something was above him and behind—something that he realized in a flash of insight was more terrible and awful than anything he had yet encountered during his life. It was something more evil than Kjaz-Barbaroi and the Drum. It was just pure, total Evil. And that Evil was now looking down on him. He knew that if he were to confront it himself, he would be destroyed and die. He would pass from life to death. He realized at that moment that he was between living and dying: caught in the middle with that wicked presence above him.

He had to get out, and he realized that he could not do it on his own. "Olugbala!" he shouted. Whether it was aloud or whether it was only in his mind, he did not know.

Pachunga then became aware of some turbulence. Something was disturbing the blackness around him. Suddenly, a shaft of white light broke into the darkness like a surgeon's scalpel cutting into flesh. He had to get to that light and let it consume him. He knew that in that light were goodness, hope, love—and Olugbala.

After an eternal moment, he was through—if that is the best way to describe it. He was surrounded by light and he was aware of his heart beating rapidly inside the chest he had once again. He was also breathing. Since there was so much light, he kept his eyes mostly closed and only opened them partially from time to time so that they could get adjusted. He bit his hand carefully to see if he could still feel pain. Yes, he was still the same Pachunga. Where was he?

"Oh!" said Muriel when she discovered herself standing next to Pachunga. She, too, had to keep her eyes closed, and she wasn't quite sure whom she had bumped into. "Is that you, Pachunga?"

"Yes." Pachunga could see well by now. They were in yet another Tunnel. It was very similar to the ones of the Cave People, only it was higher and wider. It stretched fifty meters ahead of them before gradually curving to the right. "I am glad you made it," he added.

"Yeah, so am I."

Neither of them felt like talking about their experience just yet.

"Is this all there is to it?" asked Muriel when she could see. She did not know what she was expecting, but somehow she was expecting something more than just bare, stone walls and a stone floor.

"I guess so," said Pachunga. "I wonder where all the light is coming from?"

They had no torches anymore and the light around them was yellow and orange—the color of firelight. It was different from the blue-green light of the Cave People. However, there were no torches visible. It was as if the light were a part of the air they were breathing.

Muriel realized that Kasuku wasn't with them. "Where's Kasuku?" Muriel turned around and looked around quickly.

"I don't know," said Pachunga. He was concerned, but he also felt drained and tired. Was he getting old again? He looked at his arms and legs and saw that they had not changed. "I feel I don't know much right now."

"Here I am." Kasuku was right behind them.

"Good!" Muriel was relieved.

"I've just been exploring ahead some. There is only more of what we see here. This is the real Old Tunnel, though. I am sure of it."

Pachunga turned around to look at the spot where they had entered. All he could see was the wall of the cave. He put his hand to it. It was solid.

"How unusual," said Muriel. "I guess we can't go back that way."

"No, you can never go back that way," said Kasuku gravely.

"I don't understand," said Pachunga. "Do you know what happened in there?"

"I don't know much," said Kasuku. "But I do know that it was very close for all of us. Had I known what was ahead, I would have looked for some other way to escape from Kjaz-Barbaroi. Olugbala helped us out just in the nick."

"Where do you think those spirits and ghosts are that the Cave People keep talking about?" asked Muriel. She looked around trying to spot one and saw nothing.

"You aren't afraid of them, are you?" Pachunga was concerned that Muriel would be. If so, she would be in jeopardy.

"Oh, no!" she exclaimed. "Not at all. I was just curious. What is there to be afraid of?" She laughed.

Pachunga smiled. "Maybe we'll never know."

"Oh, they're here all right," stated Kasuku. "You just aren't noticing them."

"Where?" Pachunga searched as much of the Tunnel that he could to see if he had missed anything. There were no ghosts of Tall Men anywhere. There was only light and cave. There was not even a carving on the wall or a loose stone.

Kasuku dropped to the floor at their feet. "Look here."

Muriel and Pachunga got on their hands and knees right where they had been standing.

"Look very closely."

They put their faces about three or four centimeters from the floor and peered intently in the same way that one might study the eyes of an insect or inspect the grains of mica in a pebble at the beach. Muriel wished that she had a magnifying glass.

At first they didn't see anything.

"I don't see anything," said Pachunga.

"Me neither." Muriel scrunched up her face and peered harder.

"Look again. They're there."

Pachunga noticed some movement in the roughness of the hand-hewn floor. Muriel saw it, too.

As they focused, they could see tiny, tiny Tall Men and Tall Women. At least Pachunga assumed that was what they were. They could not have been more than a millimeter high.

"They're darling!" said Muriel. "How cute!"

"Why are they so small?" Pachunga did not understand. They were supposed to be big and awesome.

"They are small because they are insignificant to us right now," said Kasuku. "They don't count. Compared to Olugbala, they are nothing. If we were afraid of them, they would be big as giants."

"But why doesn't Kjaz-Barbaroi know this? Why would he have so willingly sent us here if he thought we wouldn't be frightened into joining up with him?"

Kasuku laughed. "That is easy. Kjaz-Barbaroi likes to think of himself as the center of everything. What would be big or important or powerful in his eyes is actually very tiny, unimportant and insignificant. It is almost as if it does not exist. He thought he could frighten us into going against Olugbala. Hah! How little he really knows!"

"Well," said Pachunga, standing up. "We should still be on our guard at all times. We shouldn't underestimate him."

"Yeah," said Muriel. "He's always ready to crawl out of some slimy hole and give us a hard time."

"This is true," said Kasuku. "We'd better go on. I'm anxious for some sunlight and flying room."

"I'm hungry," said Pachunga. He tried to keep his voice from complaining, but he was not that successful. It came out as a whine. His last meal felt like weeks ago.

"We should find something to eat once we get out of these caves," said Kasuku. I wouldn't mind something to eat myself."

That was not the answer Pachunga had been hoping for, but he had gone without food before and was able to put all thoughts of eating out of his head.

They went down the Tunnel for over an hour. It wound its way through solid rock without change. They saw nothing and no one. It was all rather boring really.

"Are we going downhill?" Muriel once asked. She knew that they had quite a descent until they were level with the base of the Falls. She remembered how she had had to walk all the way up.

"Yes, we are," said Kasuku. "Do you see the direction that small stream is going on our right? As long as we walk with the flow, we will always be going down."

"Unless this is one of those strange places where water flows up. I don't want to have to walk up anymore. You're lucky. All you need to do is fly or hitch a ride on Pachunga's shoulder."

"That may be so," answered the parrot. "But I would trade my wings for your hands with a thumb anytime. I can't do anything with these claws but perch or hang on to bits of food. I can only do so much with my beak."

It was Muriel's turn to whine. The subject of food had come up again. "Food," sighed Muriel. "That meal Mwenda and Mwema fixed for me had to have been days ago."

"Who knows?" responded Pachunga grumpily. He was grouchy enough that he almost answered: "And who cares?" But he kept his mouth shut.

"Days. It has to have been days."

"Shhhh!" went Kasuku. He whispered into Pachunga's ear. "Someone's coming!"

Muriel did not hear what Kasuku had just said. Pachunga put his hand on her shoulder to stop her from walking. She froze.

The Tunnel was more or less straight for eighty meters ahead of them. Then it turned left. As they stared at the turn, a man, almost three meters tall, came around the corner.

He was very old and looked the way Pachunga did at the beginning of this story. His hair was grey. His leathery skin stuck to frail bones and you could count just about every one of his ribs. The man walked cautiously and took small steps on feet that were heavily calloused and dry. It wasn't just that he was trying to be careful and keep from falling. It looked like his joints bothered him as he moved. He kept squinting and peering ahead, as if trying to see better. Perhaps he was almost blind. But the strangest thing about him was that he held a burning torch high over his head as if he needed it to see where he was going. It was odd, for there certainly was enough light in the Tunnel. Why would he need a torch?

"A Tall Man," whispered Kasuku. "A real one. I thought they were all dead. Go to the side of the Tunnel," he instructed Pachunga.

Pachunga did as he was told, though he wondered why. It was obvious to him that they were going to be noticed at any moment. What good would it do to wait at the side? And if that old man did spot them, what then? What would he do to them? What *could* he do to them?

The Tall Man came closer and closer. Though old, he still had some strength left in his large frame. Muriel almost gasped aloud when she noticed a long, straight knife hanging at the man's side.

His hand was moving very slowly toward the hilt to grab it and pull it out!

Something Startling

Kasuku kept whispering orders into Pachunga's ear. "Allow him to pass by you. Then sneak up behind him. You can do it quietly. Remember the hunting games you used to play with Baree. Grab the torch out of his hand and—well, you know what to do. If it does not make sense, trust me."

Muriel, since she could hear nothing, kept wondering why the old man with the torch hadn't spotted them. She suspected that he was not a ghost. He looked too much like a real person.

The Tall Man was directly across from them now, almost standing in the little stream that ran alongside the Tunnel. The stream was about a meter wide and only four or five centimeters deep. He was close enough to them that they could see that he was worried and extremely frightened. Perspiration dripped from his forehead and his arm shook nervously whenever he moved the torch.

They all took short, shallow breaths that made no noise. Kasuku hopped over to Muriel's shoulder so as not to make a noisy flutter from his wings. Pachunga waited until the Tall Man passed and stepped neatly behind him. The man was a hundred centimeters taller than he, but the long torch handle was within his reach. Surprise was the key factor. He knew that he could count on only one chance.

"Now!" commanded Kasuku.

Pachunga grabbed the end of the torch and tried to wrench it away from the old man—only the Tall Man's grip was too strong. What strength he had for someone his age! The long knife was instantly pulled out of its sheath!

"Argh!" went the old man.

"Pachunga!" screamed Muriel.

The Chief let go of the torch and fell backwards onto the cave floor.

"Oof!" he exclaimed as he sat down hard. It was not a very smooth move, but at least it got him out of the way of the old man's knife. It cut through the space where Pachunga had been standing. The Tall Man still had the torch and he waved it around as if trying to see his attacker more clearly. Pachunga had a quick thought. Keeping low to the ground, he scampered around the Tall Man and came up behind him once again. He stood up and touched the knife-bearing arm with one hand and grabbed the torch with the other at the same time. The man, thinking he was being attacked from his right side, gripped the knife more tightly and momentarily relaxed his hold on the torch. It was all that Pachunga needed. The torch came free and he quickly threw it into the stream. It hissed and gurgled for a second, then went out.

"Argh!" went the old man again.

"Pachunga!" screamed Muriel again.

The knife was coming directly for Pachunga. He was ready for it this time. He leapt backwards just out of its reach.

The Tall Man didn't chase after Pachunga. Instead, he held his spot and crouched down low, making himself as small a target as possible. He was also in a more mobile position this way. He was ready to jump at or away from any attacker. He turned his head around, as if listening for any sound that would give him a clue as to where anyone might be. At one point, he was looking directly at Muriel and Kasuku—but he did not react to them.

"He must be blind," thought Muriel to herself. "Or maybe it is dark in here for him, which would explain why he needed the torch. But that doesn't make any sense."

Pachunga stood a safe distance away and considered taking out his own knife. But he was so much smaller than this giant. Avoiding him would be a better defense. He, too, was perplexed about why the man did not attack him again. The man stared in Pachunga's direction. There was no recognition in his eyes. There was only a lot of fear. The man obviously couldn't see anything. Did that mean, thought Pachunga, that he, Muriel, and Kasuku were invisible? The thought pleased Pachunga. He had never been invisible before.

"Tall Man!" boomed Kasuku suddenly.

Pachunga and Muriel both started. They had never heard him speak with such authority.

The Tall Man collapsed on the ground and the knife fell from his hand. "Argh!" he croaked. "By the blessed image of Olugbala!"

Pachunga and Muriel inhaled sharply. Why did he mention Olugbala's name?

"What is your name?" Kasuku left no doubt as to who was boss.

"M-My n-name? B-By the blessed statue of Prince Baree!"

"Why does he call on Baree's statue—whatever that is supposed to be?" wondered Pachunga. "Something isn't right here."

"Just state your name," said the parrot.

Muriel was really impressed by Kasuku. So was Pachunga.

"T-Titi F-Fatoyimbo." He looked around wildly and suddenly muttered: "By the holy image of Mamosa the Elephant!" He made some strange motions with his hands.

"Well, Titi Fatoyimbo, you have no need to fear us."

"Who—Who are you?" asked Titi. "Tell me, by the sacred name of Kasuku the Parrot!"

Pachunga was about to exclaim something. This was too much. But a quick, authoritative glance from Kasuku shut him up. Kasuku knew best what was going on, and he wanted to proceed alone with the questions.

"We are but three wanderers passing through your domain," answered Kasuku. "We are going to meet with our Chief, Olugbala."

"Olugbala? By his revered statue—and the worshipful statue of Kalopa the Lion. You are looking for *him*?" Titi was puzzled. "How can ghosts be looking for Olugbala?"

"He thinks we are ghosts?" Pachunga was incredulous. "That's ridiculous!"

"That may be more possible than you would think. But we are not ghosts, just as you are not."

"Wh-Where are you?"

"Pachunga, the Chief of the Kiritiri peoples is to your left. Muriel Sniggins, a Mzungu, is with me, in front of you against the Tunnel wall."

"And who are you?" Titi was becoming more relaxed and had risen to his feet.

"I am Kasuku Brokaw (*tweep!*) Kngaka (*squawk! whistle!*), friend and companion of Prince Baree, ruler of the Cattle People!"

"No! Not Kasuku the Parrot!" exclaimed Titi. In an instant, he was flat on his face in front of Kasuku and moaning. "Hail, O blessed one! Hail!" He repeated this twice and would have done it more, but Kasuku stopped him.

Kasuku was blustering in indignation in only the way that a small, grey parrot can. "Titi Fatoyimbo!" he commanded. "Rise! Again, I say, rise to your feet! At once!"

Titi stood up. For an old man, he was getting a lot of strenuous exercise. "Huh?" He was more puzzled. And he was trembling a lot. "I don't understand."

"Titi," explained Kasuku gently and patiently—but still with a measure of authority—"there is only One whom you may bow down before. Only One. He is Olugbala, the Chief of chiefs and First Born of the Father the Creator."

Titi sagged and was motionless. His head had lowered, and he seemed not to have any strength of will left. He thought that he could refuse to believe what had just been spoken to him, but for some reason, it all made sense. Imagine that! Years and years of one way of thinking had just been changed in a matter of moments.

Kasuku allowed Titi some time of quiet reflection. Then he spoke warmly and encouragingly. "You will understand more later."

"How do I know that you are not just some evil spirit?" He really knew that Kasuku wasn't, but he needed to ask the question anyway.

"Because I spoke the name of Olugbala in reverence and love."

"But word reached my people that you and Prince Baree were killed by one of Kjaz-Barbaroi's Dark Creatures."

"So we were. But Olugbala revived us just before we were to have been buried."

"I see," responded Titi. "But how can you see where I am? If you have a torch, it is not lit. We are standing in darkness. I can see nothing since mine was taken away and thrown into the water." He looked around the Tunnel and the expression on his face changed to one of wonderment. "But wait! I think can see a little now. My eyes must be getting used to the dark."

"You mean that you *can* see?" asked Pachunga.

"You're not blind?" added Muriel.

"No, I'm not blind. I can see—but not in the dark like you."

"But it's not dark!" insisted Muriel. "It's as bright as daylight in here. We can see you perfectly."

"Then you have better eyes than I."

He continued to peer in the direction of where the voices were coming from. "Wait! There *is* more light," he said. "Now I can see your shapes and outlines. Why, Chief Pachunga and Muriel Sniggins are only a boy and a girl. I haven't seen children in an age."

"You don't have any children?" asked Muriel.

"We are a dying race. There are only eighteen of us left and we are too old to have any children."

"How sad." Muriel liked children and thought that every family should have some.

"I know," said Titi. "We could have had them once. After all, we were younger at one time. But we never married. No one really wanted to. We have been living in isolation for so long that the only people whom we know now are ourselves. Who wants to marry someone who has been like a brother or a sister all your life?" His voice became sad. Then he cheered up and was downright bubbly with enthusiasm. "Come! You need to meet my people, and I can tell them that I can see without a torch." He looked around the Tunnel again, as if still disbelieving that it was possible for him to see on his own. "It is as bright as day—whatever that is. And to think that I never knew..."

"We have met your cousins, the Cave People," said Pachunga as they walked down the Tunnel. "They, however, are not tall like you. They are very short—shorter than Muriel and I."

"How interesting," said Titi. "This will also have to be reported to the rest of my people. We had thought that we were the last humans!"

"Sadly," said Kasuku, "they have fallen into bad ways. They are now listening to the Drum and are on the side of Kjaz-Barbaroi. However, their chief, Mkumbo is his name, is now an ally, and he should be very influential with his people."

"Yes," said Pachunga. "He is going to raise an army to help us in our battle against Kjaz-Barbaroi."

"Since there was hope for me, there must be hope for them," said Titi optimistically. As he walked down the Tunnel taking long, confident steps now that he could see, his eyes grew wider as he studied every detail of the cave walls. Muriel and Pachunga had thought they were relatively ordinary. To Titi, the colors were magnificent. "I never knew that there were so many shades of yellow and orange! And the other colors—the red, the browns and the blacks—how wonderful!"

"You will see even prettier colors than these," said Kasuku, "if you ever reach the outside."

"The outside?" questioned Titi.

Pachunga laughed. "Of course. Where do you think we came from?"

"We had been taught by our parents that you would die. That there were those who could live outside, but would die in the caves—just like we could live in the caves, but would die if we went outside." A thought came to him. "I must tell everyone about these new things!"

It wasn't long before the Tunnel began to widen. Torches burned in holders every so often on alternating sides. Underneath them were five or six replacements in bins. They were ready to be used when those burning were finished.

"Kanoti is the Torchlighter for my people," explained Titi. "It is the most respected job in our tribe. I wonder how the old man is going to feel when he learns that he doesn't have to light the torches anymore..." Titi's voice faded into a whisper. He began to be concerned about the way the Tall Men were going to feel when they learned about this change in their thinking and believing. "Once they see, they will believe," he said aloud, though he didn't realize he had been heard.

Just as Titi was about to announce that they were almost there, another very large, but old and bent Tall Man came into view ahead of them. He looked older than Titi by a number of rainy seasons. This new old man carried a torch and walked painfully as if every step were an effort.

Titi's face beamed when he saw his friend. "Kanoti! Old one! I have something important to tell you!"

Now you must remember that all Kanoti could see was the little light that was being given off by his own torch and the other torches that were sporadically placed along the Tunnel. His eyes were even worse than Titi's. Age had caused them to become cloudy and weak. All Kanoti could figure out was that someone, who was not carrying a torch, was calling his name. He was well aware of the spirits of his ancestors who inhabited the Tunnel—and he was terrified of them. He always had been, and he had lived his life fearing that they would take over and convert the remaining Tall Men into ghosts. If he came into contact with any of them, he would die. Now, of course he could not recall ever having seen any spirits of his ancestors before, but he knew they were there. And the voice that called his name out of the darkness was all the proof that he needed.

When Kanoti heard his name specifically called—he became convinced that if he stayed a moment longer, he would cease living. So he did the most logical thing he could think of.

He turned and ran.

Well, he kind of ran. It was the best that he could do at his age, although it was amazing that he was able to go as fast as he did. He was in danger. They all were in danger. He had to get back to protect them all from this possible attack.

"Argh! Ghosts!"

"Kanoti! It's Titi!"

Kanoti did something that was very brave from his perspective. He stopped running and turned towards the voice that was speaking to him. With a quavering voice, he yelled, "Go away in the name of the blessed statue of Kalopa the Lion! Stay away from us! We aren't doing you any harm!"

With that, he turned again and raced away as fast as his aching bones could carry him.

Titi was hurt. "Now I wonder why he did that? I've known him all my life."

"Remember that he could not see you," said Pachunga.

"Yeah," said Muriel. "You probably scared the bejabbers out of him."

They walked on in silence for several more minutes. Finally, the Tunnel turned yet again and led into a large, circular cavern. The ceiling was high above their heads—at least a hundred meters or more. Every bump, crack, hollow, and formation was brilliantly lit by the light that came from nowhere. Titi's eyes were as wide as those of Pachunga and Muriel.

"I never knew that this room was as large as this." His voice echoed all around. "When Kanoti and I were boys we tried to climb one of the walls into the darkness above, but became too scared and didn't go very far. Someone must have explored it, though we don't know who. At one time, our race used to live in a larger section of the cave system. But in recent times as our numbers became fewer, we have only been living in the central section—near the Temple of Departed Souls."

"The Temple of Departed Souls?"

"Yes! It is the most magnificent part of our civilization. It is dedicated to all the great souls who have passed on before us. It would be better for you to see it first, rather than to have me try to describe it."

Muriel noted that the room was empty. "Where is everyone?"

"Why, they should be—" Titi looked around the cavern. "This is strange. There is no one here. This is where we all gather during the wake period."

"Where'd they go?" asked Pachunga.

"They must have gone back to their rooms. I don't understand why."

"Maybe they're hiding from us," suggested Muriel.

"That's probably right."

"We are strangers to them," said Kasuku. "Or maybe they think that we—including you—are ghosts."

"Impossible!" protested Titi. "I am more alive than I've ever been—since I met you all. Me, a ghost?"

"They don't know that," said Kasuku.

"That Kanoti!" Titi went on. "He's probably the one who got them all alarmed and warned them that we were coming. Who knows what he said about us. I never did like him."

"Now Titi," said Muriel. "Don't talk like that. Of course you like him. Remember how you felt when Pachunga took away your torch."

"Yes," said Titi. "But he gets excited so easily and it doesn't take much to frighten him. That torch lighting job of his, too, is the most important thing to him. He'll do anything to protect that job."

"We would all be easily frightened," said Kasuku, "if we lived in darkness all our lives."

"Look!" exclaimed Pachunga. "None of the torches around the room are burning!"

"They *really* are frightened then. Putting out the torches has never been done as long as I have been alive. It is a signal of an emergency or expected danger."

As they talked, they knew someone was listening to them. Muriel was getting tired of always being spied upon. The rest of the Tall Men were probably making up their minds as to whether the voices they were hearing through the darkness came from real creatures, or whether they were the spirits of the Departed Souls.

Titi was very anxious. He did not like the quiet that he heard around them. Yet he didn't know what to do about it. Should he shout something to his people in hiding? Or should he patiently wait for them to come out? He knew that though timid, his people were also very curious and wanted to learn new things. It wasn't often that something different happened.

Kasuku helped make the decision. "Come," he said. "Let's go visit the Temple of Departed Souls. You have aroused my curiosity."

Titi brightened. "That is a good idea. The rest will come out when they see that we are safe and that we mean them no harm."

Titi led them across the cavern and through one of several doors that led to the other parts of their cave system. Like the entrance to the Old Tunnel, this entrance to the Temple was surrounded by stone carvings.

"Look" said Pachunga. "There is a carving of Mamosa the Elephant. And here is Kalopa the Lion. And here—why, it looks like it's supposed to be you and Baree, Kasuku. But you're not a departed soul, yet."

"Since these statues and carvings bear the images of the most holy," explained Titi, "we must worship them." He led them into a long corridor that went to the Temple itself. "Come, the Temple is just ahead. I can't wait to see it in the light. It should be even more wonderful."

They walked down a broad, high-ceilinged tunnel that was fifty meters long. Every bit of wall and ceiling had heads and bodies carved into it. Some told stories of battles or life in the outside. They could not have added another figure. Ahead of them, in the Temple, Pachunga, Muriel, and Kasuku could see some large statues. They couldn't tell what they were, though.

"Why, it's dark!" said Titi when he reached the entrance.

"It is?" asked Muriel.

"I can see everything very well," said Pachunga. "Let's go in, Muriel."

They both went in. Kasuku remained on Pachunga's shoulder. Titi stayed outside.

"Oh my!" gasped Muriel when she saw an immense statue in the middle of the Temple.

"Don't say anything," said Kasuku.

"But, it's—" said Pachunga.

"I know that and you know that, but I bet Titi doesn't."

"Wait!" called Titi from outside. "Let me get a torch first."

"No, Titi," said Kasuku. "Then you would only be seeing the Temple in the way that you always have been seeing it. Come in here."

"But I can't see anything!"

"Come!"

Titi came. He walked very slowly. After fifteen small steps, he stopped. He had his arms stuck out so that he wouldn't run into anything.

"Titi," said Kasuku warmly. "A while ago, you said that it was necessary for your people to see first. Then they would believe. I am sorry to say that for most of us it doesn't work that way." He spoke in a way that an older, wiser teacher would speak to a young student. "What is in this Temple?"

"Well, there are the revered and sacred statues, images and icons of Mamosa, Kalopa, Prince Baree, you, of course, and most importantly, the all-worshipful statue of Olugbala."

Pachunga couldn't contain himself any longer. "But, it's not—!"

"Shhh!" said Muriel sternly to Pachunga. She hit his arm.

"Ow!" said Pachunga.

"You deserved it," said Muriel sternly.

Kasuku continued. "Titi, what did I tell you about whom you should worship and revere?"

"Why, Olugbala only. When I realized that, I began to see."

"Right. But what do you think of these statues in here?"

I-I guess I shouldn't worship them anymore, particularly the ones of the Departed. But what about Olugbala? What about him?"

"You cannot worship his image, his statue, or his icon. You must worship only him. He is Real. He wants your reverence for him personally—not for some statue that is a poor imitation of him—not for something that is made of wood or stone, or even silver and gold."

This all made a lot of sense to Titi. It went along with what he had accepted as truth back in the Old Tunnel. He just needed to have it explained to him. "Ah," he said. "I can see it all clearly now." And naturally, that strange light filled the entire Temple for him.

Titi looked at the huge statue that was in the center of the Temple. In front of it was a large stone altar. His eyes filled with fear.

"Why, it's not—it's not Olugbala. It's—It's Kjaz-Barbaroi! Oh, no! You mean, after all these years...?" He couldn't finish. He stood in shock.

"Yes," said Kasuku. "Because your torches are not very bright, you couldn't see the statues that well. You have been worshipping the statue of Kjaz-Barbaroi, not Olugbala. Kjaz-Barbaroi—through the Drum—has tricked you into thinking it was of Olugbala."

They would have stood in the Temple for some time talking about this. Pachunga and Muriel would have tried to comfort Titi, and he would have said that it was even more important that he speak to his people. Pachunga, too, wanted to know what the altars were used for. And Muriel would have begun to feel impatient and angry—and would have said something about it.

Only all this could not happen, because something else happened first.

Kasuku, with his very good ears, heard some whisperings and stumblings in the entrance to the Temple that was behind them. It sounded a lot like a group of people trying to sneak up on them unnoticed. He whispered in Pachunga's ear to be still. A warning glance to Titi and Muriel silenced them. They all waited quietly without moving.

Who was coming?

THE MEETING

There were three of them. Kanoti came first. Then there was an old woman who was followed by another old man. They came into the Temple bending forward at the waist and walking in single file. As they crept along, they tried hard to be quiet. But the harder they tried, the more noise they made. They obviously had not had any experience sneaking around.

Since they carried no torches, they could see nothing. They kept tripping over their own feet and over each other. Many times, they would bump into the wall with their bodies, and sometimes they would bang their heads. Each of them would have been much happier if he or she could have been somewhere else.

"Watch it!" exclaimed Kanoti in a loud whisper.

"Shhhh!" scolded the old woman. She put a crooked finger to her wrinkled lips. Her "Shhhh" was kind of airy because she didn't have any teeth.

"You're both making too much noise," said the old man. His voice was louder than the other two because he couldn't hear very well.

Then Kanoti tripped.

And the old woman stumbled right behind him. And the old man bumped into them both.

"For goodness sake!"

"By the blessed image of Baree!" exclaimed the old woman.

"Shhhh!" went the old man.

They swatted each other a few times with their hands.

"Enough!" ordered Kanoti. "No more of this. We have things to do."

"Can you see anything?" asked the old woman.

"How, by Mamosa's sacred trunk, do you expect me to see anything? It's too dark!"

"I'm too old for this sort of thing!"

"Stop complaining!"

"Where are they?"

"How should I know?"

"Ouch!"

"Watch that!"

"My toe!"

"What's it doing there?"

"We're doomed for sure!"

"I don't like this at all...I don't like this at all."

Kanoti stopped after he had passed about two meters into the room. The other two, not being able to see him stop, collided into him, of course.

"For the—!"

"Shhhh!"

None of them moved.

There was silence.

"Are you ready?" asked the old man.

"Yes," said Kanoti. He tried to sound brave. "Of course I am."

"Well, go ahead then," snapped the old woman. She always sounded cross when she spoke.

Kanoti stood up to his full height. In his hand he held a small statue of Mamosa the Elephant. He held it in front of him to protect him from the evil spirits he was convinced were in the room. He chanted for a few moments and bowed and raised his head up and down.

"Oh—wah—nah—gah—mah—moh—sah—kah—soo—koo—oh—loo—bah—lah—mah—lah—wah—lah—kun—gah—lah—wah—nah—tawh—boo!"

Nobody had any idea what he meant.

Then Kanoti's lips quivered. Whatever it was that he was about to do, it was something that he did not like. He inhaled to puff up his chest and to give himself enough air to make his voice stronger. But this only made him cough. He tried again, but did not breathe quite as deeply. With all the courage that he had in his old, frail body, he bellowed weakly: "Ghosts!"

His voice echoed around the Temple.

Kasuku signaled for everyone to be quiet.

"They're not answering," said the old woman.

"Perhaps they fled in fear," suggested the old man. "They should know that this is a holy place."

"Nonsense," said Kanoti. "They're here. I can feel 'em."

"So can I," said the old woman.

"Ghosts!" bellowed Kanoti again. "Spirits of the Departed Ones, speak! By the power of the Holy Beak of Kasuku the Parrot, I command you to speak!"

"Rubbish!" said Kasuku.

"Ahhhh!" went Kanoti. He held the small statue of Mamosa higher.

"They're speaking!" said the old woman.

"What did they say?" asked the old man.

"I don't know," she said. "I don't want to know." She made a lot of rapid, funny motions with her hands.

The sound of Kasuku's voice caused Kanoti to back up against the wall. The old woman and the old man backed up with him. Kanoti did manage to look proud of himself for making the ghost speak. "If you insist on calling us ghosts," said Kasuku, "I don't know why we should speak to you."

"It is speaking even more," observed the old woman.

"It doesn't sound bad," said the old man. "It sounds quite reasonable."

"Don't be a fool," said the old woman. "I know about ghosts, I do. I have to chase them out of my room at night before I go to sleep. They are very persistent and very smart. One of them asked me to marry him, he did."

"That wasn't a ghost. That was Lulo."

"Well, he's the same as a ghost he's so old," insisted the old woman.

"Shhh!" Kanoti was not happy with all their chatter. It was distracting him. He addressed Kasuku again.

"Spirit of the Departed Souls, by all the power in the all- worshipful statues of Olugbala and Kalopa the Lion, I command you to flee from this place at once!"

"We will do no such thing," said Kasuku with some indignation. "We happen to have been invited here by one of your own group."

"And WHO of US would EVER do that?" demanded Kanoti. He didn't think it was possible that one of his tribe would invite ghosts for a visit.

"Titi Fatoyimbo," said Titi.

"Blessed holy sacred image of Prince Baree of the Cattle People! They've killed Titi!" The old woman's eyes bulged out of her face. "And he's been turned into a ghost!"

Kanoti, who was already scared, became even more so. He imagined himself being changed into a ghost right then and there.

"No, I am not dead," said Titi. "I am more alive than I have ever been. Kasuku the Parrot is here with me, as well as Pachunga, Chief of the Kiritiri peoples, and Muriel Sniggins, a Mzungu—whatever that means. They are journeying to meet Olugbala. Since I met them in the Tunnel, marvelous things have happened to me, and I have learned much."

"He's mad," commented the old woman.

"He must have gone to the Outside," said Kanoti.

"No, I am not mad," said Titi. He stared directly at Kanoti, though Kanoti was not aware of it. "Kanoti, you have known me all my life. Together, we have administered our tribe. Go tell the rest of the group to meet me in the Big Cavern so that I can tell you all that I've learned."

"Ghost!" screamed Kanoti all of a sudden. "You speak lies and blaspheme the images of all the Departed Souls!"

"Beware of the spirits of the departed souls," warned the old woman. "Let us get out of here before they corrupt us all!"

The old woman and Kanoti turned and left the Temple, stumbling and tripping and cursing everything as they went.

The old man remained.

"Lituli," said Titi. "You are not going?"

"There is something about the way you speak, Titi, which tells me you are saying the truth. I don't hear very well. I am an old man, but I know that you are not a ghost. I can't see you—but I know you are you. Kanoti will try and cause trouble—to turn everyone against you, no doubt. I'll see what I can do to get everyone to come to the Big Cavern."

"Thank you, Lituli. Thank you."

With that, he turned and left.

* * * *

Seventeen of the last eighteen Tall Men in existence squatted in a semi-circle on the floor of the Big Cavern in front of Titi, Kasuku, Pachunga, and Muriel. Special torches on stands usually reserved for the various feast days of the more important Departed Souls had been brought in to light the large cavern for those eyes that could not see because of the darkness. The Tall Men were noticeably divided into two separate groups. Kanoti, the old woman, and several of his supporters were on one side of the semi-circle and the rest of the tribe was on the other with a gap between the two.

The old Torchlighter was not happy. He couldn't make up his mind whether he should be frightened of his visitors, or whether he should be angry with them for threatening to weaken his power. He had convinced himself that any change would be bad for him—no matter how logically presented.

Lituli was all by himself on the opposite side of the semi-circle. He was also the closest to the visitors. Lituli was the one who had brought the others into the Big Cavern only because the rest of the group was willing to trust his judgment. Because of this—and for other obvious reasons—Kanoti gave Lituli some hateful glances every now and again. This was his poor attempt to try and persuade Lituli to go over to his side. It wasn't working at all, particularly since Lituli couldn't see him very well.

The ones in the middle had gasped and muttered when they had first seen Pachunga, Muriel, Kasuku and Titi in the torchlight. They had exclaimed cries of alarm and had called upon the Departed Souls to protect them. They were confused, too. They hoped that Kanoti or Titi would make things clear to them. They anxiously looked back and forth from Kanoti to Titi and back to Kanoti again. Their frequent glances at Titi showed that they had many doubts. Was he a ghost—as Kanoti claimed—or was he the real Titi? A few were beginning to think that he must be the real Titi because they observed that he was not behaving like a ghost. He looked too solid and he wasn't spending all of his efforts trying to spook them.

Kanoti and the old woman would not have been at the meeting at all if they hadn't thought that they would be accused of being cowards. "Too scared to face the ghosts, eh?" they imagined their fellow tribesmen as saying. They also wanted to hear what Titi and this "fake" Kasuku the Parrot had to say so they could refute it and banish them all for blasphemy and heresy.

There was more to it than that, however. Kanoti could not forget that his authority with his people would be lost if there were a change in the way things were. This was not true, but it was what he was thinking, nevertheless. He was the Torchlighter—the Tall Man who held the most responsible position of the tribe. He had been chosen for the job since birth and trained since his youth. It would not have been respectful to his father—now a Departed Soul of the Next-to-Highest Order—if he were not able to do the job anymore. Also, he knew that his image was to be carved into the Temple wall as being the Last Torchlighter, so that if any new eyes throughout ages happened to chance upon the Temple, they would see him along with Olugbala, Kalopa, Mamosa, Prince Baree—and the "real" Kasuku.

The ones in the middle felt confused about the visitors. As yet, they had not heard Kasuku speak, so some said that he was just a pet that belonged to Pachunga. Kanoti, with great wisdom, had said that there was a spirit who had taken the form of the Blessed Bird and claimed to be him. It was not really him and it was very evil. They were warned not to pay attention to the crafty words it might speak. Due to this doubt, none of the Tall Men threw themselves down on the floor in front of Kasuku when they first saw him. Many, though, were worried what the consequences would be if it ended up that Kasuku was, in fact, Kasuku.

Pachunga and Muriel could also be real, they thought. If so, it meant that they were not the last men and women to inhabit their world. They called themselves a name that does not translate very well into English. It means something like: "After we go on to the world of Departed Souls, there is not going to be anyone else." In simplest terms, they could be called the "Last Tribe." They were called the Tall Men only by those who had heard about them through their reputation and the telling of the history of their world. They did not call themselves "tall." To them, everyone else was short. They couldn't help staring at Pachunga and Muriel. They had not seen a boy or a girl since they had been children themselves. The women would have loved to dote on them and fuss over them. And even Kanoti found himself wishing Pachunga were not a ghost. If he were real, he would train him to be his successor as the Torchlighter. The other men would teach him how to catch cave fish and cave crabs, how to raise their special mushrooms, and how to carve images and statues from stone.

After everyone had had a chance to look at everyone else, Titi straightened himself up and began to speak.

"My fellow members of the Last Tribe, you who are the remnant of what was once a great and powerful civilization..." He shortened his introduction considerably, because Tall Men usually speak for five or ten minutes at the beginning of every speech. They flatter everyone in the audience—and themselves as well. This way, speeches took a long time, but strangely enough, they never got bored. "...just a while ago, some visitors from the Outside introduced themselves to me. And though I was afraid of them, they spoke to me and opened my eyes to the light that is surrounding us all right now. Because of my old beliefs, I could see things poorly—and only with a torch. Now, I can see all things clearly.

"Our beliefs are something I once considered to be the Truth—yet they are only a shadow of what is Real. I persuaded myself that they were right, when actually they were very, very wrong. Because he can explain things much better than I, I present to you now Kasuku the Parrot, friend and companion to Baree, Prince of the Cattle People."

"He's lying!" shouted Kanoti suddenly. "They are dangerous! Beware of what he says!"

"Oh, Kanoti," said Lituli in his usually cranky voice. "Sit down and be quiet. It cannot hurt us to hear them out." He was becoming tired of Kanoti's objections to everything.

"Yes," said someone from the middle group. "Let's hear what they have to say."

Several of the men and women nodded their heads in agreement.

Kanoti mumbled a few words to the old woman and squatted once again. He did not like it when he was not the center of attention.

Kasuku flew to the top of a stand that did not have a torch burning in it and began to speak.

"Men and women of the Last Tribe," he said, speaking in a clear, strong voice.

"No, he is not a pet," thought some of the men and women.

"I can see after examining the objects of your worship that you are a very religious tribe. You have signs of it everywhere: statues, images, and icons of all those who have been particularly blessed by Olugbala. And you even have images of Olugbala himself.

"But this I proclaim to you regarding him whose statues you worship: that he who is the most blessed and first born of the Father the Creator is too great to dwell in temples made with human hands. He cannot be trapped in wood, stone, silver or gold. He is Real. He is alive. He is to be sought only by those who wish to know the Truth. He cannot be something that is formed only by the thought and imagination of men.

"Men and women of the Last Tribe, the age of darkness and misery is coming to an end. I beg you to become participants in the light that surrounds us all. Open your eyes to see it."

Kasuku's speech had the effect that you might imagine. Many of those in the middle group looked stunned. It was not as though Kasuku had said a lot of words—but what he said spoke to them all. Lituli squatted on the floor with a strange smile on his face. His eyes were opening wider and wider as he thought about the real Olugbala.

"I—I don't—It's—It's true!" Light filled his vision and surrounded him. It almost tickled him with its soft fingers.

Several more began to see as well. And they all started talking excitedly with one another. Some stood and walked around the Big Cavern staring at the walls and ceiling and at each other.

"You're crazy!" Kanoti screamed. "You're all mad and under a spell more powerful than you know!" He took the old woman by the arm. "Come! Let's get out of here before we, too, come under the spell!"

"No!" said the old woman. "Stay here and see the light with the rest of us. This is all truly wonderful!" She began to walk around the Big Cavern with the rest and ask Pachunga and Kasuku many questions.

"I—DON'T—BELIEVE—ANY—OF—THIS!" shouted Kanoti. "You are all fools! You are all insane! You will all perish and suffer an eternal punishment for this! Beware!"

But nobody was really paying any attention to what he was saying.

Kanoti snatched a torch out of a stand and ran into the Great Temple. He wanted to console himself there and think of what he would do next. He knew that there had to be some comfort he could get there. Perhaps he would receive some sort of guidance. Yet in a moment, a thought came to him as suddenly and as swiftly as a spear coming from the strong arm of one of the Cattle People warriors. It pierced his thoughts and momentarily stopped the beating of the Drum inside his head.

What if they were really right after all?

The Cave of Perpetual Sorrow

Titi was the only person to see Kanoti disappear down the cave that led to the Great Temple. He would have to see him later. Right now, everyone of his tribe was so overcome by being able to see that they were talking quickly and excitedly. They were behaving more like small children at a birthday party than old folks over ninety.

"This is the day that light came into our world!" announced Lituli. "We must have a feast!

"With music!" said the old woman.

"With drums!" said Lulo.

"And dancing!"

"Our best food!"

With those, and some more suitable exclamations, they all returned to their dwellings to begin the preparations. They remembered fondly the feasts of their youth.

Titi spoke to Pachunga, who stood to one side with Muriel and Kasuku. "You will stay, won't you?"

"Only for a short while. We must be on our way."

"I will guide you the rest of the way when the time comes. It is not that far. Nor will it be a difficult trip—especially since we can all see so well now."

"Th-Thank you very much," said Muriel. She yawned rudely and loudly. "But—But for the..." She yawned again.

"Come," said Titi in a grandfatherly tone of voice. "You are all very tired. I can show you where to rest until the festival begins. You, Muriel, can stay in the cave of my sister, Nola. Pachunga, you may rest in mine." He looked at Kasuku and became doubtful. He'd never had to offer lodging to a parrot. "Kasuku, I don't—"

"I'll be happy somewhere out of the way in a dark, quiet corner," he said. "But with all this light, I guess dark is impossible now."

Titi led them to the places where they were to sleep. After they were all settled, he walked slowly back to the Big Cavern. The rest of the Tall Men were rushing around the cave system like ants as they got ready for the feast. Whenever Titi met one or two of them, they would grab hold of his hands and jump up and down a few times. Titi tried to participate in their joy, only he could not. Thoughts of Kanoti kept coming back to him. Sure, the old Torchlighter had been acting stupidly. Titi should just tell him to go jump and then forget all about him.

But Kanoti was still Kanoti. He was someone whom Titi had always loved and respected. They had been close friends all their lives and were constant companions. Titi knew that he could not ignore his friend. He had to go to him and talk with him. Titi hoped that Kanoti would change his mind about everything and join them in the feast.

Titi was presented with a lonely and sad sight when he entered the Great Temple. Torches burned everywhere. Kanoti had gathered together all that he could find. Smoke rose in black columns to the top of the cavern and escaped through ventilation cracks in the ceiling. If Titi could have seen the Temple through Kanoti's eyes, he would have seen that in spite of the number of torches, it was still very dark.

All Titi could see of Kanoti was his skinny brown legs sticking out from the space between the old, crumbling statue of Kjaz-Barbaroi and the massive stone altar in front of it. He was flat on his belly worshiping the statue that he believed to be of Olugbala.

"Oh, blessed, holy, sacred and revered statue of Olugbala," he wailed. Few sights are sadder than seeing a man at the end of his years crying and calling out to a statue that will never answer. He repeated the chant no one knew the meaning of: "Oh wah-nah-gah-mah-moh-sah-kah-soo-koo-oh-loo-bah-lah-mah-lah-wah-lah-tawh-boo!"

Titi walked on silent feet across the damp, smooth floor and rested his hand on the shoulder of his friend.

"Kanoti," he said softly.

"Olugbala? Olugbala, is that you?" A crazed look crossed Kanoti's face. He lifted his head and tried to peer through the darkness at the statue. In doing so, he noticed Titi squatting beside him. "Oh. It's you," he said plainly. He turned himself around and sat against the altar.

Titi took a deep breath. This was going to be difficult.

"Old one," he said.

"Yes, old one," responded Kanoti. That was how they addressed each other when they wanted to be the most personal.

"How long have you known me?"

"Almost since the day you came from your mother, and she became a Departed Soul in birthing you."

"Have you ever known me to lead you astray?"

"No." His answer required no second thought.

"Have I ever lied to you?"

"No, old one. Not since we were boys and you didn't know the evil that you were doing."

"Then why would I lie to you now?"

"Because—!" snapped Kanoti viciously. Then he realized that there now was no reason to be angry with Titi. He knew that Titi was Titi and that he was not a ghost. He had known that since he had talked with him in the Temple before the meeting in the Big Cavern. Kanoti knew, too, that Titi was right and that he was wrong. Why would Titi try to mislead him? That was very unlike him. Titi was known among his people for having the integrity and honesty of Mamosa the Elephant. And Kanoti had seen—if only briefly—the faces of his people as they saw this light that came from who-knows-where. There had been in their faces a reflection of Olugbala that was much deeper and closer to the real face of Olugbala than any of the faces the stone carvers had made. It was true all right. Kanoti knew that he had been in the dark all those years.

He could go with Titi and accept the truth, or he could stay right where he was, shivering from fear in the dark shadows of a statue that was no greater than the lifeless rock from which it had been hewn.

Kanoti was about to admit to Titi that he, the Last Torchlighter of the Last Tribe, was wrong and that his friend was right. He almost said to Titi: "Yes, old one. I've been wrong all this time. I'm sorry for the trouble that I've caused you."

And Titi would have embraced him and said, "That is all right, old one. You are forgiven. You caused no trouble. Olugbala is victorious in the end." They would have risen rather unsteadily because their knee joints would have been stiff and returned to a festive celebration with Kanoti being one of those honored.

But Kanoti did not allow for this to happen.

Titi did not know this, but Kanoti had begun to hear the Drum once again. It had been silent during their conversation, but now it returned—stronger than before. Kanoti had asked for it back because it was something familiar to him. He knew what it was. In a way, he was like a pig given the opportunity to live in a clean, dry barn rather than wallowing in the mud and his own filth—and then rejects the barn to return to the mire only because it is something familiar and safe—not something new and different.

Kanoti wished immediately that he hadn't invited the Drum back. He had never known it to beat so painfully. It hammered inside his head with such a din that he thought that if he heard it for a moment longer, he would go mad. But he would *never* admit to his people that he had been foolish and wrong. He would *never* face his people in shame. And he didn't want to be the Torchlighter anymore. They, especially Titi, could all stuff it. They were so smug in the assurance of what they now claimed to believe. What was there to believe in anymore? All he could be sure of was the Drum. His mind was crowded with feelings of anger, pride, resentment—and they grew stronger and stronger as the Drum beat more loudly. It wouldn't stop. He didn't want it to stop.

Titi noticed that Kanoti's eyes had changed. They were dark now. Before, they still contained a spark of life and hope. But now, the pupils had become small black dots and his dark brown irises reflected the orange torchlight in a hyena-like manner. This was not the same Kanoti. This was someone who had just lost his soul.

"Kanoti," he said again softly, putting his hand on the Torchlighter's shoulder.

With a snarl and a growl that sounded exactly like a Dark Creature, Kanoti leapt to his feet and shouted: "No! No! I won't! I won't do it!" Clutching the small stone statue of Mamosa tightly in his fist, he raced down a small, narrow tunnel that receded from the immense statue of Kjaz-Barbaroi. At the entrance to this tunnel, symbols and pictures of people perishing warned anyone getting close not to pass into the cave. Kanoti didn't pay any attention to them. As he ran down the passageway, he bumped into the walls, bruising his flesh and scraping his skin. He felt nothing. He was being pushed into madness and driven forward by the pounding and beating of the Drum that was splitting his head apart.

And then Kanoti stepped on air and began a long, downward plunge into deeper and darker blackness.

Anyone who had studied the cave system of the Tall Men would know that the name of the cave Kanoti had entered was called the Cave of Perpetual Sorrow. The reason for this name is simple. Anyone running down it in the dark—and it is always dark—would find themselves in a state of perpetual sorrow. About one hundred meters from the entrance is a hole so deep that the noise of anything hitting the bottom cannot be heard from the top.

Titi didn't just squat there and let Kanoti run down the tunnel to his chosen death. He made a brave effort to grab him, but missed. If only he had been younger! In the process of missing Kanoti, he hit his right arm against the rock floor and broke it. His forehead also hit the ground hard, and he blacked out.

Kanoti fell for a full five minutes. Then he stopped falling very suddenly. If you had been at the bottom with eyes to see the spirits of the Departed Souls, you would have seen that Kanoti's spirit was very surprised after his body had been turned to mush. Kanoti knew instantly that he had done the wrong thing, and it was too late for him to do anything about it. Before he knew it, he was with some of his ancestors—though he didn't know that they were with him—in a place where Olugbala and the Father the Creator are not. He did not become a ghost in the Old Tunnel as expected. All this time the Tall Men had believed that the actual spirits of the Departed Souls haunted the Old Tunnel. They didn't. Those spirits were actually evil beings who had taken the form of those who had departed. The real spirits, which were now locked away in an infinitely small space, were outside of Olugbala's domain and had put themselves beyond the reach of the Father the Creator.

Titi gradually came to and couldn't decide whether his arm hurt more than his head, or his head hurt more than his arm. He tried to lift his head. It hurt so much he fainted. He awakened again a short while later. This time, he didn't faint when he raised his head. Black patches in front of his eyes grew larger and nearly smothered the light around him. He forced those black patches away. The effort upset his stomach and he threw up. He told himself he would not black out again. He propped himself up with his good arm and pulled himself to his feet and managed to throw up a second time—this time, on the statue. The symbolism of what he did brought a weak smile to his lips. If only it had been the feet of the real Kjaz-Barbaroi!

Titi looked at the face that towered above him. "You!" he tried to scream. He didn't make much sound. His head hurt too much. He shook his good arm at the face and thought about what had happened. It seemed unfair that Kanoti had done what he did. Why? Why did he do it? Where had Olugbala been? He could have saved things at the last. If ever there had been a time when he was needed, it was then. Could he not have come in an instant, shown himself to Kanoti, and thus saved him from eternal despair?

Yet Titi realized that Kanoti had known about the real Olugbala during their conversation. In many ways, Olugbala had shown himself to Kanoti. Kanoti had known who he was already. It had been his own choice to do what he did. Now he was going to have to live with that choice.

Olugbala was still in control, too. And besides, here was Titi blaming the statue for what had happened. It was not the statue that had made Kanoti jump. It had been Kjaz-Barbaroi himself.

"Drat him!" If he, Titi, ever saw him, he'd tear him apart faster than a Dark Creature ripping apart the flesh of a zebra.

At the exit from the Great Temple, Titi turned and looked one last time at the statues, altars, and other carvings. He looked at all the torches Kanoti had put around them. All but one had gone out, but this last one flickered, then died down to smoke. The last torch of the Last Torchlighter was extinguished. Titi knew that he would never return to this cavern.

He forced his eyes to focus again on the statue of Kjaz-Barbaroi. He thought that the blow to his head was making his eyes play tricks on him. At first, it looked as if the statue were laughing at him. But then the malignant smile faded as the statue began to crumble. This was for real. All the other carvings in the Great Temple started to fall apart as well. Slabs of rock, the size of tables, fell from the bigger statues and crashed to the floor. They sent up clouds of dust that filled the air and made Titi choke. The last thing Titi saw before he turned and staggered painfully away was the statue of Kjaz-Barbaroi falling forward toward the central aisle of what was once the Great Temple of the Last Tribe. The old man was chased down the passageway by the dust and a noise that sounded like an earthquake. When he reached the Big Cavern, the ceiling of the passageway collapsed, too, filling the entire area with broken rock.

"Where have you been?" someone demanded as Titi stumbled into sight. People pressed around him.

"The whole cave! Is the whole cave going to fall?" someone else shouted. He started running in circles with his hands on his head.

"No," said Titi. "The rest of the cave won't fall down. It is only the Temple. We have no need for it anymore."

"What happened in there?"

"What was all that?"

"Where's Kanoti?"

"It's been hours since we last saw you," said Muriel.

"Look! He's hurt!"

Some were too afraid and too concerned to ask sensible questions. All they could say was: "Oh, my!" or, "Oh dear!" or, just, "Oh! Oh!" and "My! My!"

Titi held up his good arm to quiet the rabble. "Let me sit down and I will tell you everything."

He carefully walked to some flat rocks that served as benches and sat on one. The rest squatted in front of him. He was surprised that he had been knocked out for such a long period of time. Pachunga, Muriel and Kasuku were already well-rested from their naps.

There was a long story to tell, and Titi shortened it even more by not recounting fully what had happened to Kanoti. He implied only that Kanoti had not been able to escape. Yet since the people all knew Titi and Kanoti well, they suspected something else had gone on in the Great Temple that Titi did not want to talk about. They had too much respect for him and for his position to ask him further questions. The old folks had lived long enough to know that some things are better kept as secrets.

While Titi was recounting his tale, Muriel came forward and insisted on looking at his head and arm. Though she appeared to be a young girl, she had gained a lot of experience in first aid when she had traveled all over the globe in search of Meaning and Truth.

"You don't need to trouble yourself about this," said Titi. "It's nothing serious."

"It may not be serious. You are going to live no matter what I do. But it does need some attention."

Titi laughed warily, though it hurt his head. "Then look after me, my little friend. May your touch be as gentle as your eyes."

"Fiddlesticks!" spouted Muriel. She was never much at accepting compliments. After requesting some strips of cloth and pieces of flat wood—which are hard to come by in caves—Muriel had Titi all fixed up.

"I could swear that it was time for the celebration to start," said Lituli.

"Let's get on with it," said the old woman. Though she no longer walked in darkness, she still had some of her impatience.

"And why not?" asked Titi.

Almost immediately, the Big Cavern began to echo with the sound of festive drumming and the high-pitched singing of the old chants. Pachunga recognized some of them from the time of the Battle of a Thousand Cries. He joined in when he could. He even got Muriel to dance in the circle. She clapped, jumped up and down and danced with everyone else. In addition to drums, two Tall People played guitar-like instruments and one blew a wooden flute. The drum sticks beat so rapidly that they produced a blurry, rhythmic noise.

Pachunga had not heard so much music played in Olugbala's honor in years. It thrilled him. For several long moments, he was able to forget about the ordeal of his trip and the plight of his people. Instead, his mind was filled with the chants that sang of the greatness of Olugbala, and the entire cavern was filled with his sweet breath.

It was Kasuku who broke in to spoil the fun. But Pachunga and Muriel knew that it was really time to go. The music and festival stopped. Titi made a farewell speech. Pachunga reminded him to take heed of Olugbala's call to battle against the Dark Creatures. And he expressed confidence that they would be all be meeting together in the near future.

"Look out for Chief Mkumbo of the Cave People," Pachunga said. "He is preparing for battle as well."

"We certainly will. It will be nice to meet out little cousins."

They embraced each other and the trio departed.

Since Titi was injured, Lituli led the three travelers down the remainder of the cave system until the Old Tunnel came to an end at a large pile of rocks. Thinking that their trip might have been in vain, they all stared at the rock pile and became disheartened.

"Oh, no," groaned Muriel.

"All this way for nothing!" complained Pachunga.

"Cheer up!" said Kasuku. "Look at the top!"

Sure enough, there was a small opening. It was not large enough for a Tall Man to pass through, but they would have no difficulty.

"Well, this is it," said Pachunga. He saluted Lituli in the way of the Kiritiri people.

Lituli bent over and touched his hand on Muriel's cheek. She kissed him on the cheek and he looked at her in surprise. He found it pleasant.

"In my country," she explained, "Er, in my tribe that is a sign of love."

"How odd—but how nice," he said.

"Good-bye for now," said Kasuku. "We'll see you all later outside."

"Yes!" said Lituli. "Imagine that! We can go outside with no problem!"

Kasuku saluted Lituli with his wing. The three of them then turned around and scrambled up the pile of rocks to the escape hole. Already they could smell the thick, green air of the outside and feel the warm strokes of the sun on their faces.

As sad as they were to leave the Tall Men behind, it was great to be out in their own world again.

THE BOULDERS

Out of the small hole they crawled, squinting in the bright sunlight of midday, which they hadn't seen in a long time. Or so it seemed. Muriel had been in the caves a lot longer than Pachunga and Kasuku. She had forgotten what it was like not to have a ceiling over her head or to be enclosed by stone walls. The day was so bright that they could not, at first, look at the blue sky above them. Although the caves of the Tall Men had been illuminated by the light of Olugbala, there was a difference in the sunlight that took a few minutes to get used to. It was a different color or something.

Just below them was the beginning of a large field of vine-covered boulders. It stretched on before them and did not stop until the horizon. At the point where the Great Grassland must have begun, they could see the root-like tops of baobab trees and other, scrubby trees that fluttered in heat-distorted air.

Nothing could be heard because of the roar of the Falls. Even though it was more than a thousand meters behind them it still smothered every sound. Pachunga tried to see the top where his adventures in the caves had begun. But the clouds of thundering water-smoke that billowed skyward prevented him.

Stretching off toward the horizon on their left as far as they could see was a cliff higher than the Falls. Pachunga remembered the Cattle People of Prince Mwailu, whom he had seen up there when he had been fighting the vultures. He wondered if they were observing them all right now. He half expected their spears to come raining down on them. To the right, starting about two hundred meters away was more jungle. Pachunga knew from his study of the terrain when he was at the top of the Falls that the jungle continued on to the Great River for about a day's journey. Then it followed the river on both sides as it turned South.

Kasuku studied the boulders in front of them and looked to the left. They could travel across them, which would be the shorter distance to the Great Grassland, or they could travel along the base of the cliff to the North for a day or two. They would miss the boulders, but they would also have a lot more walking to do.

Pachunga was assessing the situation, too. "What do you want to do?" he asked. He had to shout the question.

"I don't know," said Muriel. "It looks like hard work no matter which way we go."

"What?" asked Pachunga. He couldn't hear her very well.

Muriel put her mouth close to Pachunga's ear. "I just thought of something. The entrance to the caves that I went through is over there." She pointed to a place at the base of the cliff. "If we go anywhere near, there may be Dark Creatures or bad Palace Guardsmen. They'll shish-kebab us with their spears."

"What's shish-kebab?" asked Pachunga.

"Roasted meat on a stick."

Pachunga got the connection. "Then let's get on with it," he said, facing the boulders.

"I wish I had my helmet," shouted Muriel back into Pachunga's ear. "My northern head isn't used to getting baked by this equatorial sun."

Pachunga knew what to do to take care of it. "Let me help you."

He took out his knife, and before Muriel knew what was happening, he had cut off less than half a meter of material from the bottom of the wrap-around dress she was wearing. He then took the cloth and made a turban on her head. The dress now reached down to her knee. Since the wrap-around had originally gone down to her ankles, it was easier for her to walk.

"Ready?" asked Pachunga.

Muriel nodded her head yes.

"Just breathe this air!" he exclaimed.

"It's great to be outside again where I can really fly!" said Kasuku.

They descended a couple of meters to the boulders and began to walk over them. It was not easy going. They were vine-covered, and the stiff, dark green, triangular leaves, tough stems and stalks meant that their footing was not secure. There were large spaces between the rocks, which meant that they had to climb, slide down, or jump into the space—then climb up again. It would have been easier if the boulders had been either closer together or more spread apart. Then they could have either hopped from boulder to boulder or walked between them.

The rocks that had no vines or had large bare spots were the most hazardous. Because mist from the Falls settled on them whenever the wind blew from the South, they were covered with slippery moss. Where the mist gathered into pools, there were slimy green algae.

The water in the pools tasted clean. Since the day was hot—and felt all the hotter since the caves had been cool—they frequently had to stop for drinks. Muriel did mention something about stagnant pools, but she drank the water anyway. It was either that or be thirsty. She had learned enough about the tropics to realize that unless she were on the top of a very high mountain, there was no such thing as truly cold and pure water.

The pools were also the perfect place for breeding mosquitoes. They pestered Pachunga and Muriel continually. Muriel was thankful for the numbers of iridescent and green lizards that hid in miniature caves or under leaves. In some of the swampy places between the rocks, frogs and toads sat motionless and stared at the travelers. All of these animals ate many of the bugs that bit them. But they weren't eating enough. The bugs were relentless. Muriel soon was beyond letting the pests bother her. They were a fact of life, just like the humid heat which they could not get away from. "You can't let these things get you down," she kept saying to herself.

Kasuku was thankful for the opportunity to give his wings some exercise. Caves are not the best places for parrots to fly. From time to time, he would go straight up into the air so that he became just a tiny grey speck. Most ordinary parrots, as you well know, cannot fly as long or as high as Kasuku. But then, he was not an ordinary parrot.

By the time the sun was setting behind them at the top of the cliff they had not left far behind, they could see that they had traveled three-quarters of the way across the field of boulders. They were finally out of hearing distance from the Falls, though they could still see them. The setting sun turned the white mist into clouds of orange and yellow. It was one of the most beautiful sights that Pachunga had ever seen.

"Don't you think we should stop for the night?" asked Pachunga.

"I'm with you on that," said Muriel. Her bright wrap-around was damp with perspiration and her white legs were streaked with green algae and black grime. Her turban was falling apart, her feet scratched and sore. She wished that she were a boy so that she could only have something around her waist like Pachunga.

"Ohhh," she moaned as she sat down on a boulder and tried to wash her legs off in a pool. Enough was enough.

"I—We—" Pachunga stopped. He wanted to say something, but he wondered if he should.

"What is it?" asked Kasuku.

"I, uh, I—" Pachunga tried again. Then he blurted it out. "I was just wondering about Kjaz-Barbaroi. He must know by now that we are not trapped inside the Old Tunnel."

"I'm sure of that," said Kasuku.

"Then that means that we are not safe from an attack," said Muriel. She began to look all around her, peering into the shadows underneath the boulders.

"Of course," said Kasuku, "we've been in danger all along—even in the caves of the Tall Men."

"It's odd," whispered Pachunga, "but I did not feel any danger until now. I wasn't thinking of anything happening to us."

"That's the way it should be," said Kasuku. "You remember how it was when we first went into the Old Tunnel. As long as you were not afraid of the ghosts you were not in any danger. It may have been easier not to be afraid, because you were in some dark caves—a strange place where you would expect evil spirits to lurk and to haunt you. You were frightened into not being afraid. That was for your own protection. Here, out in the open, it seems safer because it is more open. We're just finishing a bright, beautiful day. We think that there is less chance of a sneak attack. So you are not frightened into not being afraid."

Pachunga couldn't quite follow what Kasuku was saying. The bird was getting philosophical again. He knew that it must have made some sort of sense, though. Kasuku was not like other parrots who just said whatever popped into their bird-sized brains.

"What should we do, then?" asked Muriel. She didn't quite catch Kasuku's reasoning, either.

"We'll have to stand watch. Olugbala will protect us, but we must remain alert. As you both have learned by now, Kjaz-Barbaroi can be a very crafty adversary."

"Up in the North, we'd say he is as sly as a fox," said Muriel.

"Or that he wants to devour us like a roaring lion," said Pachunga.

"We'll have to take turns being night watchmen. One of us will have to be awake all night."

"I'll take the first watch," said Pachunga.

"Good," said Kasuku. "When the constellation of Kalopa the Lion is half-way across the sky, wake me up and I'll finish out the night."

"What about me?" demanded Muriel. "Shouldn't I be pulling my own weight, too?"

"Well," said Pachunga doubtfully. "You're only a—"

"Listen, kid," said Muriel clenching her fist and waving it in front of Pachunga's nose. "I just hope—I just hope that you were not about to say, 'You're just a girl.' I'll take the third watch. And that's final."

So it was. After a quick meal of dried blind cave fish and dried mushrooms that Lituli had given them for their trip, Muriel and Kasuku fell fast asleep. Pachunga forced himself to stay awake. He concentrated on his surroundings and listened for any strange sounds. Bit by bit, he pushed away the last shreds of sleep. The sky was perfectly clear, and he spent the time looking at the different constellations and shooting stars. There were a lot of them that night. He enjoyed especially the constellations of Kalopa the Lion and Mamosa the Elephant. And on this clear night, they seemed as if they were watching over the threesome.

At the appropriate time, he woke up Kasuku, who kept a good watch. His turn also passed without incident, though just before he awakened Muriel, he got the feeling that the entire night was not going to pass without something happening. It was too peaceful. The night creatures, who normally would have taken an interest in him, were trying too hard not to pay any attention to the strangers going through their territory. In fact, by now they had all disappeared. It was much too quiet. That was not normal. It was a silent warning. But what was the warning about? What was going to happen? He decided that he was not going to get any more sleep that night.

Muriel came awake suddenly and sat straight up. Something was gently pinching her toe.

"Oh! It's just you, Kasuku."

"It's time for your watch. Everything went well, but keep alert. Something is going on."

"That's just what we need—more excitement. I wish that this night would be over with."

"And I likewise," said Kasuku. "But for now, it's off to the world of my dreams." He gripped a tough vine with his claws and buried his head under his wing. Through a space, he watched and listened. He would not sleep.

Muriel still felt groggy from having just been awakened out of sound sleep. Her thoughts were not clear. It also seemed like she couldn't see very well. Later on, if she tried to think about it, she would wonder whether some of the things that happened were real, or whether they were the remnants of a dream.

In the dark, humid night, it seemed as though the entire field of boulders was coming alive. Shadows moved and danced between them. The rocks themselves appeared to be moving. But not very much. There was only a wiggle here or a quiver there—or a shake here and there.

Muriel rubbed her eyes and stared at every rock that appeared to be moving. Yet whenever she looked straight at one, it didn't move at all. The only times that she *thought* she saw something move was when she turned her head away and saw it out of the corner of her eye. Her head turned to the right, then to the left. She moved it faster and quicker as she tried to catch one of the boulders moving. But they were all still. It must just be her imagination, so she decided that she wouldn't be bothered by it at all and tried not to pay any more attention. Boulders moving on their own? That was ridiculous! But her attention was fixed. It had become a game, and she felt as though the stones were mocking her, teasing her, and laughing at her. Yet she could never see a boulder moving if she looked directly at it.

Her fear moved to anger and frustration. She didn't like being picked on, especially by something as unlikely as boulders. She wanted to call Kasuku for help, but she remembered that Pachunga had indicated that she should not go on watch because she was a girl. No, she would have to stick this one out alone—unless it got really bad. For the time being, the boulders weren't doing anything to harm them. They were just moving. She thought. But then, maybe they weren't.

Then she began to hear the noises. They didn't come that often at first, but they sounded like one big stone thumping against another one. Again, like the movements that she thought she was seeing out of the corner of her eye, the sounds came from behind her or beside her. They never came from in front of her.

Tick-tick-tick-tap-tap-knock-knock-crack—CRACK!

A boulder in front of her moved. She saw it with her own eyes. She was not imagining it or dreaming it. It was for real this time.

Knock! Knock! Thud! Crack! Tap! Thud! Thud! Smash!

Muriel wished that she were only in the middle of a dream.

"Kasuku!" she screamed. "The—the rocks! They—they're m-m-moving!"

It would be hard to describe the horror that Muriel felt then. Boulders just don't start moving on their own. They went up and down, knocking and crashing into each other.

Kasuku puffed up his chest and took command. "Come on! Follow me!"

Muriel pulled a sleepy Pachunga to his feet just in time. A boulder bounced on the spot where he had been lying down.

"Wh—What's going on?" His eyes couldn't focus on the rocks in front of him. They should not be moving. But they were.

"Stay right behind me," said Kasuku. "Don't do anything else!"

The boulders were now moving up into the air about three meters and bouncing like marbles dropped on a stone floor. Then they went higher. Some started going sideways, as though flung through the air by a giant sling-shot. Many of them collided with loud, pulverizing explosions and broke into sharp, stony fragments.

All around them as they fled, the boulders crashed and cracked and bounced. Pachunga felt as though he were in some kind of avalanche. Only the rocks weren't just falling down. They were falling *up* first.

134

The one advantage was that with the boulders moving more up in the air than down on the ground, there were fewer rocks for them to climb or stumble over.

Strangely enough, the boulders had missed them so far. Both Pachunga and Muriel felt that at any moment, their heads and bodies were going to be turned into paste and mixed into the broken fragments of rock and chewed-up vines.

They continued to run through the rocky storm. The boulders were missing them and missing them—and missing them. They ducked and swerved and veered and pushed themselves out of the way of the projectiles that were launched at them. The more they maneuvered, though, the more they were hit. These weren't direct blows—just enough to bruise their backs or arms and scrape their skin.

Kasuku flew ahead of them. Muriel was doing an admirable job. Even though she was wearing that wrap-around, she still moved swiftly and easily—though there were many close calls. Kasuku stayed a couple of meters in front of her. And the weird thing she noticed was that he stayed flying in a straight line. He never once served to the left or right, but kept up a steady speed. The boulders—and some just brushed the tips of his wings—kept missing him entirely.

The noise was terrible. The darkness was terrible. The sparks that filled the air from colliding rocks were terrible. As they fled in fright, they had no idea of the direction they were running. Were they running back toward the center of the boulder field, or were they running in the direction of the Great Grassland?

Those questions came to Pachunga. But there was nothing—*nothing!*—that he could do about it. He was not going to turn around and run in the opposite direction in case Kasuku was wrong. All he could do was trust in the parrot and his sense of where to go—and trust in Olugbala.

When was it going to end? They ran and stumbled and sometimes fell—but were immediately back on their feet again. Muriel would recall later that it was the noise that was the most frightening—and added to that was the fear that they might have been running in circles.

Then it was over. There were no more boulders around them. There was just the rough, dry coarseness of the long grass of the savannah that pricked their bloody feet. They collapsed onto it, coughing and wheezing and sputtering for several minutes. None of them could speak clearly.

"Wh—Wh—?" began Pachunga.

"Wow! Hoo—!" attempted Muriel.

Behind them, the boulders quieted and were still. A breeze blew over the field and brought with it the strong smell of crushed vines. It was not pleasant.

"I—I don't understand." Pachunga was finally able to get a complete sentence out.

"How did all of that happen?" asked Muriel.

"No doubt Kjaz-Barbaroi again," said Kasuku. He was perched calmly on the branch of a small gum tree.

"But none of the boulders hit us." said Pachunga. "At least not very much." He rubbed some tender spots on his arms and legs. They would be bruises by the time the sun rose.

Kasuku shook his head and his penetrating look at Pachunga made him feel small. "All this time following Olugbala and you still don't think of him?" Kasuku's voice was firm and convicting. One of his eyes gleamed from the brightness of their moon which had risen during their run through the field of boulders. "Remember that he is protecting us as we go along. The magic of Kjaz-Barbaroi will have no effect on us—unless we ask for it."

"Well, I would never do that!" said Pachunga. The thought of allowing Kjaz-Barbaroi to influence him through choice was upsetting. "Who would ever be that crazy or stupid—especially once he's met Olugbala?"

Kasuku gave Pachunga a long look in the moonlight. "Just remember the Drum," he said softly.

Muriel peered at the eastern horizon. There was the faintest glow of light reflecting off some distant clouds. She knew that it was only a short time until morning.

"There's not much time until morning," said the parrot. "You two lie down and go to sleep. I'll keep the rest of the watch."

"Not on your life!" protested Muriel. "It's still my turn. I should be the one to finish."

"As you wish," said Kasuku. He knew that he wouldn't have any problems sleeping.

Pachunga curled up in a ball on the dry grass and hoped that there weren't any driver ants around or any other biting insects. He wanted to have a good night's rest.

Muriel sat down and leaned against the trunk of a scrubby tree. She had no idea what kind it was. The stars above her faded in the growing light of dawn in the East. Above her, silhouetted against the sky, Kasuku slept on a branch. His head was placed comfortably under a wing. This time, his sleep was for real.

Pachunga was breathing heavily and deeply. And before Muriel knew what was happening to her, she, too, was sleeping soundly.

THE GREAT GRASSLAND

The sun had already climbed high in the sky by the time Pachunga awakened. He had not expected to sleep that long, and he wished that he had managed to awaken sooner. There was a lot of traveling to do. He rolled over onto his back and felt the hot sun on his face. The last of the morning breezes came from the East and picked up the smell of dry, sun-scorched grass and the occasional odor of animals not familiar to him. This was Prince Baree's territory–his lands–and he hoped he would run into him soon.

As he lay there, he wondered how many bruises he would discover when he tried to stand up. The grass, though not soft and lush like some of the jungle grasses back in the Village, was still comfortable. It had made it easier for him to sleep without reminding him of the places on his body that had been struck by the boulders. He felt some of the bruises on his legs. They were not bad. Pachunga hoped they would only be felt for a day—or less. He remembered how quickly his wounds from the vultures had healed.

But for the rustle of the breeze in the leaves of the tree where Kasuku had spent the rest of the night, there was no other sound. However, high in the air above them, Pachunga noticed six black vultures circling. But they were behaving like ordinary ones—not ones that wished to do him or the others any harm. Pachunga realized that they would descend on them only if he and Muriel had failed to awaken. He was sure that they were disappointed that the still forms lying on the ground were not potential carcasses that would have given them something to eat.

Off in the distance through the spaces in the tall grass and bush, he saw several pairs of hyenas' eyes. They were almost invisible, for the markings on their fur hid them in the scrub. They, too, were hoping for a meal of old meat. At the same time, the hyenas and the vultures were probably serving another purpose besides just hanging around looking for breakfast: they were watching Pachunga, Muriel, and Kasuku and reporting their movements to Kjaz-Barbaroi.

Pachunga waved his hand at the hyenas to shoo them away.

They turned their heads and were seen no longer. Perhaps somewhere, lurking out of sight was an old lion deciding whether the two humans on the ground were worth eating.

The Chief rose to his feet with more ease and less pain than he expected. Muriel was still asleep at the base of the gum tree. Pachunga stared at her for a few moments. She had proved to be a good companion and had quickly become his friend. He knew that there was a lot more they would share together before everything was finished.

At the moment, he was hungry and thirsty. Where was Kasuku? He would be able to make a suggestion as to where they could find food and water. That bird had a nasty habit of disappearing whenever Pachunga needed him most. He searched the surrounding trees and shrubs and could not see him anywhere. There was nothing to be concerned about—yet. If he were gone a long time, though, Pachunga wondered how they would cope without him.

He felt they would be in serious difficulty, and—. He stopped thinking those thoughts. They weren't very helpful, and they certainly weren't getting him his breakfast and something to drink.

All the water that Pachunga and Muriel might ever have wanted for the rest of their lives was visible twenty kilometers away at the Falls, but it was too far away to be of any good to them. Pachunga had to find food and water all within close enough range so that he could keep an eye on Muriel. He had decided that he would let her sleep. Who knew how much sleep any of them were going to get within the next few days or weeks? As a warrior, he had learned to sleep whenever the opportunity came up and for however much time was available.

He walked forward a few paces, keeping his eyes open for anything he might see on the ground. He didn't know enough about the bushes of the Great Grassland to risk eating some of the berries growing on them. In a few places he saw some cacti, and Baree had told him once that certain kinds were edible. If only he could remember which ones. They had eaten one close to the Great Desert, and it had been sweet and moist inside.

He noticed some old acacia trees ahead of him. The trunks were thick and their fern-like branches spread out in wide circles. They looked different from the ones he knew were growing farther South. Those had branches that grew upwards and had purple flowers. He headed for the trees. Once there, he noticed several medium-sized blue and black birds. They had long tails and became excited when they saw Pachunga coming. Kasuku was with them.

"Good morning," said Pachunga when he saw his friend.

"Ah, you're up," said Kasuku. "Just catching up on the latest gossip. Those birds are full of it, you know."

"What do they have to say?"

"Well, for one, they are amazed that we survived the boulders. It is a wonder we came out alive. It is the first time they had known anything like that to happen. They told me they've written a song about it so that the event will be remembered in history. I'd translate it for you, but I still don't think it would make any sense. And of course, they've exaggerated it a lot."

"Save it for when this whole thing is over. There'll be plenty of quiet moments then for long stories and songs."

"They also said they were given quite a fright by the whole episode."

"They were—! What about us?" Pachunga laughed. "What else did they have to say?"

"Give me a chance. They said some animals here are very nervous. There is a rumor of an upcoming war—and hearing the Drum beating from time to time has just made their panic worse. A large herd of wildebeests came by yesterday. With their usual gloom, they complained about Kjaz-Barbaroi's recruiting methods. They said the Dark Creatures were using force to get them on their side. Some were even tortured."

Pachunga thought introspectively about his own people and some of the things that had happened to them because of Kjaz-Barbaroi's tactics. "He won't have a faithful army if he has to do that sort of thing. Armies don't fight their hardest when they are terrified of their generals. They fight for causes that are far greater than they are and out of respect for their leaders. Then you see warriors who are ready to go the extra step and take desperate chances. Were there many wildebeests that went with Kjaz-Barbaroi?"

"No. None. The few who were tempted would not leave the herd. They will be there for us when the time comes. That's Kjaz-Barbaroi's major weakness. He's convinced himself that he's going to win—when he's lost the battle before it has even started."

The birds ignored the human speech of Kasuku and Pachunga and continued to peck the dirt looking for food. The sight of them hunting for breakfast reminded Pachunga that he had had nothing to eat since the previous evening.

"What's for breakfast?" he asked. "I'm starved, and I want to save the food that the old woman gave us for an emergency. The Grassland is not like the jungle. It doesn't have the same kinds of food."

"Yes, but there is still plenty of it if you know where to look. Follow me."

Pachunga was concerned about Muriel. Perhaps she was already awake. Also, he didn't know how safe it was to leave her alone. "What about Muriel?"

"Don't worry about her. She is being carefully guarded."

"By the vultures and hyenas?"

Kasuku looked disgusted. "Of course not. You'll meet him soon enough."

"And if she wakes up?"

"We're not far from her, and it has not been that long."

"But—"

"Don't worry about her, I said. She's safe."

Kasuku told Pachunga to go straight through the acacia trees. They were only a meter taller than Pachunga, and he had to duck frequently to keep from hitting the branches.

"I discovered these this morning while you were sleeping," said Kasuku. "One of them should make you and Muriel a fine breakfast."

"What are they?"

"See for yourself. They're right in front of you."

Lying on the ground in a shallow trough were four of the largest eggs that Pachunga had ever seen.

"What hen laid this?"

"It was no chicken," said Kasuku.

"That's right. What are they called? Ostriches. I've eaten these eggs before with Prince Baree. The ostrich is that big bird that runs—but doesn't fly."

"Correct. They don't do well in the jungle. Out here in the open is their homeland. Perhaps you'll see some off in the distance. They are very shy and run extremely quickly. We use them for messengers at times. These eggs were recently laid."

"We'd better go back to Muriel," said Pachunga. He couldn't keep her off his mind and was just standing up with the egg when he heard Muriel scream. His body became rigid and he dropped it. With a thud, it broke on the ground, spreading clear white and yellow yolk into the sandy soil.

"Muriel!" He turned and raced through the acacia trees back to their overnight camp. The birds scattered as he ran by them. When he saw Muriel she was apparently unharmed, standing straight up. Her face was white.

"Are you all right?" he asked.

"What is it?" asked Kasuku.

"It—it—it was a lion—the b-b-biggest lion I have ever seen!"

"Ah, yes," said Kasuku. "I thought so. That's why I wasn't worried about Muriel. The wildebeests were right after all. Kalopa the Lion is back."

"Kalopa?" Pachunga didn't think he'd heard right. "*The* Kalopa? That's impossible. You don't mean it."

"But it has been an age since he was last seen," said Muriel.

"Yes, it has been an age," said Kasuku. "Remember that nothing is impossible for Olugbala. The three of us are testimonies to that." He flew to Pachunga's shoulder. "The time of battle must be closer than I'd thought. Olugbala would not have brought Kalopa back if it weren't of the utmost importance. Did you see where he went?"

"No," said Muriel. "He was in the long grass. I-I just saw him staring at me. His eyes were so fierce—so savage. Then he went away."

"Well, I wouldn't worry about him. Fierce though he is, his anger is only for our enemies. Woe be to any creature who would ever try to stand against him."

"Are you feeling better?" asked Pachunga.

"Yes, I think so," said Muriel. She still looked shaken. "I was just surprised."

"Kalopa wouldn't have let you see him unless he wanted you to," said Kasuku. "He was probably just letting you know that he is here to protect us."

"Enough of this," said Pachunga. "I'm hungry. We can talk while we get the food ready."

"What is it?" asked Muriel.

"I, uh, dropped it," said Pachunga. He was embarrassed. "I heard you scream and—"

"That's a fine thing," she said. "Does that mean we have nothing to eat?"

"No, there's more." He looked at Kasuku. "Why don't you show Muriel where they are while I get a fire going?"

"Can you tell me what we're having for breakfast?" Muriel was getting exasperated herself. She felt grumpy from the long night.

"You'll see," said Pachunga. He was being as cagey as Kasuku.

About an hour later, Pachunga and Muriel were eating fire-cooked ostrich egg. To them, it tasted better than ordinary chicken eggs. And one was certainly enough to feed them both.

"Now for water," said Muriel. "I'm parched."

"Me, too," said Pachunga. He brushed off a crumb of egg yolk from the side of his mouth and wiped his hands on the grass. "But where do you suppose we'll find it in this hot, dry place?" He knew that any hope of finding water in the field of boulders would be impossible after what had happened there in the night. And he had no desire to return there anyway. The next time he saw a field of boulders, he would avoid it at all costs.

"Follow me," said Kasuku simply. He certainly wasn't being direct that morning. They picked up their few belongings and followed Kasuku's directions to continue East. They left the acacia trees behind and walked up and down small hills that had appeared flat from far away. They saw the herd of wildebeests off in the distance. They wavered and moved fantastically in currents of heat that rose through clouds of dust kicked up by their hooves.

As they walked, they saw a small herd of common elands running away. Once they surprised a pair of crowned cranes that took off in heavy flight in the direction of the Great River from which they had strayed. Karoo thorn trees were abundant as was the spekboom tree and the boerboon tree, which was pretty in the blooming season because of its scarlet, lantern shaped flowers. Kasuku, who had spent considerable time in the Great Grassland with Prince Baree, would have named them something different in the language of the Cattle People. These names came from the Bazungu, who had explored the area for their governments.

Pachunga and Muriel were bothered the most by the dry heat and the direct sun which fried their skin. It sucked the water out of their bodies until their mouths and lips felt as parched and dusty as the soil they trod upon. The sunlight that glared off the light brown and light grey terrain made their pupils small black dots. The minute, unseen particles of dust kicked up by an occasional breeze stung their now bloodshot eyes and grated against their throats.

"Where's the water?" demanded Pachunga. His temper became shorter with every step he took. The Drum began to beat in time to his walking.

"It's right in front of you," said Kasuku.

Pachunga looked around. The only thing of significance he could see was a large baobab tree. There was nothing that looked as if it would produce water.

"Now, look, Kasuku. I'm getting awfully sick of your darn— *moralizing*—and constant cagey answers to my questions. You haven't answered a single one directly all morning. And you usually have something to say about Olugbala this and Olugbala that—"

"Pachunga!" said Muriel. She didn't like what he was saying.

"And don't start telling me about the Drum. I am sick and tired of it. Do you hear? Sick and tired of it!" The strain of their trip and no water was beginning to show up in Pachunga's behavior.

"Pachunga!" said Kasuku firmly, but softly. "Pachunga, I didn't know that I had been offending you this way. Forgive me if I have been. I had no idea."

"Oh, you really haven't. It's just that—"

"Pachunga, each of us has been under a lot of pressure," said Muriel. "It's to your credit that you've put up with as much as you have."

"I know we have been," he said. "I only wonder from time to time if it's worth it."

"We all do," said Muriel. "You're not the only one to think that way. There have been many times in the past few days when I've wondered myself what it is we are doing. We're supposed to be meeting Olugbala. Yet, we don't know where. We know that there is going to be a battle against Kjaz-Barbaroi. We don't know when. Soon. That is all we keep hearing. Be alert. Be ready. Be watchful. Be watchful for what?"

"Watchful for those times that Kjaz-Barbaroi thinks he has us in his grasp," said Kasuku. "Watchful for the coming of Olugbala. This means all the time—not just the times when we feel like it. We are now working for Olugbala and have to be ready for what he wants us to do—no matter when or where it might be. That was the responsibility that we each took when we decided to follow him. You don't have to accept that responsibility, though. You can tell Olugbala you don't want to serve him right now."

"No!" said Pachunga definitively. "I would never do that!"

"Me neither," said Muriel. "Look at all he's done for us."

"Yes," said Kasuku. "I knew you'd say that. You see? You really do want to follow Olugbala."

Pachunga walked over to the baobab tree near them. It was very old and looked like something the Father the Creator had mistakenly planted upside down—that is, if he were capable of making a mistake, which he isn't. Its branches looked exactly like roots that twisted through the air. The trunk was about three meters high and less than two meters wide at the base. Its hide was very withered and gnarled and tough.

Pachunga thought that it was the ugliest tree he had ever seen. He said so. "This is the ugliest tree I've ever seen. I didn't really pay any attention to them the last time I was here."

"That may be so," said Kasuku. "But I'd much rather look at this tree right now than any other."

"This is where the water is?" Pachunga walked around the bottom and examined it. He couldn't see anything that resembled water. All he got was the feeling that the tree was very old and had seen a lot. It had stood on that spot for more rainy seasons that those of him, his father, and his father's father combined.

"Yes," said Kasuku. "It's right here." He flew to the top of the trunk and perched on a short, broken branch that was next to a round, dark hole in the side of the tree.

Muriel noticed for the first time small indentations carved into the side of the tree where someone could place their feet as they climbed. These foot-holds were so weathered they blended in with the trunk and could not be seen at first.

"Here, Pachunga," she said. "You can get up this way."

"You go ahead, Muriel," said Pachunga. "I can wait." He was still feeling badly about his outburst.

"Thanks."

She climbed up the side. Hanging on to a wooden peg just inside the opening was a tiny string made from braided palm fibers. The Mzungu needed no further encouragement. She pulled the string slowly. There was something heavy at the other end. Presently, a smooth, hard gourd full of water emerged.

"Well, I'll be!" she said. She drank what she wanted and held the dipper for Kasuku.

She laughed.

"What's so funny?" asked Kasuku.

"You," she said.

"Why?"

"Your eyes and head do crazy things when you drink water. It's adorable."

Kasuku chuckled.

"I suppose it's because you're a bird and can't swallow. I'd drown if I had to drink like that." She took another drink.

"Whose water is this?"

"See the mark?" asked Kasuku. "It's just above the hole."

"Yeah." She saw some slanted lines slashed into the tree.

"This water belongs to the Cattle People. That's how I knew that it was here. The Prince and I would take a drink whenever we passed by. Normally baobab trees don't have such an ample supply like this. You have to press the water out of the wood. But this one was turned into a water storage tank by the Cattle People. So not all baobab trees are

146

like this. You'll find ones like this throughout the Great Grassland. I'm hoping I can remember where most of them are."

"It's been here that long? Wow. Where are all the Cattle People now?"

Kasuku turned his head around and viewed the surrounding savannah. "They are all around."

"Where?"

"In places where you cannot see them. They have been traveling with us since breakfast."

"These are the good ones, right?"

"Yes, they are on our side—not Prince Mwailu's."

"Good, I—"

"Hey, Muriel!" It was Pachunga. They had forgotten all about him. "Is there going to be any water left by the time it's my turn to drink?"

"Oh, Pachunga. I'm sorry. Here, come up."

"Thanks."

Pachunga drank his fill and looked at the herd of wildebeests still on the eastern horizon. Like the setting of a flat, brown and dusty sun, they disappeared over the edge of the Great Grassland. There were no other signs of wildlife. Not even a bird could be seen. The sense of danger came to all three of them at the same time. He tried to locate the Cattle People, but he couldn't.

Pachunga climbed down from the tree. "I don't like this."

'"Nor do I," said Muriel.

"Look!" said Kasuku.

Beyond the scrawny, mostly-dead tree came a couple of flashes of tan and white. One flash of color was noticeably higher than the other one. As Pachunga focused his eyes on them, he discovered that the white and tan flashes were two pith helmets. Behind the helmets were eight porters carrying wooden crates. Some of the crates lay on their shoulders and upper backs, and a couple of heavy ones were attached to long wooden poles so that the weight could be shared by more than one man. From time to time, they would stagger under the load.

A disgusted, distasteful and hateful feeling filled Pachunga's heart and his hand went for the handle of his curved knife. The two helmets meant Bazungu. One helmet higher than the other one meant something else: those two Bazungu were Snipe and Snippet. Pachunga felt the hatred flow through his body like burning acid. As he felt it, the Drum beat louder and louder. While pulling his knife out of his belt, he crouched down and began to creep silently through the brush towards his enemies. This was his opportunity for revenge.

"Pachunga!" cried Muriel softly. "Where are you going?"

"Pachunga!" commanded Kasuku. "Don't listen to it! Don't listen to the Drum!"

Pachunga forced himself to ignore Kasuku's warning. But then he really didn't need to try so hard. The pounding of the Drum beat so loudly that all other noises were drowned out.

THE ENCOUNTER

From his days as a warrior fighting against the Dark Creatures, Pachunga had learned how to move silently through the dense brush and undergrowth without making a sound. Snipe and Snippet were walking in a straight direction from the South to the North. Pachunga circled around to his left so that he could intercept them a couple of hundred meters from his previous position where Muriel and Kasuku were. He constantly kept them in his sight, knowing that while he could see them, they would not be able to see him. He was too swift—too quiet—too much the experienced hunter. Wouldn't they be shocked when they saw him? He would be the last human they would see before his knife did the work that was necessary.

Boom! Boom! Boom! Boom!

As he neared them, he saw Snippet's bloated red face and Snipe's long, cruel grey lips. He remembered that it was Snipe who was most likely responsible for the deaths of Mwema and Mwenda. He had been the one to alert Mkumbo's Palace Guard after Muriel had diverted them. Seeing them in person—and not just hearing them in voice only—for the first time since he had fled the Village of the Kiritiris made him remember all the things that these two men had done to his people. How many deaths were they responsible for in the mine?

He held the knife tighter in his hand and thought how wonderful it would be to cut them open like slaughtered warthogs. These two Bazungu were going to pay for what they had done to him and the Kiritiris. They would pay, all right. And he would get such delicious

149

pleasure from doing it, too. They were going to suffer just as he and his people had suffered.

It was sad that Pachunga could not see that what he was doing was exactly what Kjaz-Barbaroi wanted him to do. By listening to the Drum, he was separating himself from Olugbala. So what if the two Bazungu were killed? Kjaz-Barbaroi didn't care. They, like all his subjects, were easily expendable. And Pachunga hated them with all the hate he could muster. This hatred did not come from Olugbala. It came from Kjaz-Barbaroi. Kjaz-Barbaroi grew stronger on hate, and Pachunga had forgotten that the only way to defeat him was to love those who were under the tyrant's control. Love was something Snipe and Snippet had difficulty understanding. It was something they had given up on. In their current state, it would have confused them and confounded them. It would have broken down their defenses and made it possible for them to be defeated.

Yet love was further away from Pachunga's thoughts than anything else. He was too intent on doing away with Snippet and Snipe. And he had decided exactly how he was going to do it.

* * * *

Muriel began to run after Pachunga a moment after he disappeared into the tall grass and shrubs.

"No!" cried Kasuku. "We cannot go after him now. It will only make things worse."

Muriel's distress was evident in her eyes. Nothing good was going to come out of this. For one thing, Pachunga was listening to the Drum. For another, she knew Snipe and Snippet. She knew that they had guns and knew what they could do.

"They'll shoot him. Does he know that?"

"He should know it—if he remembers. The two Bazungu used guns when they were in the Kiritiri lands. It was what gave them their sense of power and strength and superiority. Without the guns, they are nothing. Pachunga, though, in his mood, probably feels that he can stop anything—even bullets."

"Can't we do anything?"

"Yes," said Kasuku. "Listen to this."

* * * *

150

Pachunga crouched down low behind some bushes that hid him from the trail that Snipe and Snippet were following. His plan was a simple one. All that he had to do was jump out and surprise them. He knew them to be such wimps and cowards that they would be at his mercy. And he felt very strong now—the strongest he had ever been. Hate was giving him a lot of courage. They would shrink back in fear as if he were Kalopa the Lion himself.

Their weak, simpy voices reached Pachunga's ears, though he could not understand what they were saying. His brown body was slick as though covered with oil. Pachunga had to control his breathing so that he wouldn't make any sound. Strength and power flowed through him and he knew that he would not be beaten. His would be the victory.

Boom! Boom! Boom! Boom! Boom!

The voices of Snipe and Snippet grew louder, and Pachunga could understand what they were saying. The porters followed along behind them. The strain of their burdens could now be seen on their faces. In a few moments, thought Pachunga, they would not be slaves of the Bazungu anymore.

"The Boss (which was their name for Kjaz-Barbaroi) seems to be upset these days," said Snipe. "Must be on account of Pachunga."

"Oh, yes. It must be," said Snippet.

"That geezer is long gone, I'm sure," said Snipe. "He could never have survived the Old Tunnel."

"Oh, yes. I'm sure he didn't. They say there is no exit and that it is full of deep holes."

"He probably fell down one of those holes and got smashed up by the rocks," said Snipe. He was perplexed. "But the Boss is still convinced that he's alive and that he escaped—" He tripped over a stone and nearly fell. "Drat this place!" he cursed.

His distraction was just what Pachunga needed. He was tough. He was strong. He was over six feet tall and had the strength of Mamosa the Elephant. This was the moment. It was *his* moment.

"Ah-*hah*!" he cried as he jumped out at the Bazungu.

"What's going on?" Snippet's pudgy face went white.

"No—!" exclaimed Snipe. He tried to get his rifle in a position so that he could aim it and pull the trigger. The strap got tangled around his upper arm and shoulder. As he struggled with it, he kept his good eye focused on Pachunga. A look of astonishment came to him. "Why, he's only a boy." He stopped struggling with his rifle.

"Oh, yes," said Snippet. "It's only a boy." He tried to relax, but he saw the knife that Pachunga was holding.

"Huh?" thought Pachunga. He'd forgotten that he was as young as he was. When he realized this, he didn't feel quite as strong as he had—nor as invincible. His enemies wouldn't know this, though. He continued to move the knife in a menacing and threatening way.

"Children," said Snippet. "We keep running into children."

"Why are they talking so much?" wondered Pachunga. He wanted to get the business over with. Which one should he take out first? Snipe. The answer was obvious.

"Children," said Snipe, "should not be carrying such big knives." He spoke warily and slowly. Although the boy in front of him was only twelve or thirteen, he didn't know how well he could use the knife. He was holding it expertly enough. And he did appear to be serious about it. The road of caution was always the better route to take. "They might hurt themselves." Snipe did not feel that he was saying anything original. However, he might have been encouraged to say something more dramatic had he realized that his words were going to be in a story.

"Oh, yes," said Snippet. He was in full agreement with Snipe—as usual. "They might hurt themselves."

Snipe studied Pachunga's knife closely. "That knife—I've seen it before." Snipe was a mercenary, and it was his job to know all that there was to know about weapons. "Boy," he said authoritatively, "where did you get that knife? It looks like Pachunga's. And what's a Kiritiri doing all the way out here, anyway? Shouldn't you be working in the mine?"

"Yes, boy," said Snippet. "Where'd you get that knife?" Snippet tried to look imposing, though he didn't do it very well.

Something needs to be said here about the porters—the men carrying the heavy loads. When they saw Pachunga jump out and confront Snipe and Snippet, they sighed with relief. It meant they could put down their boxes and bags and take a rest. They were Cattle People, though you wouldn't have known it to look at them. Since they had been made slaves by Snipe and Snippet, they'd had their shields and spears taken away from them. The only clue that they were Cattle

People—besides being tall and slender—was the diagonal scarring that they had on their chests.

These particular Cattle People were not on the side of Kjaz-Barbaroi. They were on Olugbala's side. As Snippet and Snipe continued to talk to the strange boy in front of them, they began to get the feeling that they were about to receive their freedom.

Until they saw the lion.

And he was no ordinary lion. He was huge. His brown eyes shone bright and alert—and betrayed a superior intelligence. His broad nose wrinkled and his large jaws were firmly set. He walked slowly up the trail behind Pachunga. With each step, the powerful muscles in his body rippled under his dusty coat.

Snippet and Snipe were so interested in Pachunga and his knife that they didn't notice the lion behind him.

Then one of the porters screamed.

Then Snipe and Snippet saw the lion.

Then the lion roared.

Well, he didn't actually roar. He really yawned, though it sounded like a roar to the two Bazungu. With many shrieks, wails and cries, Snippet, Snipe and the porters scurried down the trail away from the lion.

That is, all the porters but one fled. The one who remained was a boy Pachunga's age.

Pachunga didn't notice the boy, though. He was too busy turning around and slashing whatever it was behind him with his knife. The lion pulled his nose out of the way just in time.

And he roared—for real this time.

Snippet screamed off in the distance.

Pachunga dropped the knife on the ground and took one step backward. He wanted to say something, but he was too afraid. It was not fear for his life, however. He was afraid because of the power of Olugbala that he sensed coming from the lion. He stared into his eyes, and the lion stared back. There was recognition there—though Pachunga knew that they had never met until then. The lion knew who he was. He was just waiting for Pachunga to recognize him.

The Drum stopped.

"Kalopa," said Pachunga. "I am staring directly into the face of Kalopa the Lion."

"I thought you would recognize him," said the boy who had been standing quietly behind Pachunga all this time.

That voice was familiar. It brought back a thousand memories all at once: fishing in the Great River near the Village, hunting in the Jungle, and fighting against the Dark Creatures at the Battle of a Thousand Cries. The voice was one that he knew. All the feeling that Pachunga had experienced when Kasuku had flown through the window of his hut several weeks before came back to him again.

"Baree," Pachunga said quietly to himself before turning. "Prince Baree."

He now looked at him. A smile slowly replaced his doubt and wonder. He longed to give him a hug.

Baree held open his arms, grinning broadly, and they embraced enthusiastically. Pachunga had feared momentarily that Baree might have been a ghost, but this wasn't true. The Prince was solid. He was flesh and bone. He also had a small scar on his chest where the spear had entered eighty-one rainy seasons before.

Baree was about a centimeter taller than Pachunga, although he was a lot skinnier. While Pachunga was broad-shouldered with just-developing muscles, the Prince was sinewy and lean and weighed about five kilograms less. He had been trained to be the prince of his people from the time he was born, so he was the most skilled in the use of bow and arrow, the spear and the other weapons of hunting and battle. Although he appeared to be only thirteen, he had spent the last eighty-one rainy seasons on Olugbala's Mountain. If the battle against the Dark Creatures went well, Baree would be named head of a council of chiefs and princes for the region.

"Baree, Baree, Baree," repeated Pachunga.

"Pachunga, Pachunga, Pachunga," echoed Baree.

"It's good to see you again!"

"After all this time!"

"And to think that Kalopa the Lion—" Pachunga stopped. He turned to greet Kalopa, only the lion had disappeared.

"Where'd he go?"

"He is around," answered Baree. "It's just that he is from a time so long ago when things were really wild, he has problems being with humans. It's not that he doesn't like us—he loves everyone. He's just so big and snarls so much when he talks that it's hard for people to relax when he's here."

A flapping flash of grey settled on Baree's shoulder. The normally inseparable pair were reunited once again.

"Well, old friend," said Baree. "It's good to see that you're back safely." He tried to glare at the parrot, but it was impossible. He smiled. "Did you stay out of trouble?"

"Er, most of the time," said Kasuku.

"He was the most ill-mannered parrot I have ever known," said Pachunga. "He was always getting us into trouble."

"Kasuku," said the Prince sternly, "Is that true?"

"Well, you know how these long trips can be," said Kasuku. "You have to do something for entertainment." He looked very meek and had lost some of his usual parrot pomp and stuffiness.

Pachunga laughed. "Actually, it was more the case of him keeping me out of trouble. Who knows what would have happened if it hadn't been for Kasuku? I would have blown everything by now if I'd been given the chance."

"Pachunga?" came a breathless cry from up the trail. "Are you okay?"

"I'm fine, Muriel," said Pachunga. He turned to greet her. "Did you think I wouldn't be?"

"Well, with Snipe and Snippet having guns and Kalopa the Lion—"

"He's on our side," said Baree.

"I know, but nonetheless—"

"It was all my fault," the Chief said quietly. He didn't want to look his friends in the eye when he spoke, but he forced himself to. "Never have I felt such hatred. And I would have killed them, too! I know I would have at least tried."

"We know," said Kasuku. "That's why Kalopa had to stop you."

"I appreciate that—more than you'll ever know."

"You'd do the same the same for us," said Baree. "if you had to."

Muriel looked at the boy who had just spoken. This was someone she didn't know. "Who are you?" she demanded.

"Oh! I'm sorry," said Pachunga. "This is Prince Baree of the Cattle People."

"But I'd heard that—" She stopped herself when realized whom she was addressing. "Uh, you are?" Now she was feeling embarrassed. "Er, your highness," she said. She tried to curtsy, only she didn't do it very well.

"Baree is fine," said the Prince. "Only Kjaz-Barbaroi gets hung up on titles."

"Thank you," she said quietly. She still felt self-conscious.

"How did you get here?" asked Pachunga.

"I joined the other porters to try to prevent Snipe and Snippet from reaching the camp of Kjaz-Barbaroi. They were hoping to rejoin him there. If I could have distracted them—and—"

"Well," said Pachunga, "we seem to have done that."

"Not quite," said Kasuku. "They might try something. This is a very important delivery they are trying to make."

"All is not lost," said Baree. "It never is when Olugbala is arranging things. We have to get the supplies they are trying to take. Even if they were to get them back again, the porters have fled. This will hold them up a lot."

Baree went over to one of the crates and pried off a few of the top boards with Pachunga's knife. "Look at what they were bringing." He picked up something heavy that was wrapped in thick, oily paper. After unwrapping it, he showed what was inside to Pachunga. "You know what this is?"

"No, I don't. It is something the Bazungu have made."

"I know what it is," said Muriel. "It's part of a gun. Snippet and Snipe were transporting rifles then up to Kjaz-Barbar—"

"Yes," said Baree. "And with these in the hands of the Dark Creatures, there is no telling what might happen. There are not many of them—but these are enough to cause some trouble and to make things rough for us."

"We must—" There was a sharp crack that echoed across the Great Grassland. Muriel didn't finish her sentence. Instead, she forgot all about what she was trying to say as she suddenly and abruptly twisted on one leg before falling to the ground. She gazed at her upper leg. A large red stain started growing on her wrap around. A look of astonishment came across her face before she fainted.

There was another crack, and a piece of wooden box next to Baree burst into little splinters.

"Down!' commanded Baree. "They're shooting at us!"

He and Pachunga dropped to their bellies.

"Kasuku! To the air! Find out where they are!"

The bird flew straight up into the sky like a peregrine falcon.

More shots were fired. They pressed themselves down into the ground.

"How's Muriel?" asked Baree.

Pachunga was in a better position to crawl over to her. He looked at her carefully. What he saw made him feel better. The bullet had not gone into her leg. It had only made a small groove on the outside.

"She'll be okay," he reported. "Though she won't be able to walk well for a few days. Ayyy! We'll have to get her someplace where we can clean it up and bandage it. But how?"

Baree didn't answer. He was thinking quickly and waiting impatiently for Kasuku to get back with his report.

Snipe and Snippet continued to shoot at them. Since they couldn't see their target, they were shooting wildly. Even still, some of the bullets were still coming very close.

Kasuku dropped from the sky like a shot goose, but broke his fall with his wings so that he landed gently on the ground between the Chief and the Prince.

"Snipe is behind a termite-eaten baobab tree about two hundred meters to the front and left. Snippet is about fifty meters to Snipe's left. I don't know why they are firing at us from such a distance. We don't know how to use the rifles."

"What's it like behind them?"

"It's all open field. There is no place to hide or make a sneak attack from the rear."

"That means you can't signal my warriors and have them come in from that side."

"I wouldn't want to risk it, anyway. The warriors only have spears, and I think you would lose too many of them because of the Bazungu's own rifles."

"You're right," said Baree.

"And behind us here?" asked Pachunga. "What about a retreat?"

"We can't do that with Muriel the way she is," said Baree. "And we don't want to leave them those guns if we can help it."

Muriel groaned.

"Shhhhh," went Pachunga in her ear.

The ground exploded centimeters from her head from a bullet fired by one of the two Bazungu. Pachunga yanked her back and put her behind one of the crates.

"Wh—What?" she asked.

"Don't talk," he said. He ripped some cloth from her turban and wrapped it around her thigh. He hoped that it would stop the bleeding. "Everything's going to be fine."

"What about Kalopa?" asked Baree.

Pachunga had forgotten about him.

"He's in the thick brush about forty meters to the left of Snippet," answered Kasuku.

"Can't he attack them?" asked Pachunga.

"The two are spread out too far. If he were to go for one, the other one would shoot him. Kalopa is not bullet proof."

They really were in an awkward situation.

Baree looked reflective for a moment and motioned for Pachunga and Kasuku to come close to him. "Watch this," he said in a very low voice. He took a small wooden whistle that hung from a leather cord around his neck and blew it. A long, high-pitched and shrill note sounded and traveled quickly over the scrubby savannah.

"Now all we have to do is wait," said Baree.

The whistle reached the ears of someone who recognized the signal.

He knew what to do.

Snipe and Snippet

Snipe cursed the bugs that were biting him and the heat that was causing his forehead to sweat. He was most uncomfortable. Why did he choose an ant colony to hide behind? From a distance—particularly since he had been running from the largest *blankety-blank* lion he had ever seen—the big, old rotting tree trunk had looked like the ideal place. It was also close enough to those boys and that girl that he could keep an eye on what they were doing.

But when Snipe had planted himself behind the tree, he discovered that hundreds of insects with pincers the size of pliers were there with him. They were driving him crazy. He wanted to brush them away, only he didn't want to make any unnecessary movement. And he also wanted to wipe away the sweat that was filling his eyes and burning them. Because of all these irritations, he was having difficulty aiming and firing his rifle. He wasn't getting the bullets anywhere near his target —except for that first shot that decked the little punk girl.

He was pleased about that. For the moment, it was the only thing that had given him any satisfaction. That girl, Muriel, had taken one of his bullets. He didn't like to shoot children—especially white ones—but the Boss had said that she was one of the enemy and was helping to make a royal mess out of everything. "Make sure you get them all if you see them," he had hissed. "Kill them slowly and painfully."

Snipe had questioned at the time whether or not the white girl and Pachunga could have survived the Old Tunnel. Kjaz-Barbaroi had snarled quietly in response to that question: "Keep your eyes open for them." He had said this only to Snipe. It was a secret between the two of them, and Snippet was not to be included in it. "Snippet—that whimpering coward—won't have the guts to kill them when the time comes. He will only want to capture them. If he stands in your way, you know what to do."

Snipe had only smiled.

Well, the girl was suffering right now. If he could keep them pinned down with his rifle, she would slowly bleed to death. What a way to go! He wondered who the boy with Pachunga's knife was. Clearly the old man wasn't around anymore if the kid has his knife. But what was a Kiritiri doing all the way out here? The other boy—the one who had been one of his porters—was also confusing him. He questioned who he really was and what he had been doing as a porter. He obviously had been in charge of the other porters by some kind of concealed arrangement. He also had not run away when the lion had appeared. The whole thing was mystifying. And then there was that grey parrot. Some of the Kiritiris had seen it when Pachunga had escaped from the Village. A couple of them had claimed that it had been Kasuku the Parrot, who had been a pet of some boy prince of the Cattle People decades ago. That was, of course, ridiculous native hogwash. He was certain of it.

His thoughts drifted back to the wounded girl again. She reminded him of one of those girls who had refused to go out with him when he was growing up in the North. Her type had to suffer—as he had suffered.

Snipe had been whipped continually by his father, starved by his mother, and his older brother used to tie him up and stick toothpicks up his fingernails for the slightest offense. His teachers always paddled him, and the other boys had despised him. Soon, the only way that he had learned to survive was to make those who had antagonized him and tortured him suffer, too.

He had escaped from reform school at the age of seventeen by setting it on fire. The only place he could think of going was South—into the jungle. It was a good place to disappear from the law and nobody asked any questions once you got there. It was in the jungle that the Company had found him—penniless and half-mad from malaria and dysentery. They had rehabilitated him when they recognized that he had one good talent: meanness. The Company had needed somebody with that talent to take care of their nastier bits of business. Those working in the mines had to be kept in line. And because this was "legitimate" employment, Snipe never thought of himself as only a hired gun or professional killer. He saw himself as a mercenary—a soldier of fortune.

Snipe thought again of the boy with Pachunga's knife. *Who was he?* The face was almost familiar—besides the fact that all the people around here looked alike to him. Snipe knew that he had met him somewhere before. The boy had certainly met him before. Those brown eyes had shown recognition and hate. Was he some Kiritiri kid seeking revenge for the death of his father or something? But then, how would he have escaped from working in the mine? The only one whom he knew who had escaped was Pachunga.

Could it be that boy was he? The more he thought about it, the more he realized that it had to be Pachunga—or maybe his son. But Snipe knew that the old coot had never had any sons. That left only one possibility then.

But it wasn't possible.

And Snipe felt as if he were going mad.

People grow older. They do not grow younger. Granted, a lot of mysterious and funny things were happening—things that he could not understand as being possible—especially with Kjaz-Barbaroi around a lot more than he used to be. This was a very kooky continent. "No!" he thought to himself. But it had to be true. Nothing else fit. That boy had to be Pachunga. And as a boy, instead of as a doddering old man, he was going to be a lot more dangerous to them.

* * * *

Snippet was in a different situation from Snipe. He didn't have the other Mzungu's natural meanness, but he was learning about it quickly. He had not been hired by the Company to do the nastier bits of business. However, he seemed recently to be doing more and more of it ever since the Boss had started to call the shots.

Snippet was a geologist. He had his Ph.D., in fact, and his specialty was in precious metals such as gold, platinum and silver. He also knew a lot about precious stones and gems. He was such an expert that he could look at a piece of ground, take a few samples of rock and soil and decide how much gold was lying beneath the surface. While meanness was the food that kept Snipe going, the one thing that kept Snippet living in the jungle and working for the Company was greed.

Of course, it had not always been so. Snippet, when he had been a boy, had been a large, pleasant and roly-poly child. He had had a broad, round, pink face, brown deer eyes, and a warm, innocent personality. He had liked games, friends and working on model battleships which he would proudly display on a shelf in his room. Since he actually was intelligent and had an active imagination, he could think of many different games for himself and his companions to play. He had been quick to tell an amusing story and his interest in his friends and his concern for them made him very popular. His brothers were the only ones who gave him a hard time—mostly because they were jealous of the popularity he enjoyed. He had been completely different from the way that he was now.

All had been going well until the economic depression. His father lost his job and started to drink a lot of whiskey—a bottle a night. In order to put food on the table, Snippet found it necessary to start working in the afternoons following school and on Saturdays in a jewelry store owned by a man named Snoot. Actually, Snoot owned not just one jewelry store. He owned a whole chain of them that ringed the city in the suburbs and dominated every major borough in town.

Snippet's job had been to work in the main store in the center of the city. He was messenger boy, sweeper, window washer, wastebasket emptier and brass polisher. Snoot and the other employees constantly reminded him of this. His hourly wage was equal to that of someone being paid eighteen cents an hour today. There was no minimum wage. This paltry salary didn't help his attitude towards his job, either.

There had been something about working in Snoot's jewelry store that had gone to his head. Being surrounded by all those precious metals—not to mention diamonds, rubies, emeralds, amethysts, opals and sapphires—had made him sort of crazy, according to a report made to the police later by his mother. "He hadn't had much since his father lost his job," she had said. "We were very poor, you know."

Greed took the poor lad over and he had decided that his one goal in life was to become richer than Snoot. He wanted much more gold and many more diamonds. How he achieved that wouldn't matter at all—just as long as it was the quickest and easiest way.

Greed made him endure Snoot's snobbishness. Greed made him work hard to go to the university to earn his doctorate in geology. Greed got him a position in the Company in their mining subsidiary. Greed brought him to the tropical jungle and the dry bush that were rich in the treasures that he sought. And greed led him to Kjaz-Barbaroi who would provide him with more wealth—so he had promised—than Snippet's greedy little mind could imagine. Snoot would be very small town by the time Snippet returned. And he would go back in triumph, too. Perhaps he would buy all of Snoot's stores with his petty cash.

Unbeknownst to Snipe, Snippet had made a special deal with Kjaz-Barbaroi. Snippet knew that Kjaz-Barbaroi knew that he was much more intelligent than Snipe. All Snipe was good for was using his hands, or his guns, or his knives to make other people's lives miserable or over with. He though only in terms of "kill or be killed."

"Snippet," Kjaz-Barbaroi had confided in him one day back at the domain of the Cave People, "there is something that you must do for me—and you cannot tell anyone about it—particularly Snipe."

"Yes, boss. What is it?" Snippet had said this like an eager child being offered a trip to an amusement park.

"Pachunga is still on the loose. He has passed successfully through the Old Tunnel and is currently wasting his time with a bunch of old people called the "Tall Men." Snipe is going to want to kill him when he is captured. Pachunga must not be killed. Don't let Snipe do that. Kill him if you have to in order to prevent that from happening. Bring Pachunga to me alive, and I will give you so much gold and diamonds that they will smother you. Heh-heh-heh-heh-heh-heh-heh-heh-heh-heh."

Snippet had laughed so hard at the thought of being smothered in gold and diamonds that he hadn't stopped to think what Kjaz-Barbaroi had really meant.

The only question now was where to find Pachunga. For some unknown reason, the Boss had ordered them take some crates full of weapons over to his headquarters. Snippet couldn't understand why it was that they had to hurry and do that. Unless, of course, Kjaz-Barbaroi had known that theirs and Pachunga's paths would end up crossing in the Great Grassland. How Kjaz-Barbaroi would have suspected that, Snippet did not know.

The only clue that they now had to Pachunga's whereabouts was that young boy with Pachunga's knife. He would have to capture him and—though it was something he didn't want to do—torture him to find out where Pachunga was. Snipe could do all that, come to think of it. But was Pachunga dead or alive?

What Snippet did not know was that Snipe now knew who and where Pachunga was. If Snipe were to tell Snippet that Pachunga was now that boy with the knife—and Snipe was not about to do this— Snippet would have never believed him. Snippet was a scientist. And at the university he had *never* been taught that it was possible for old people to become children again. If Snipe were to tell Snippet what it was he had deduced, Snippet would have accused Snipe of clouding the issue. A cloudy issue was something that Snippet would not have wanted. It was not scientific.

Snippet could not make up his mind what to do next. He didn't like the idea that Snipe was aiming his rifle so close to that boy with Pachunga's knife. What if one of those bullets killed him and made it so that he could not answer any questions? Snippet might never find out where Pachunga was. He would never be smothered in gold and diamonds as a reward. *Ohhhh*, he thought. Life was not easy.

Snippet had the luck, which he believed in strongly—however unscientific it was—not to be hiding behind an ant colony like Snipe. He wasn't firing his rifle nearly as much as Snipe was. And when he did shoot, he made a point of aiming high so that he would not wound anyone. He just wanted to scare them into not running away. What was the expression that they used in war movies? He was trying to keep them pinned down. That was it. Perhaps they would surrender if they thought there was no escape.

Snipe, on the other hand, was still shooting to kill, though he couldn't see anyone since they were all lying on the ground behind the crates of ammunition and guns. A thought slowly worked its way into the conscious part of his mind, much in the same way a worm crawls through sludge at the bottom of a sewer pipe. When the thought registered, Snipe cursed his stupidity. His hiding behind the ant colony and shooting blindly was just wasting time and bullets. He should have been thinking of a Plan and putting it into action.

Snippet, whom Snipe did not like, would have to be told what part in the Plan he would have. That meant a couple of things. Snipe would have to stop shooting his rifle—which he didn't want to do—and run across to Snippet. What if those boys had spears or arrows? What if they discovered the box of grenades? There were only ten of them, but one was all that was necessary to put Snipe into forever-ever land. Snipe wasn't ready for that just yet. What if they had a—had a *tank*? "Get a hold of yourself, Eugene," he said to himself. "They wouldn't have a tank." What if Snippet thought that Snipe were an enemy and shot him?

Now that was a real possibility.

Putting together all of his courage—which wasn't much—he sent off one last slug and ran the short distance to Snippet. His body was low to the ground. He zigged and zagged like a Marine at boot camp. When he was several meters from Snippet, he clutched his rifle against his chest and dived. He slid across the sandy soil on his chest and arms, ripping open his shirt and getting all sorts of scratches and bruises. He should have gone into a tuck and roll, only he had forgotten about it.

All this bravado had not been necessary, of course. Although Snipe could not have known this, Baree had been talking with Kasuku, and Pachunga had been checking up on Muriel's wound. There really wasn't anyone paying that much attention to either Snipe or Snippet at that moment.

Snippet quickly turned when he heard Snipe hitting the ground and watched his partner come toward him. "I should be covering him," he thought. "That's what they do in books and on Westerns." He fired his rifle once or twice.

"What's the scoop?" asked Snippet after Snipe had pulled himself together following his cinematic plunge.

"I've got a Plan."

"Oh, yes," said Snippet. "It's always good to have a Plan."

"We've got to figure that they don't know how to use the guns, right?"

"Right."

"And they don't know about the grenades, right?"

"Right."

"And they are just little children, right?"

"Right."

"And we are adults, right?"

"Right."

"So we should know better what to do, right?"

"Right."

"And we are bigger than them, right?"

"Right." Snippet thought a moment. "They—" he said.

"Huh?" asked Snipe.

"Oh, nothing," said Snippet. He hated bad grammar.

"So you can walk right over there and shoot them, right?"

"Right." Snippet thought again. "Wait! Who? Me? No!" He certainly would not.

"Sure," said Snipe. "I'll cover you. I'll be hiding right here the whole time."

"I'll bet you will," thought Snippet. Then he said aloud, "But they have a knife."

"So what? You have bullets. Use them."

"I think we should capture them."

"Why should we do that?" Snipe saw that Snippet wanted to do exactly what Kjaz-Barbaroi had said he would do. The coward. He should be shot. Then he remembered that Snippet would be shot, and the best time to do it would be when his back was turned. Perhaps he could persuade him to leave his gun behind.

"Ahhh," thought Snipe. "Now I have a better Plan." He made a show of changing his mind and sounding reasonable. "Okay," he said. "You don't have to shoot them."

"Huh?" asked Snippet. He thought Snipe would be insistent.

"I just thought of a better Plan."

Snippet looked doubtful.

"All you have to do is leave your gun here. They won't attack you when they see you aren't armed."

Snippet looked even more doubtful. "They won't?"

"No, they won't. Then, while they're distracted by you, I'll whip around behind them and sneak up on them. They'll be cooked geese."

"But—But—" Snippet didn't like this new Plan at all. He could see his fortune in gold and gems going down the drain. Kjaz-Barbaroi had said that he should shoot Snipe if he had to. Was this the time to do it? His faced turned white thinking about it, and he started to shake.

Snipe thought that Snippet was trembling in fear about having to go unarmed in his encounter with Pachunga. Had he known that Snippet was thinking of shooting him, he would have been more concerned. The shaking person in front of him nauseated him. "Do it!" he said strongly to Snippet. To make his command stronger, he waved the end of his rifle under Snippet's quivering nose and grabbed Snippet's rifle, throwing it on the ground.

Now that he was unarmed, Snippet saw that he did not have a choice in the matter. He placed his chubby hands on the ground to push himself up into a standing position. He was about all the way up when he froze. The muscles in his chest tightened so quickly that all the air was forced out of his lungs. His eyes became big and his body began to quiver. He didn't dare move back into a squatting position or sitting position. He stayed motionless and tried to keep from gasping aloud for air.

Somewhere behind him was a presence with a strength that Snippet could perceive even with his back to whatever it was. He felt that there was a very large pair of eyes behind him, peering intently at him. He could feel the gaze piercing his back and passing through the center of his heart. Those eyes saw him as an enemy. Those eyes had a strong and dangerous creature behind them. Those eyes were angry with him and wanted to do him harm.

Snippet was not alone in this experience. Snipe felt the powerful look of the eyes and realized that they belonged to the lion they had seen behind Pachunga. Snipe became afraid. He was more than afraid, he was possessed by fear. He began to shake and tremble and sweat even more than Snippet —which is quite remarkable.

The image of the awesome beast grew greater and greater in their minds. It was not only its size and strength that was frightening. It was not only its mouth full of long, white teeth. It was its power. That lion was getting power from someone, somewhere else. Snippet decided that his thinking about the lion was not very scientific or rational. But science or reason didn't matter now. What mattered was how he felt—and he felt terrified. He dared not turn around and confront it face to face. It was there. He was certain of it.

He also decided that if something didn't happen soon he was going to scream.

Nothing happened.

So Snippet screamed.

Snipe whirled around at the same moment and fired every single round that he had left in his rifle into what he thought would be the lion right behind him.

There was no lion.

His bullets just went into empty grassland.

There was nothing behind them.

* * * *

"What was that all about?" asked Pachunga.

"I don't know," said Baree. "Maybe Kalopa's just doing his thing."

"I hope he's okay," said Muriel weakly.

"He'll be fine," said Baree. "This is all a game for him."

The three of them were huddled together behind the crates. Pachunga and Baree covered Muriel to protect her. This had been part of Baree's instructions after he had blown the whistle. Kasuku rested lightly on Baree's back. He remained ready to fly at the right moment.

Pachunga was unaware of it at first, but through his left leg and thigh that were touching the ground, he could feel the earth begin to vibrate. His good ears began to pick up a sound far away and behind them all. Something very big was coming their way. Whatever it was, it was a large and destructive force. He pressed himself closer to Muriel and Baree. The three of them grasped each other's hands and squeezed tightly.

"He's coming," murmured Baree quietly more to himself than to the other two.

* * * *

Snippet and Snipe collapsed to the ground and looked in astonishment at the emptiness behind them.

"Wh-Where'd he go?" asked Snipe. He was dumbfounded.

"I—I d-don't know," responded Snippet.

"Well, they aren't going to get away with this!" said Snipe. He was very angry and shoved more bullets into the empty magazine of his rifle.

"Get your gun!" he hissed at Snippet.

* * * *

The vibrations in the ground increased. They could all hear a low, rumbling sound.

"It will be easier if we keep our eyes closed, I think," said Baree.

An elephant trumpeted loudly.

"It's Mamosa!" shouted Pachunga. "It has to be Mamosa!"

"Yes," said Baree, "he's coming!"

"May Olugbala help us all!"

Snippet's Decision

It took a quarter of an hour for the heavier dust to settle. It took several hours more for them to spit it out of their mouths, blow it out of their noses and cough it out of their throats. The destruction around them was awesome. Nothing in the immediate vicinity looked the same as it had been. Imagine ten bulldozers rampaging a field and you might get a picture of what happened. The old, termite-eaten baobab trunk, behind which Snipe had been hiding, now lay in thousands of grey, pulpy splinters. The surviving ants were feverishly trying to assess the damage. All the brush and trees were mashed into the ground. And the sweet and sour smell of sap from larger trees mingled with the odor of hot dust and the musty smell of forty-four elephants.

Pachunga squatted in a daze. Muriel lay on the ground next to him. Around them, fragments of wood varying in size littered the area or were mashed into the ground. It was all that was left of the crates. The contents were strewn in a large circle. Infrequent miniature cyclones, formed by the breezes crossing the plain, caught pieces of grease paper and twirled them around in circles. During the next rainy season, the pieces of rifle, the grenades and the ammunition would sink out of sight into the mud. They were no longer a threat to the allied forces of Olugbala.

Off by himself, surveying the entire scene like an aging field marshal, stood a very large and strong bull elephant. Pachunga had never seen one quite that size until then. His massive forehead sagged down over the top of his head. His long nose was as thick as the trunk of a tree.

He stood more than five meters high. And the sight of his long, tapered and curving tusks would have made Mamosa an ivory hunter's life pursuit.

Meanwhile Kalopa was walking through the herd with Baree accompanying him. Kasuku was back in position on Baree's shoulder. Pachunga did not understand what it was they were doing. The lion was going to certain elephants—and *licking* them. He wished he were closer to see better. But at that moment, with the ground still shaking and roaring in his memory, he was too dazed to stand up and walk over to Kalopa to find out what he was doing. He'd learn soon enough.

Kalopa reached one young bull that was lying on his side. Pachunga had thought it had been killed by either Snippet or Snipe. But then his trunk had moved and his ears had twitched reflexively to scare away bothersome flies. Kalopa spent the longest time with this one, gently licking the elephant's forequarters. Baree, with Kasuku, stood close by and watched with grave concern. Even Mamosa took a few ponderous steps closer to get a better view of one of his fallen soldiers.

Kalopa finally stopped licking and backed away a few steps. With a loud trumpeting noise to celebrate, the elephant was suddenly on his feet. He was well!

Baree said something to Kalopa. They both turned and walked toward Muriel and Pachunga. The lion moved gracefully and proudly with a sense of purpose. Pachunga could not help but feel afraid of him again, although he knew that he had no reason to fear him. He was on their side.

Muriel chose that moment to moan. The wound in her leg, though not bleeding, had become inflamed. The bandage around it was covered with crusty dirt, and the wound did not look healthy. Something would have to be done to it, though Pachunga wondered what it would be. If he had been back in the Village, he could have had the tribal doctor dress it with herbs and bind it tightly with a cloth. He wished that they at least had some water. Then they could clean it and put on a fresh bandage.

Baree arrived ahead of Kalopa. "How's the wound?"

"It's not that good," said Pachunga. "It's not deep, but it will go bad if we don't do something."

"It's fine," said Muriel. "All I—all I need to do is rest awhile."

"She's lost a lot of blood," said Pachunga. "And has not been talking clearly."

"Do you want to see what Kalopa can do?" asked the Prince.

"Kalopa?" questioned the Chief.

"Yes," said Kasuku.

Everything clicked in Pachunga's mind.

"So that is what he was doing with the elephants."

Baree smiled. "You don't learn very fast, do you?" He then turned serious and said, "Stand back and give him some room."

Muriel opened her eyes and looked directly at Kalopa. Her fear turned to trust. All it took was one glance from him and she knew that everything would be all right.

Kalopa slowly approached Muriel and stuck out his long, pink tongue. As he licked the wound, Muriel could feel his tongue's soothing roughness. It was a much more pleasant sensation than she had thought it would be. The cloudiness in her mind disappeared and immediately she was in another place walking side by side with Olugbala.

He was just the way he had appeared in the desert, though his face was brighter, his eyes livelier and he was laughing and talking to her in such a way that let Muriel know that she was getting his full attention. She was the only one who mattered at that moment. What he said to her was fascinating and gripping and seemed to last forever, although she later could not remember much of what they were talking about. Olugbala's eyes held her so intently and so pleasantly that she was unaware of her surroundings. She could have been in a building, in a meadow or even underwater or deep space. Where she was did not matter. All that mattered was that she was with Olugbala and that she finally felt that she was Home—that her long search for Meaning and Truth was at an end.

Olugbala then became very serious and told Muriel some bad things that were going to happen. It shocked her when she heard this, and she began to cry.

"All things will work together for good in the end," Olugbala said. "But now it is time to return." He smiled warmly.

She tried to smile in response, but she was still feeling very sad and wished she had a handkerchief. She sniffed loudly. "How am I to do that?"

"It's not difficult," he said. "Watch." He took a step forward and touched her lightly on the shoulder. "I'll be seeing you later."

His smiling image faded, and the next thing she knew, she was standing on her feet, encircled by her friends.

"Wha–? Wow!" The feeling of being in Olugbala's presence was still very strong.

Kalopa smiled.

"How do you feel?" asked Pachunga.

"Uh, great!" she said. "I-I don't know how to describe it."

"Look at your leg," suggested Baree.

She looked down and saw that there was not even a mark on her thigh. Her flesh had been healed of the bullet wound. "It's gone!" she exclaimed. "I knew it would be."

Kalopa started to walk quietly away without adding to the conversation or claiming any credit. He'd done the job he was supposed to do. Now it was time to do other things.

"Kalopa!" called Muriel when she saw he was leaving. "Uh, thanks."

He stopped and turned his head slowly to face her and gazed at her soundlessly. His tail flicked at a few flies. "Don't thank me," he said. "Thank the One who gave me this ability. I could not do it without him." He continued walking and found a spot about sixty meters away and plopped down gracefully, though wearily, to the ground. He studied one paw and began to lick it gently.

"Well," said Baree. "What do you think we should do with our prisoners?"

"Prisoners?" asked Muriel.

"Yes," said Kasuku. "Snippet and Snipe."

"I'd forgotten all about them. Where are they?"

Baree took out his whistle and blew. Mamosa started to walk toward them, and two elephants moved out of the herd and joined them. Lo and behold, Snippet was held securely in the trunk of one elephant and Snipe was being carried in the same way by the other. As they got nearer, Pachunga could see that Snipe had an angry, indignant look on his face. Snippet, however, was screaming and carrying on in a way that was not suitable for a man of his age and responsibility. He did have his

Ph.D., if you remember. The poor geologist looked as if he expected to be boiled alive and eaten.

"Ohhhhh!" he whined in his usual high-pitched voice. "Do something!" he whimpered to Snipe.

"Shut up, you fool!" growled Snipe. He had decided that the best way to handle everything was to remain tough. He would not give in to anything.

"We should have just let them go and gotten out while we could!" wailed Snippet. But then he remembered that if he had let them go, he would have lost the opportunity to capture Pachunga and become smothered in diamonds and gold by Kjaz-Barbaroi. So much for his returning home in triumph. All was lost. Everything he had worked for had now been done in vain. He wailed even more.

"What are we going to do?" he babbled. "What are we going to do?"

"I told you to shut up, you idiot!" Snipe glared at him.

Snippet struggled to calm himself, but he was not successful. He moaned as quietly as he could, which was not very quiet.

What was Snipe to do with such an incompetent moron? He was in something of a quandary. Should he tell him, or shouldn't he? It might make Snippet shut up for once, though he doubted it. He muttered softly to Snippet: "Don't worry. I have a solution in my right boot."

"What are you going to do?" Snippet was suddenly very interested and stopped his blubbering. Snipe's strategy appeared to be working. This conversation, of course, was taking place while they were being carried in the trunks of two elephants, so it made it very strained.

"You'll see. When I give the signal you run."

"What kind of signal?"

"You'll know it when it happens."

"Run where?"

Snipe's face became even more pained. He hated working with amateurs. "Stop asking so many questions! Who the heck cares? Run anywhere, as long as you get away. Run home to your mama for all I care!"

"Maybe there's some hope after all," mumbled Snippet to himself. "But how can we run when we're being carried by these elephants?"

Snipe rolled his eyes and once again cursed the bad luck that had paired him up with Snippet. "They're sure to let go of us sometime, idiot. What are we going to do? Spend the rest of our lives wrapped up in the trunk of a dumb animal?"

Snippet was quiet. Snipe was probably right, and if he weren't, saying anything more was not going to help the situation.

The two elephants listened with interest to Snipe and Snippet. Had the Bazungu realized the abilities of their captors, they would have kept their mouths shut. But whoever heard of elephants understanding human speech? Mamuko, the first elephant, winked knowingly at the second elephant, Mambimbo. Mamosa had been listening, too.

"Where do you suppose these elephants came from?" asked Snippet.

"Who knows," said Snipe flatly. He'd had enough of Snippet. He had things to think about—like Escape.

"They must be trained for the circus, huh?" Snippet went on. "Do you see the size of the tusks of that big one? Never have I seen such ivories. If only I had my gun. They're worth millions, I betcha."

Snipe did not give Snippet any answer. He knew that his only chance for escape and survival would be if he went alone. He couldn't have Snippet slowing him down or botching everything up. Perhaps he shouldn't have told him his plan. Maybe it would have been better to have kept it a secret—his own personal, private secret.

The two elephants unrolled their trunks and gently deposited the Bazungu in front of Baree. Snippet began to shake. Pachunga, who was standing with Muriel, was reminded of Chief Mkumbo in the caves.

To Snippet and Snipe, the silence seemed long before anyone spoke. But more was going on than they realized. Mamuko went up to Mamosa and whispered something in his ear. The old elephant signaled silently to Kasuku to come over. He flew from Baree to Mamosa's right tusk and perched as best he could on the smooth ivory. Kasuku listened carefully to what Mamosa whispered. Then he flew back to Baree and repeated the message in his ear. Baree nodded his head imperceptibly.

Neither Snipe nor Snippet knew what was going on. They stood up stiffly and brushed the dust off as best they could. If Snippet's mother had been present, she would have scolded him for looking like he had crawled through a bush backwards. Snipe's eyes went quickly from

Baree to Kasuku to Mamosa to Pachunga and then to Muriel. He was astounded when he saw Muriel.

"What? I thought I put a slug in you!"

"Yes," said Muriel. "But that's all right. I forgive you." She spoke sincerely. Her words were not trite or smug.

"But you should be—" He did not want to talk about it. Too many strange things were happening. He was beginning to feel like he was in the middle of a three-ring circus—and that he was one of the clowns.

"Kalopa licked the wound and it was healed," explained Muriel.

"Who's this Kalopa?" demanded Snipe. He looked at Pachunga and Baree. None of them looked like the witch-doctor type—though you could never tell with these people.

"That lion behind us."

"You—You l-let that thing lick your leg? He could have chewed it off!" Snippet was astounded.

"Never," said Muriel. "would he have done that. Not when he's on your side. He has a special gift from Olugbala and—"

"Olugbala!" exploded Snipe scornfully. "More mumbo jumbo." He gave Muriel a long, hard stare. "You're one of us. How'd you come to believe in this whacky religion?"

Muriel felt anger rush through her when she heard what Snipe had said. "Don't be angry," her inner voice told her. "You'll say something foolish and will only be playing his game. Keep calm and love him." These were unusual thoughts for Muriel. Before she had met Olugbala, she would have enjoyed ripping apart the mercenary with her sharp tongue. She spoke slowly. "I have met Olugbala personally—after Kjaz-Barbaroi and his soldiers left me to perish in the Great Desert. Meeting him was the happiest event of my life."

Snipe was tempted to say something rude, such as, "Maybe the sun was too hot and it fried your brains," but Muriel's tone of voice kept him quiet. Her words were disturbing, and the sooner he could make his escape, the better off he would be.

Snippet, on the other hand, found that he was not so much disturbed as moved by what Muriel said. He liked the part about meeting Olugbala being the happiest event of her life. In one brief moment, he felt ashamed of the life that he had been leading and all the greed he had felt. Diamonds became like glass to him and gold like iron. He saw that he had not been leading a happy life. When Olugbala's name had been mentioned, he had been given the impression or image of a kind of wealth or riches that were far more meaningful than what he had been seeking. These thoughts were troubling—but he thought them anyway.

Baree watched Snipe intently. He studied his eyes and was amazed at how easy it was to figure out what was going on in the Mzungu's mind. Any moment now, Snipe was going to make a move to his boot and pull out a knife. Baree moved the left side of his mouth as a signal to Mamosa.

The moment came. Snipe didn't think that his plan was a very good one—he would have loved to have had a machine gun—but using his knife was the only resource available to him. It had gotten him out of jams before. While talking with Muriel, he had moved closer to her a little step at a time. She hadn't noticed. He was ready, *now!* He plunged his hand into his boot and pulled out a long, thin knife. It was made of good steel and reflected the sunlight in a way that made it look even more deadly.

"Look out!" shouted Muriel. The knife was coming toward her, but not at her. She knew his plan. He was going to take her hostage.

"Argh!" went Snipe, lunging at the brat. He just about had her. His free hand reached for her shoulder and—

A strong force flicked the knife out of his hand before he knew what was happening. Mamosa had done the job properly with his trunk.

"Darn it!" How could his plan have failed?

"Snipe," said Baree in his most regal voice. He stood erect and faced the Mzungu. Even though Snipe was taller, Baree's noble carriage made him seem the greater in stature. "We have no intention of keeping you and Snippet prisoner."

"Huh?" asked Snipe. He was convinced he hadn't heard right. Then he thought that they meant to kill them both. He knew the rules of the game.

"If you want to leave us, that is fine by us. We don't want you to feel you have to escape by force or with a possible loss of life."

Snipe was even more confused. Baree was not playing by the rules. "What?" It was all he could say.

"You're free to go if you wish."

"They're crazy," he thought to himself. Then he realized that there had to be conditions. There were always conditions. "What are the conditions?" he asked aloud.

"Conditions?" laughed Baree. "You Bazungu are always alike. Everything is a deal or a contract. There are no conditions. We have no need to keep you as long as you remain our enemies. You'd only get in the way and slow us down."

"Why don't you just kill us, then?" To Snipe that was the logical thing to do. He'd do it himself without even a second thought.

"That is not our way," replied Baree. He took one step in Snipe's direction. "I am going to give you an option, though. You may join Olugbala and us and help us fight against Kjaz-Barbaroi and the Dark Creatures. Or, you may go. It's up to you."

Now Snipe was really flabbergasted. There was a surprising turn every moment that he prolonged his conversation with this boy. He was obviously young and inexperienced. Boy, would he learn later about the hard facts of life.

"Never!" he exclaimed. He spat on the ground. "That's what I think of your monkey religion!"

Baree ignored Snipe's last comment. "Think about it. Only by joining us can we really give you your freedom. By letting you return to Kjaz-Barbaroi, we are actually condemning you to your deaths."

Snipe now knew that this kid wasn't making sense. "They're all nuts. They've all gone bonkers." But for some reason, he couldn't quite convince himself that this was so. He almost asked the boy what he meant by that last statement, but decided against it. He realized that the answer would include more of that phony Olugbala stuff. Instead, he thought deeply about Mzungu Matters, which took a lot of effort for him. His expression changed. "What kind of a salary would you pay?" If they paid him more than the Company, he'd consider going with them. He had no loyalties other than to himself. He was a solider for hire, after all. His services went to the highest bidder.

Baree laughed. "We pay no salary. There is only the joy of serving Olugbala."

Once more, Snipe was astounded. "No salary? Well then, that settles it. I'm cutting out of here."

"We'll be sorry to see you go," said Muriel.

"Hah! I'll bet you'll be. You'll be *very* sorry to see me go."

Snipe laughed meanly and unpleasantly.

"Give him his knife," said Baree. "And Snipe, remember this: we will always be available to you should you change your mind."

Pachunga handed Snipe the knife.

Snipe smiled cruelly. "Thanks, kid." When he grasped the knife, a sinister glint came into his eyes as he looked at Pachunga. "Er, should I say, *Pachunga*." He stared into the eyes of the boy chief. Yes, this was the old geezer, all right. He thought of killing him then and there. He could do it very easily. But when he looked over Pachunga's shoulder, he saw the big lion lying on the ground gazing at him from a distance. It was almost as if the lion could read what was on Snipe's mind.

"Don't try it," said a voice inside his head. "Don't even think about it." The image of the huge lion came into his head.

Snipe shuddered. He thrust the knife back into his boot with a cocky flourish that hid his fear and anxiety. He turned abruptly and walked in a northerly direction toward Kjaz-Barbaroi's camp. He kept Kalopa and the elephants well away from him. After walking almost a hundred meters, he realized that he had been going alone. Without looking back, he yelled, "Snippet!"

Snippet began to shake. He hadn't said a word and had been hoping that Snipe would continue to forget about him. For the past few minutes, all he had been thinking about was Olugbala and the 'happiest event in all my life' that the little girl had described. Then Snipe had called the boy, 'Pachunga.' And Snippet knew that was correct. He didn't know how he knew it. It was just true. Very confusing thoughts whirled in his head and he tried to sort them out. Now Snipe was calling him. Should he stay where he was? He really wanted to. Or should he go with Snipe? What of Kjaz-Barbaroi? Snippet shook even more when he thought of him. What would Kjaz-Barbaroi do with him if he were caught fighting with the enemy forces?

"Stay!" "Go!" "Stay!" "Go!" These commands went through his mind. If Olugbala were as great as he was supposed to be, perhaps he would protect him from Kjaz-Barbaroi. He clenched his fists and squeezed his eyes shut. He moaned. "Ohhhhhhhh!"

Forces within him and forces without him were fighting over him.

No!" he screamed finally. "I won't go! I'm staying! Yes! I'm staying!"

Snipe did not react to this. When he heard Snippet's response, he started to walk North again.

So it was. Olugbala's army was now increased by one.

THE FORCES GATHER

Snippet was so overcome by his decision to follow Olugbala that he grew faint. The blue sky and brown grass in front of him began to wobble up and down and turn circles. He staggered to the left, then to the right—then to the left again. Muriel thought that he looked like a bowling pin about to topple over.

"Ahhhhh!" he wailed. He started at a low pitch and ended with a high-pitched squeal. When he finally did faint, his body went limp and he fell backward.

Just before he hit the ground, Mamosa caught him in his trunk and lowered him gently.

Muriel went to Snippet. "Dr. Snippet? Dr. Snippet, are you okay?" She lifted his heavy head and put his helmet under it.

He came to. "Yes—Y-Yes, I think so." He swallowed once or twice with difficulty.

"We're glad you've decided to join us," said Pachunga. He felt that it was important for him to say that. Just a few hours before, he had wanted to kill him.

"Yes, welcome," said Mamosa.

Snippet couldn't believe that this circus elephant had just spoken to him. If the truth were known, he really could not believe anything that had happened to him up to that point. His decision to leave Snipe and Kjaz-Barbaroi was something that bewildered him. What had he done?

"May we get you anything?" asked Kasuku.

181

That was a parrot speaking, too, wasn't it? First it was an elephant. Now it was a parrot. He felt his head spinning again. Maybe he had been in the sun too long. He closed his eyes and moaned.

"Don't faint again!" said Muriel. "Take a sip of this." She had found his canteen and put the bottle to his mouth. Since Snippet was lying down, more water dribbled down his chin than into his mouth. It was warm and tasted like the chlorine tablets he had put in it to purify it. He spat the water out.

"Ugh, no thanks," he said. "Help me up — uh, please."

Baree and Pachunga pulled him to his feet.

"I think I feel better now."

Baree congratulated Snippet on his decision. "You have now made the most important choice of your life. We commend you. You have recognized Olugbala for who he is and you have accepted him. May you serve him well."

"Serve him?" asked Snippet. "I don't serve anybody!" Why did he say that? He didn't mean to.

"You don't?" asked Pachunga. "What about Kjaz-Barbaroi? Did you give him orders, or did you do everything he told you?"

"We are all servants of something or someone else," said Kasuku. "Even Olugbala, whom we serve, serves us. The important thing is to find the right One to serve."

"Here! Here!" said Mambimbo.

"Yes! Here! Here!" said Mamuko. Although he was a very nice elephant, he never was very original in what he said.

Snippet took all this congratulating, back-slapping and 'Welcome to the Club' very well. Though he was perplexed by it all, he was happy to belong. Everything felt right about it, and he had not experienced such warmth and acceptance since he had been a boy. If only he didn't have so many questions.

Pachunga watched Snippet carefully and felt a chill of suspicion sweep over him. What was Snippet's motivation for coming to their side? Was this part of a sinister plan of Kjaz-Barbaroi's? He decided that he would have to keep a special eye on him and that he would tell his suspicions to no one. The rest would accuse him of not accepting Olugbala's ability to change people's lives. Ever so faintly the Drum started to beat. Kjaz-Barbaroi didn't like to lose followers.

"Dr. Snippet," said Muriel. "What—"

"Call me Oscar," he said. "I'm really not as stuffy as I try to be sometimes. Or, just Snippet will do. I've heard that often enough."

"My name is Muriel Sniggins. I—"

"Any relation to *the* Sniggins family?" asked Snippet.

"Why, er, yes, but—"

"But you own half the Company!" exclaimed Snippet.

"What?" demanded Pachunga. "You?" He looked at Muriel with new eyes. "Say it's not so!"

Muriel glared at him with a hurt expression on her face.

"Can't you give me any credit for anything, Pachunga? I don't own it anymore."

Pachunga looked properly chastised and relieved all at the same time.

"And that was before I met Olugbala, anyway. When Elmer Sniggins, my second hus —" She stopped and looked at the amazed and confused look Snippet was giving her and decided not to explain her relationship to Elmer. It was too soon to tell him that she was a younger version of what she had been. Snippet would not have understood at that point. "I mean, when Elmer Sniggins died, I, er, we sold out our interest in the Company. We don't have any part of it anymore. I didn't like their business practices."

Snippet was glad to hear what Muriel said. If he did get into hot water with the Company for joining up with Olugbala's side, she might—or her father or uncle—be able to vouch for him. She would know someone important.

"Introductions are in order," said Muriel. "This is Baree, Prince of the Cattle People, and Kasuku, the parrot. Mamosa is the elephant—the big one —and Kalopa the Lion is lying down over there. We're all happy to know you."

"I'm Mambimbo," said Mambimbo, not to be forgotten.

"And I'm Mamuko," said Mamuko. "We're happy to know you, too."

"And I likewise," said Snippet. "However, the last time I saw you, Pachunga—if that is who you really are—you were an old man."

"Olugbala made me young again," said the Chief.

"Oh, I see." Snippet seemed to accept this, but his mind was becoming overloaded by so many new thoughts, that all he could do was accept things as they were without thinking too hard. It was easier that way. And if none of this were real, he'd find out soon enough anyway.

Baree studied the sun which was becoming larger and redder as it approached the western horizon. There was only about an hour of daylight left.

"What are we going to do now?" asked Muriel.

"We must go to the Well of the Wildebeests and set up camp," said Baree. "The women of my tribe are there already preparing food for us. We cannot stay here. It is too much out in the open. Also, there is no water."

"We will hold a council there," said Mamosa. "We must decide how we will defend ourselves against the enemy."

Kalopa wandered over slowly to join the group. Snippet nearly fainted again when he saw him approaching. Muriel assured him that he was a friend, though Snippet wouldn't allow the lion to get near him. It would take a long time, he thought, before he'd get used to the idea that Kalopa was safe.

"We must call everyone together to go to the Well," said Kalopa. He lifted his head without warning and roared so loudly that the sound must have carried all the way to the Great Desert.

"Am I glad he's with us," Snippet muttered to himself. To Muriel he asked, "Are you sure he won't bite?"

"Positive," she said with certainty. She recalled the rough gentleness of his tongue that had cured her of her bullet wound. "Yes, I'm sure."

Mamosa lifted his trunk and trumpeted. Pachunga remembered the first time he had heard that sound just before the stampede. The elephants—who were eating their supper several hundred meters away—grouped themselves together and marched toward their general.

Baree now put his whistle to his lips and blew three short blasts. The shrill sound reached ears that were waiting for their leader's signal. Gathering shields and spears, the warriors left the seclusion of the bush and walked across the churned up ground and broken stalks of grass that had been destroyed earlier by the elephants. They carried their spears and shields with purpose and wore the stripes of battle on their faces and chests. War was in the offing.

Snippet, Pachunga and Muriel watched in amazement as dozens of lions and lionesses appeared out of the long grass and joined the Cattle People warriors. They walked around and under the legs of the elephants and formed a large pride next to Kalopa.

Pachunga thought of the young men in the mine who were once his warriors. If only they were available to respond to his own call to battle! How eagerly their fathers had joined him in the Battle of a Thousand Cries.

Baree inspected his soldiers. There were a hundred and thirty-one of them. At one time, he could have commanded five hundred, but many had left him for Prince Mwailu, who had made them empty promises of honor and glory. Where was that rascal, anyway? Baree did not want to fight against his own flesh and blood, but he knew the time would come when he might have to.

Pachunga looked at the setting sun. The day was getting old. He was about to turn his head away, when he saw some figures walking in a hurry toward them. Two were very short and one was very tall. The short ones were almost running in order to keep up with the powerful strides of the tall man.

"Two Cave People and a Tall Man!" he shouted to the group.

The three men stopped a safe distance away.

"Friends or foes?" asked Pachunga.

"We are your friends if you are with Olugbala," said the Tall Man. "We are two Cave People and a member of the Last Tribe."

It was Titi!

"Titi, you made it! You are most welcome!" said Pachunga.

"Thank you," he said politely.

"You're not the only ones?" asked the Kiritiri Chief when they were closer. "Where's Mkumbo?"

"Our Chief is with the rest of the warriors," said one of the Cave People. "We are not the only ones. There are ninety-five of us ready to fight for Olugbala."

"That is more than we could have hoped for!" exclaimed Pachunga. "Olugbala be praised!"

"We are ready to receive our instructions as to where we are to proceed."

"We are all meeting at the Well of the Wildebeests," said Baree. "It is an hour's walk due East from here."

"Titi," said Muriel, "how's your arm?" She noticed the sling.

"Not so bad that I won't be able to slay a few Dark Creatures!" he said.

"Nonsense!" she said. "Come here and let Kalopa take care of it."

"K-Kalopa the Lion?"

"Yes, he'll fix you up."

"*The* Kalopa?"

"Yes, of course," said Muriel matter-of-factly. "Who else would it be?"

"Whatever you say, granddaughter."

Muriel led him to Kalopa and in a few moments the arm was as good as new.

In fact, after the experience, Titi looked stronger and even more ready for what was ahead. Never had he felt so strong.

"We must march," said Mamosa. He spoke to the Cave People. "Greet your Chief for us and give him Prince Baree's instructions. Go with Olugbala—and with haste."

"Yes, we will," said one of the Cave People. "Until the Well of the Wildebeests!" The two turned and walked quickly back in the direction from which they'd come.

With the setting sun behind them making long shadows in front of them, the warriors, elephants and lions made an imposing scene as they walked across the Great Grassland. Muriel had climbed up onto Mamosa's back—at his invitation — and hung on tightly to his leathery neck. Pachunga was on the back of Mamuko, and Baree and Titi rode Mambimbo. They, too, held on as best they could. Snippet was on the back of another bull elephant. He tried very hard to look happy and at ease, but it was obvious that he was not having a good time. He'd trade an elephant for a Land Rover any day. Kasuku alternated between resting on Baree's shoulders or flying high in the air to act as scout. They could never let their guard down because the forces of Kjaz-Barbaroi were all around them.

Snippet had much that he wanted to say about what he knew of Kjaz-Barbaroi's plans. He was not quite sure whom he should talk to, though. There were obvious leaders: Pachunga, Baree, Kalopa and

Mamosa. But they were most likely not the real leaders. Two were boys, one was an elephant and another a lion. Titi, while a grownup, was too much of a newcomer to confide in — and he seemed just as new to all of this as Snippet was. He decided that the adults in charge would be at the Well of the Wildebeests and he could tell them Kjaz-Barbaroi's plans when they got there.

* * * *

Snipe's feet were hurting him. It seemed as if he had been doing nothing but walking. He had spent all day walking with the porters as they carried the ammunition from the river, and since he had left Snippet, he had been walking very quickly toward Kjaz-Barbaroi's camp located South of the Land Where No One Dares to Live. His heavy leather boots rubbed against the sides and tops of his feet and were making blisters. His arches felt sore, and the muscles in his legs ached. He was thirsty and had no more water. And although it had become cool since the sun had set several hours before, he was still perspiring profusely. A cloud of gnats and flies circled his face and tried to land in the damp part of his eyes to drink. His skin itched and a rash was developing. He longed for a cold drink and a cold bath and knew that he was going to get neither.

His mind was bothering him as well. Snippet's desertion seemed very perplexing. He was not supposed to do something like that. It didn't make any sense at all, and Snipe couldn't figure it out. He began to have doubts himself about what he was doing. Things were just getting too weird, and he had learned from experience that if things were no longer predictable, he needed to clear out as quickly as possible. It was too dangerous otherwise. He wanted to convince himself that he was doing the right thing and that everything was going as planned. It was right because it was right for him. He muttered aloud to himself, "Yeah, right, Snipe. That's not true and you know it."

On the other hand, if everything went as well as it was supposed to, he would have the opportunity to be richer than anything he had ever dreamed of — rich enough to buy an island somewhere in the tropics and live out the rest of his days in peace and luxury. He liked money. It could buy you anything he wanted. And right now, he didn't have as much as he needed to retire.

He kept feeling more and more apprehensive as he got nearer and nearer to Kjaz-Barbaroi's camp. He voiced his thoughts again. "But, Eugene, you are doing what is right for you. You are the only one that matters. As long as you continue to be paid, then everything will be okay."

If this were so, why was he feeling...*so afraid?*

It would only be a short time until he reached the camp. He would report to the Boss everything that he knew. He convinced himself that he was going to be rewarded for his efforts. He knew where Pachunga was, and he thought that he knew what kind of troop strength they would have. All they had were the porters, the two boys, Snippet and the girl. Huh. What a small number! They would clean them up in no time. Of course, there were the elephants. But what could they do? He knew they were trained, but it seemed impossible to him that they would be able to fight in a battle. Maybe there were a few more Cattle People around that he didn't know about, but they would not be many. It was all going to be an easy victory. The little tribal insurrection would be squashed and he would be guaranteed more workers for the mine. Snipe thought that the Boss was going to find all this information very helpful.

Off in the distance, he could see the campfires and torches of the camp. It was huge. There had to be almost two thousand soldiers there made up of Imperial Guards and the Cattle People of Prince Mwailu. They wouldn't need the guns and ammunition they had lost, after all. Yes, the Boss was going to reward him all right—especially since he had shown such good sense not to accept the kid's offer. He hurried on, ignoring the dust, the discomfort of his feet, the irritations on his skin and the doubts that were growing stronger.

Snipe was met by two Imperial Guards as he approached the outer perimeter. They snapped to attention and held their spears in a ready position.

"Who goes there?" growled one.

"Snipe," he said. "I have news for the Boss."

They both smiled viciously and drool started flowing from between their sharp, pointed teeth.

"You should never have come back," one said.

"Huh?" Snipe was confused.

Then he was even more confused as the two guards did an unexpected thing. One grabbed Snipe's left arm and the other grabbed his right. They held him tightly.

"Hey!" he exclaimed. "What's going on? Unhand me, you idiots! You don't know what you're doing!"

"Silence!" ordered the first guard. He hit Snipe in the face with the end of his spear. Snipe's nose started to bleed.

"We take no orders from traitors!"

"Traitor? I—?"

"Shut up!"

Snipe received another blow to his head that dazed him and made him think silly thoughts.

The guards dragged him into the camp. Dark Creatures, milling around and getting bored because there wasn't much action, perked up when they saw Snipe. They gathered around him.

"Here comes the swine!"

"Illegitimate son of a camel!"

"May he die slowly and cruelly!"

"Burn him!"

"Cut him into pieces!"

"Cut him into pieces–then burn him!"

"Burn him then cut him into pieces!"

This was getting too repetitious.

"We'll have a feast tonight!"

They punched him and spat at him. By the time Snipe reached the central bonfire, his clothes were torn, his nose was bleeding even more and he had bruises all over his body. What had he done to deserve this? It had to be some kind of a mistake — some terrible misunderstanding.

Kjaz-Barbaroi was conversing with Lieutenant Ngaba when Snipe was brought to him. The guards threw him down at his feet. Kjaz-Barbaroi was obviously not in a good mood when he turned to look at the human groveling and whimpering before him.

"Y-Your H-High—" Snipe started to say.

"Shut up, dog!" ordered Ngaba. The lieutenant gave Snipe a kick in the ribs. Fortunately for Snipe, Dark Creatures don't wear boots, so it was not a serious blow. It did hurt, though.

"Piece of filth," said Kjaz-Barbaroi to Snipe. "Why did you come here?"

"The-There m-m-must b-b-be some m-m-mistake—"

Ngaba kicked Snipe again. "There are no mistakes! The Emperor does not make any. Ever!" He was in a screaming rage. "Answer his Imperial Allworshipful's question, slime!" Ngaba could get a little carried away with titles for Kjaz-Barbaroi sometimes.

One of the guards jabbed him with his spear. Now that really hurt.

Snipe screamed.

"Speak!" shrieked Ngaba. He was having a good time.

"I—I h-have n-news—"

"News?" asked Kjaz-Barbaroi. "You have brought no news. I know it all already. Snippet has become a traitor. You lost the shipment of arms that we have been waiting for. And you did not kill Pachunga, even when you had the opportunity to do it. They are now gathering their forces at the Well of the Wildebeests and have become a much stronger opponent to my will. Dog! Vermin! Piece of cattle dung! You have failed. I have no more use for you!" He turned away from Snipe and spoke to Ngaba. "Dispatch him—slowly."

"As you will, Your Excellency," said Ngaba. He signaled the guards to take Snipe away.

"No!" pleaded the mercenary. "You don't understand! It's—"

No one paid any attention to what he was saying. He was dragged off and not seen by anyone ever again.

Kjaz-Barbaroi continued his conversation with Ngaba as if he had never been interrupted. "Tomorrow we fight at the Hills of Separation," he said. "Have everyone ready. Instruct Prince Mwailu of our plans."

"As you will, Your Supreme Highness."

A Special Mission

It was already dark by the time they reached the Well of the Wildebeests. Torches and cooking fires lit by women of the Cattle People provided a beacon as they walked across the Great Grassland. They had encountered no one during the last leg of the trip. The march was made in silence. Each person or animal was alone in his own thoughts as he contemplated what morning would bring.

No one wanted to say it aloud, but each knew that their army was smaller than the combined armies of Kjaz-Barbaroi. The only consolation lay in their firm belief that Olugbala alone was greater than any army Kjaz-Barbaroi could muster together.

As they approached the outskirts of the camp, the women and children rushed out to greet them. They lined the entrance and clapped their hands as they sang songs. A leader called out: "No say lah-wam-bu!" and she was met with the response: "Oh-loo-bah-lah- lah-wam-bu!" They were greeting them in the name of Olugbala. Some were dancing, and others bent over and told their children exactly who Kalopa, Mamosa and Pachunga were. It was the first time they had seen these famous creatures.

Baree called together the leaders of the different groups once the humans had dismounted from the elephants. "We will have to hold a Council of War as soon as possible. We need to determine our plan of action for tomorrow. But first, we must drink water and refresh ourselves."

"Where are all the adults in charge?" asked Snippet. "I have something to tell them."

"Adults?" questioned Pachunga. "Surely, Oscar, you remember that I am your elder by one generation."

"And I am the same age as Pachunga," said Baree.

"And I'm actually Elmer Sniggins's widow—not his daughter," said Muriel.

"What! You, too?" asked Snippet. "I don't understand how it's possible!"

"With Olugbala everything is possible," said Kasuku.

"Oh, yes, I suppose that's true. Er, I think." He looked doubtful once again. "But why doesn't Olugbala make me young? I wouldn't mind it."

"Perhaps Olugbala needs you the way you are," said Baree. "He does everything for a purpose."

That idea made sense, though Snippet was hoping that he could be changed. Maybe it would happen eventually. "Anyway, the information that I have is that Kjaz-Barbaroi is encamped several hours North of here. He has gathered together all the armies that are allied to him and is planning on attacking you all tomorrow."

Baree already knew this, but he was thankful that Snippet felt he could volunteer it. "Thank you, Oscar. That is what we had figured, but it is nice to hear it coming from another person."

"I'm thirsty," said Muriel. "Does anyone have any water around here?"

"We certainly do," said one of the women. "Come with me and I'll show you where you can drink."

"We will meet at the central fire when I blow my whistle," said Baree.

The small group broke up and went in different directions. Snippet was thirsty himself, so he went with Muriel. He was very confused by everything that he was hearing and seeing, and began to wonder about what he had gotten himself into. He had doubts and wished that Snipe were around so that he could ask his advice. Snipe frequently made sense, and he had been living longer in this part of the world. Muriel seemed comfortable enough around these foreigners. Even though he was told that he was accepted, he still felt like an outsider. He didn't know what role he was supposed to have. If only there were someone he could talk with. But with whom?

After he had gotten his drink and washed his face, he wondered what he would do next. Muriel was talking happily with the women who had shown them the jerry cans of water, and Pachunga and Baree were having a conference. For some reason, he was feeling very sentimental and was experiencing other emotions he did not understand. He left the group unnoticed and walked outside the camp. It was darker there, and he felt that he could think better if he were alone. He decided that he wanted something, but he didn't know what it was. He wasn't hungry. He wasn't thirsty. He didn't want diamonds or riches anymore. He decided that he didn't want Snipe's advice—it was always bad. He certainly didn't want Kjaz-Barbaroi. He recognized the tyrant now for what he was and shuddered to think that he had once obeyed him and followed him so readily. What did he want?

"What do I want?" he asked aloud in the language of the North. It had been so long since he had spoken his own language that the words sounded strange and out of place in the middle of the Great Grassland. "Tell me, what do I want?" he asked again. He thought about it some more. He desired joy—peace—love—truth—acceptance—belonging.

"Yes, what do you want?" asked a voice next to him. The voice spoke to him in Snippet's language and not in the Common Speech.

"What?" asked Snippet. He turned to his right and saw a man standing close to him. He couldn't see his face because he was in shadow.

"What do you want?" repeated the man. Something about the way he spoke told Snippet that this man could answer his question. He was reminded of a melody—such was the quality of his voice. And the voice spoke of wealth that was greater than any diamonds or gold or kingdoms or governments.

"I don't know what I want. I only want." He thought some more. The man permitted him. "How do you know my own language so well? There aren't many down here who do, you know."

"I know all the languages of men and animals," he said. "I made them."

"Oh," said Snippet. What the man just said didn't sink in.

"I also know what you want."

Snippet's heart jumped. "Tell me! I can't figure it out."

"A while ago, you were given a choice. You had to choose between going with Snipe and returning to Kjaz-Barbaroi or remaining here with Prince Baree and the rest who are on my side."

Snippet was astonished. "So you're Olugbala? I didn't really—"

"You didn't really think I existed, did you?"

"I hoped you did! But no, I didn't, I guess. But I did know that I didn't want to go back with Snipe. I was afraid to."

"You made the right choice. That path would have led to your death."

"And Snipe? He's—He's not dead r-right now?"

There was a long, silent moment—a moment filled with deep sadness.

Olugbala's voice was very heavy and sounded tired. "No, he is dying." There was another pause. "Now he is dead."

"Oh." Snippet didn't know whether to feel sad or not—but he could somehow feel Olugbala's sadness. Olugbala obviously did not want Snipe to die. And he felt a strange sense of emptiness in thinking about Snipe. It was like sorrow for a missed opportunity. "But why did he die?"

"That is not for you to know." Olugbala stepped into some light that came from the camp. "I came because you called me."

Snippet could now see his face. It was young. It was old. It knew everything about everything and everyone. Snippet could tell that each event in every history was etched into his brown skin.

It all began to fall into place. "When I chose not to go back to Kjaz-Barbaroi, I knew of you, but I never imagined you as existing and breathing. I never imagined that I could have a conversation with you like we are having right now." He stopped to think. "Now I know what I want!" he exclaimed. "It's you! It's not just some idea like liberty and justice that I've been told to believe in. It is accepting you as you *are*, Olugbala."

"Yes," he said. "Now you are beginning to understand."

Snippet had a sudden thought. "I mean, you are real, aren't you? I am talking to you, aren't I?"

Olugbala laughed. It was comforting and loving. "Of course I am real. I am not a ghost or only a spirit as some have tried to claim."

"I thought so."

Snippet was talking with Olugbala very easily, as if he were his closest friend in all the world. He thought about how Pachunga, Muriel and Baree had all received their youth again.

Maybe now that Olugbala was right there, he would make him young again if he asked him. He was just about to ask Olugbala about this, when he thought of another question he should ask first.

"What am I to do for you?"

Olugbala smiled again. "You will serve me in a way you never would have thought possible."

"I will?"

"Yes. Kjaz-Barbaroi has brought four hundred Kiritiri young men to put in the front lines of his armies to confound Pachunga and weaken his allegiance to me. If that happens, Pachunga will be put in a situation where he would have to fight against them and allow Mamosa, Kalopa and Baree to fight against them as well. It is too strong a test for him. I am sending you back to Kjaz-Barbaroi's camp to speak to the Kiritiris on my behalf and give them the opportunity to join forces against Kjaz-Barbaroi. I—"

"You—you want *me* to go to Kjaz-Barbaroi's camp? I-I will be—" he interrupted.

"You must do it. There is not much time, and you are the best person for the job. You must leave immediately."

"But—"

"Oscar!" said Olugbala sternly. "Am I not who I am? Do you not trust me to protect you and guide you? I will not fail you. My commitment to you is forever. I will be with you."

Forever...Who had ever made a promise to Snippet like that? No one. "But will I fail you?" It seemed a real possibility.

"I will tell you the words to speak. Already you are a stronger man. You will not fail. Go. *Now!*" With that, Olugbala turned away and disappeared into the darkness.

Snippet was left alone. A strong, dry wind blew into his face from the East. It refreshed him and made him feel better. He had found what he was wanting, and now he knew what he had to do. And there was not time to go back to the Well to tell the others what he was going to do. Looking at the polar star to find his bearing, he walked steadily to the North. He would not fail. He was sure of it.

* * * *

"Where's Oscar?" asked Muriel. She hadn't seen him since they had gone to get water.

"I thought he was with you," said Pachunga.

"He was, but then he left me and went for a walk."

Baree spoke to one of his warriors. "See if you can't find Doctor Snippet. Ask around to learn who saw him last, if you have to. He couldn't have gone far. We need him for the Council."

Baree turned and looked at the assembled fighters. "We need to review our troop strength. I have one hundred and thirty-one who are ready to fight."

"And I have a hundred and twenty-one lions and lionesses," said Kalopa.

"There are forty-four bull elephants," said Mamosa. "The cows have also expressed a willingness to go into battle, and I am permitting them. That makes ninety-one."

"There are twelve of the Last Tribe—including me," said Titi. He wished that he could have offered more.

"Remember that ninety-five Cave People are coming, too," said Pachunga. "They should arrive at any time with Chief Mkumbo. How many does that make in all?"

Muriel did a quick sum. "Four hundred and fifty-three. Four hundred and fifty-five, if you include Kasuku and me."

"You?" asked Pachunga. "You're not thinking of—"

"I certainly am—and the only one who could tell me I can't is Olugbala himself."

Pachunga knew that there was no arguing with her. "Okay," he said. "What about Snippet? That is one more if we can find him."

The warrior was waiting to give his perplexing news. "The last time Doctor Snippet was seen, he had left the camp and was walking North."

No one needed to be told what was in the North.

"That traitor!" exclaimed Pachunga. "Now Kjaz-Barbaroi will know how strong we are! From the moment he decided to stay with us, I knew that it was an evil plot of Kjaz-Barbaroi's. He sent him as a spy!"

"We don't know that for certain," said Muriel. "It's possible that—"

The Drum was beating.

"What would you know, anyway? You're one of them!"

Kalopa growled. "Pachunga! Enough! I agree with Muriel. We don't know why he has gone."

"Yes," said Mamosa. "He may be on a special mission."

"But why wouldn't he tell us first? Why would he sneak away?"

"We don't know that he snuck away. And maybe there wasn't time," said Baree. "And besides, he cannot tell anything to Kjaz-Barbaroi that he doesn't know already. Even our words right now will be reported to him eventually."

Pachunga could see their reasoning—almost. He still wasn't quite convinced. But he noticed Muriel as if for the first time. She was crying.

"Aw, Muriel. I'm sorry," said Pachunga. "I didn't really mean it. You've done so much for us, too." Pachunga once again was frustrated with himself. He seemed to make some mistake with every step.

"It's okay," said Muriel softly. "We're all under pressure and sometimes we do things we don't really mean."

"We need to make some plans," said Kasuku.

"Right," said Baree. "Then we will have a festival such as one that we have not seen since before the Battle of a Thousand Cries!"

Another Cattle People warrior appeared. "Chief Mkumbo and his men have arrived along with the remainder of the Tall Men."

"Wonderful!" said Muriel.

"Good," said Baree. "Bring the Chief here. We have much to discuss."

* * * *

Snippet had been walking for several hours. His legs were very tired, and he had finished the water in his bottle. As he approached Kjaz-Barbaroi's camp, his apprehension started to grow. What was ahead of him? How would he get by the guards? He didn't even know where the Kiritiris were being kept. He didn't even have a knife. All he had with him were Olugbala's instructions.

When he was close enough to survey the situation, he stopped behind a tall thorn bush. The Dark Creatures stood guard where he had originally planned on entering the camp. As it was, they were the same two guards who had captured Snipe, though Snippet didn't know this. He decided that he couldn't enter there, so he moved to his left and kept the camp off to his right as he walked around it. He stayed in the shadows and it occurred to him that his clothes probably reflected the light too well. He dropped to the ground to see if he could rub dirt into them. But it was too hard and dry.

Going further, he discovered a small stream bed that was empty of water. However, he knew that the soil would be moist several centimeters below the cracked surface. He found a flat rock and started to dig. After two or three minutes, he finally reached some mud and covered himself with it. It smelled terrible, but it did make him darker. Snippet decided that he did not need his helmet anymore, so he took it off and rubbed some more dirt on his face and arms. That was the worst part.

As he walked, he saw more guards, but the camp looked deserted around the outer edge. He wondered where everybody was, for there normally should have been a lot of activity. He would find out soon enough—once he got inside. That is, *if* he got inside. He wondered if he were going to be able to do it. He was certain that Snipe would have reported to Kjaz-Barbaroi his change of allegiance, so he couldn't just walk in like he used to back at the Land Where No One Dares to Live.

He could see from where he was that the center of the camp was lit by several large and powerful lights. He remembered that he had ordered a generator and some floodlights for the mining operation, and he assumed that Kjaz-Barbaroi was using them now.

At last! There was an unguarded section. This was where he was supposed to go in. He was sure of it. There might as well have been a sign saying: ENTER HERE. Though it was dangerous, nothing or, more accurately, no one was telling him that this wasn't the place to get into the encampment.

As he had traveled across the Great Grassland those many hours from the Well of the Wildebeests, he had discovered something that he had not noticed previously. It had started after his meeting with Olugbala. He had felt directed as to which way he was supposed to go. He couldn't explain how he was directed, but he had been nevertheless. He was counting on that guidance once he entered the camp.

He passed by the entrance and walked between a few loosely constructed huts that had been created as temporary shelters. There was no noise coming from them, and he assumed they were empty. Where was everyone? His question was answered once he had walked a few more meters.

In the center of the camp, dozens of Dark Creatures were building something very large. Those that were not involved in the actual job of building were watching with interest and anticipation. Already enough of it had been built that Snippet recognized exactly what it was that they were making. It was a huge drum. It had to be *the* Drum, and it had been moved to this spot for some unknown reason. It measured at least fifteen meters high and forty meters across. The top was made of hundreds of skins taken from the Cattle People herds as tribute. Prince Mwailu was paying dearly for his allegiance to Kjaz-Barbaroi. The question was also answered as to why there had been no guards at the point where Snippet had entered the camp.

The two Dark Creatures, who were supposed to be guarding the gate, had wandered in to watch the building of the Drum. They were leaning against a hut and drinking whiskey. The Company had made several shipments of whiskey to Kjaz-Barbaroi and his Imperial Guard. Snippet had signed the requisition order himself having learned that it was easier to maintain control. He was encouraged. It had been one of the more sensible things he had done. If the rest of the Dark Creatures were as drunk as these two guards, he would have an easier time of it.

He walked carefully by another hut and kept himself in the shadows as much as possible. He didn't really know where to go, but he knew that he would find the Kiritiris eventually. He continued to receive the same type of guidance he had received walking across the Great Grassland. From time to time, he had to duck out of the way as one or two Dark Creatures came close by or some Cattle People moved into view. It took him almost half an hour to reach the place he was searching for.

About a hundred meters ahead of him and separated from the rest of the camp was a stockade fence that was three times the height of a man. There was an entrance at the front that was being guarded by four Dark Creatures.

The Kiritiris had to be inside.

But how was Snippet supposed to get in? He was baffled. Should he walk all the way around the compound and see if there were another way in? He didn't think that would be advisable. It would take too much time. Also, this was obviously a prison. They wouldn't have more than one gate leading in. He wished that there weren't so much light. Torches and fires burned everywhere, and the light from the lamps reached all the way out to where Snippet was.

He looked for a few minutes at the guards who were in front of the gate. He wanted to see if a couple of them would leave and go on patrol. But they didn't move from their spot. The Dark Creatures were too interested in watching the work on the Drum that they could see easily from their position.

Snippet studied them some more and thought that if he waited long enough, the liquor would put them asleep. No, they weren't that far gone yet. He looked at his watch. It was after one-thirty. The usual custom for the Dark Creatures was to change guards at two a.m. or so.

Snippet could not wait. He would have to make his move.

"Go ahead," said a voice inside of him. That was the most direct communication that he had received so far since he had talked with Olugbala hours before.

He was supposed to walk up to the gate and pass through?

The Drum began to beat inside his head. That was the most ridiculous thing he could think of doing. It was an impossible mission. He would just have to return to the Well of the Wildebeests and tell Olugbala that he had not been able to do it—that it was too difficult a task.

"Go ahead!" repeated the voice more firmly. It was a command.

The Drum stopped. Snippet knew what he had to do.

He left the protective shadow of the hut he had been hiding behind and walked the remaining distance to the compound. As he approached, he noticed that the guards had not seen him—yet. Maybe they were so absorbed in watching the construction of the Drum that they wouldn't pay any attention to him. But now, he could hear what they were saying.

"The skinny white one really got it tonight, eh?"

"Wasn't that the best? He screamed and yelled like nobody's business."

"What a hero! The only time Bazungu are brave is when they have a gun in their hands."

"You're not kidding."

"Did you get a piece of him?"

"Naw, I was too late. There weren't even any bones left."

Snippet was horrified. Snipe had been eaten. What would they do to him if he were caught? "Oh no oh no oh no oh no oh no oh no," he repeated over and over to himself.

One of the guards noticed him. He would succeed or fail at this moment. "Help me," he said to Olugbala.

"Oh, it's just you," said the guard. There was no animosity in his voice—only bored half-interest. He didn't even seem to notice that Snippet was covered with smelly mud from head to foot.

"They must not have heard about me yet," he thought. He felt much better about his chances.

"The Boss wants me to speak to the prisoners," said the voice inside of him.

Snippet knew that he had to say those words. "The Boss wants me to speak to the prisoners," he said aloud. He felt no need to clarify who his boss was.

"Yeah, sure," said the other guard. "Go right in. You want protection? They're in a pretty surly mood."

"No, thank you," said Snippet. He passed by the guards.

He was through!

Once he was inside the compound, he could not see that well. The entire stockade was lit only by one small dying fire in the center. He could see the dim outline of sleeping or standing Kiritiris. They had nothing to shade them from the hot sun during the day, nor did they have anything to sleep under. There weren't even any straw mats. They were being treated like penned cattle. From what he could see of them once his eyes became adjusted, they did not look like they had been given proper food. They really weren't different from the way they had been in the mine. He was just seeing them with new eyes. There was also a horrible smell, the source of which Snippet did not care to investigate.

He was immediately filled with shame when he saw them in this condition. He knew that he was responsible for making them that way. That was why, he thought, Olugbala had sent him to speak to them. It could be no one else.

Before Oscar knew what was going on, a couple of warriors grabbed him.

"Wait!" said Snippet. "You don't understand!"

"Oh, we understand, all right, Doc-tor Snip-pet," said one of them. "You should have known better than to come here. We have been waiting for an opportunity like this. What kind of a fool are you?"

His arrival in the stockade had caused a considerable stir. Snippet soon found himself encircled by all four hundred Kiritiri young men.

"Kill him!" suggested one.

"Make him suffer as we have suffered!"

"The baboon does not deserve to live!"

"Men of the Kiritiris! Hear me out!" said Snippet with more authority and sureness than he had ever spoken previously. His voice did not show fear. "I know that you are just and honorable men. The Kiritiris are known for—"

"Quiet!" said someone in the crowd.

Snippet was silent. He stood there passively and did not try to resist the men who were holding him tightly.

"Yes," said another. "He is talking too loudly. I have a feeling that he has something important to tell us and that it should not be heard by those outside." The man who was speaking was Maringa. He was a Kiritiri who knew Olugbala and could tell that Snippet had changed. "He is right. We are honorable men. That much we have not forgotten."

"Yes, Maringa, you speak well. Remember that he is not totally responsible. We listened to him and accepted his ideas when he arrived in our Village three rainy seasons ago. We could have told him that we were not interested."

"What do you have to say to us, Doctor Snippet?" asked Maringa.

The men holding Oscar let him go—though reluctantly. They did not share Maringa's confidence that he was safe. There were still those who wanted to kill him and get it over with. Their bitterness and their anger went deep. Payment and revenge were what they wanted. And it wouldn't stop with Snippet. It would only stop when Pachunga had paid the price for betraying his people to the Bazungu. For now, they realized that killing Snippet would be too hasty an action. It would be better to hear what he had to say first—then kill him.

"Warriors of the Kiritiris—for such as you are now since we are in a state of war with Kjaz-Barbaroi—" he stopped. There was something more important to say first. "Before I continue, I want you to know—I want you—" Snippet was finding these next words hard to say. It was such an emotional moment that he had to swallow several times before he could continue. "I want you to know that I accept full responsibility for all that I have done to you over the past three years." It was out.

"I didn't know what I was...Yes, I did know what I was doing and that it was wrong and that I was being bad. I acted out of greed and thought only of myself and what the diamonds from the mine would bring me." He looked directly at Maringa. "After I finish what I am saying, you are free to do what you think is right and just according to the teachings of Olugbala—"

"Kill him!" said a warrior. "He has confessed his guilt!"

"Yes! Yes!" said a couple of others.

"No!" said Maringa. "He is speaking from his heart. He has asked our forgiveness. I have been remembering the teachings and stories of Olugbala from our youth. If a man asks forgiveness from his heart, then he should be forgiven. There is no other thing we can do. Now Snippet comes to us in the way of Olugbala. We must forgive him. And we must listen to him even more."

"Maringa," said Snippet, "how you have changed since I last saw you in the Village."

"I have changed like you have changed," he said simply. "I have returned to Olugbala once again."

"Let me tell you all this," said Snippet to the men. "Tomorrow, Kjaz-Barbaroi is planning on putting you all in front of his troops as he goes into battle against Pachunga and the allies of Olugbala. Olugbala has directed me—"

"You spoke with Olugbala?" asked Maringa. He was astounded.

"He is the one who directed me here. I could not have come otherwise."

"Your speech is getting better, Mzungu," said a warrior.

"Yes, it is getting more and more dangerous. He is lying!"

Snippet became angry. He had never spoken with more sincerity. "If I am lying, then what good would that lying serve? Answer me that, man!"

The warriors were silent. Snippet had spoken with good reason.

"It is—" Snippet could not continue. There was a commotion at the gate, and a horde of Dark Creatures came crashing into the compound.

"Where is that traitor?" growled one. "We want his blood!"

Snippet knew at that moment that this was where it would end for him. He would not escape, but there was still a chance for most of the Kiritiris.

"Go to the Well of the Wildebeests! The army is gathering there. Go with Olu—!"

A Dark Creature reached him before he could say more, but Snippet had said all that was necessary. With a quick jab of a spear, Snippet fell to the ground, dead.

But Snippet felt no pain. He was not in the Kiritiri prison anymore surrounded by screaming, attacking Dark Creatures. There was no darkness—just the bright, warm light of the sun. And there was Olugbala standing next to him. "Come," said Olugbala. "Come to my Mountain with me. You are a good and faithful servant."

Meanwhile, all the Kiritiris could see was Snippet's corpse and the Dark Creatures.

"To the Well!" shouted Maringa.

With that command, they fought the Dark Creatures. The warriors grabbed the spears from the hands of their attackers who were caught off guard by the vehemence of the response. The prisoners weren't supposed to behave this way.

The Dark Creatures were soon overrun because there were too many Kiritiris. They escaped through the gate and left the camp, running quickly and silently across the dry grassland.

Some Cattle People had heard the noise and tried to head them off, but they were suddenly called back before they could do anything.

"Let them go," said Kjaz-Barbaroi from his observation post. He had seen everything. "The battle will be ours tomorrow no matter what we do. We will defeat Olugbala once and for all."

THE HILLS OF SEPARATION

Pachunga was awakened a lot sooner than he had anticipated. It seemed as if he had only just fallen asleep after the long evening's feasting and dancing, when someone was shaking his shoulder.

"Chief Pachunga," said a voice, "You are wanted immediately."

"Huh?" he asked. He had been dreaming about battle, and was surprised—and relieved—that he was still in the camp.

"What is it?"

"Kiritiris, sir," said the voice that could now be identified as a Cattle People warrior. He had been on the night watch. "There must be several hundred—or more—and they all want to speak with you."

Pachunga's mind was going in circles. "Kiritiris?" he wondered. "What are they doing here?"

He stood up and pulled on a pair of cotton shorts the Cattle People had given him to replace his old garment. The shorts represented a permanent change in the ways of his people and those of Baree. These had come from the Bazungu and the Cattle People men and boys preferred them to what they used to wear.

The guard had already left the hut, so Pachunga followed after him. It was almost dawn, and there was quite a bit of morning light preceding the rising of the sun. At the edge of the camp, Pachunga saw his Kiritiri warriors. They were not armed, and Maringa was standing nervously in front of the group.

Pachunga stopped ten meters in front of them and studied them silently. Maringa kept his eyes lowered. Neither of them knew what to say. It was not that Maringa was amazed at seeing Pachunga so young—he had been told that already by the Cattle People guards—it was that he didn't know how to begin, especially since he had been elected by the Kiritiris to ask Pachunga's forgiveness for all the trouble and worry they had caused him.

Baree joined Pachunga, though he stood behind him. "What are they doing here?" he asked.

"I don't know," said Pachunga quietly. He knew that he would have to be the first one to speak. "Maringa," he said with his voice full of hope. "What brings you and the other young men all the way out here?"

The tension was broken.

"We came at the bidding of Doctor Snippet," said Maringa. "He came to us late this night at the camp of Kjaz-Barbaroi and told us where to find you."

"Snippet?" He was astounded. "He did?"

"And he lost his life doing it. He was killed by the Dark Creatures as he spoke to us—speared right through the heart. We only just managed to escape with little injury."

Pachunga was shocked and stunned. So that is why Snippet had gone back to the camp of Kjaz-Barbaroi. He was not a traitor. Pachunga's mind filled with regret and sadness for the thoughts that he had had about the man since he had left the Well. The geologist *had* been sent on a special mission—by Olugbala, no doubt—after all.

"We are here to fight under you," said Maringa. "You are our Chief—not Kjaz-Barbaroi. It wasn't until he took us captive and forced us to march for many days to his camp that we realized what he stands for. We beg your forgiveness. We have done much wrong, and we wish that we could have remained faithful to Olugbala like you have." His face started to twist up and it was obvious that he was trying not to cry. But he couldn't help it. His eyes glistened and his voice became hoarse and fractured. "We—we are so ashamed."

Pachunga now felt ashamed himself. It was a deep shame that came out of recognizing what it was costing Maringa and the others to speak to him this way. He was the one who should be asking for their forgiveness. They were the ones whom he had betrayed when he let the Bazungu come into the Village in the first place to start mining the diamonds. If he had not been so tantalized by Snippet's persuasive words, they would not be in the situation they were currently in. These men had showed much more courage than he had. They were the ones who had had to work in the mines. They were the ones who had been in danger of losing their identity as men of the Kiritiri.

Large tears started to roll down Pachunga's cheeks.

Maringa was confused.

Pachunga took several steps forward and then knelt at Maringa's feet. He said, "I need to ask your forgiveness. You are not at fault. I failed you as your leader and Chief. You, now, must lead our people. You are the one who is worthy of this task."

"Chief Pachunga, I cannot—"

Pachunga stood up and faced the man in front of him. Maringa was a full head taller. "Please let me finish. You are aptly named, for your name means the one who is always given the portion of food from the hunt. It signifies worthiness in our tribe, because you come from a great family. Your grandfather, Maringa the Elder, served Olugbala well and faithfully at the Battle of a Thousand Cries."

Maringa thought about what Pachunga was saying. This was an opportunity that he had never thought would happen. He was being offered the chieftainship. Would he not be more qualified to rule than this boy? Yes, Pachunga was a boy again. It was not right for him to remain Chief. He, Maringa, was better suited.

"I—" Maringa stopped speaking. He was about to accept humbly Pachunga's offer when he realized that he should not take it. It was the wrong thing to do. He knew that if he took it, it was only because of his own, personal ambition—not a desire to serve the Kiritiris. He was not the right person for the job. No, Pachunga was the rightful Chief and Pachunga would stay Chief.

Pachunga then reached for the knife that he had sheathed on a belt around his middle and removed it. He extended the knife handle first towards Maringa. It was his most valuable possession and the one thing he still had that symbolized his chieftainship.

"No!" said Maringa looking straight into Pachunga's eyes. "I cannot accept this. You are our Chief. Only you—as long as you are with us—are entitled to sit on the High Seat as Chief of all Kiritiri peoples."

It was out. He did it—and his heart felt much lighter. He kept his hands at his side and refused to take the knife.

"But I failed," said Pachunga.

"We have all failed," said Maringa. "But if we admit that we have failed and we ask for forgiveness, then you know that Olugbala gives us a new start—a fresh start. Not one of us is worthy. Our worth only comes because of Olugbala and serving him. Do you forgive us?" The question was almost a plea.

"Maringa, there is nothing to forgive you for. You have done no wrong."

"Yes, we have. And we need your forgiveness. It needs to go both ways."

Pachunga considered this. "Well, then I forgive you and forgive you and forgive you!"

Maringa broke into a broad smile.

Pachunga smiled back and put his knife back in the sheath. "Maringa, you are wiser than you know. You will be my advisor once again. I can't do this alone."

Maringa quietly nodded his assent while smiling broadly and knelt in front of Pachunga. He said very formally: "Chief Pachunga, I offer to you my service in the name of Olugbala. You may use me in any way that you desire."

"And I accept it," said Pachunga. "And I will use you!" He laughed.

Maringa stood up and turned to the Kiritiri men.

"Men of the Kiritiris, in this past night and this early dawn of day you have stood in the presence of two great people. The first is Dr. Snippet, who will be remembered with joy and gladness as our liberator—who gave his life so that we would be free. The second is our Chief Pachunga, who has demonstrated by his humility and love for all of us that he is fit to remain our leader. It is a new day today. The old is gone and the new has come. May Olugbala be praised!"

"Hooray!" they cried in unison. "Hooray for Chief Pachunga!"

Joy came over the faces of the Kiritiri warriors and they immediately burst into a song, clapping their hands together and moving as one in a simple dance to the beat.

Maringa tilted his head toward the young Chief. "You have been rightly named Chief Pachunga the Good. May you continue to be faithful in your service to Olugbala and rule us all well."

"Thank you," he responded simply. But there was no time for more formality. They needed to get organized and prepare for the battle. His mind was moving ahead to more practical matters. "You are all hungry and tired. You must eat, then rest."

Baree spoke to his guard. "See that they are fed well and that they have a place to sleep until we march. Also, arm them with the best shields and spears you can find."

As the Kiritiris filed past their Chief, he greeted them one by one and called them all by name. Pachunga's head was reeling with joy. He was to be in command of Kiritiri warriors in battle, and they were going to be an even greater threat to Kjaz-Barbaroi. When the last warrior went by, he was reminded about Snippet and felt sadness again. He had not trusted in Olugbala's ability to change lives—even though he was surrounded by people whose lives had been touched and changed by Olugbala. Even though *his* life had been changed and he had been given a new start.

Breakfast and his pre-battle preparations would have to wait. He needed to be alone to get everything sorted out with Olugbala before he could do anything else that day.

* * * *

It was time.

But there were still some details that had to be taken care of first.

Titi had requested that he and the twelve Tall Men be permitted to ride elephants into battle. "I don't mean to be asking for a special privilege," he had said. "It is only that the walk here was more tiring than anything we have ever done, and we are older people. We need our strength for the Dark Creatures."

Baree had immediately seen his reasoning, and wished that he had thought of it first to spare Titi the embarrassment of asking. He instructed the elephants to carry them. It took some doing getting the Tall Men properly mounted. Lituli had protested at first, but when it was explained to him the distance they were to travel, he consented. The twelve Tall Men looked considerably different than they had in the

210

caves. To protect their skin from the burning sun, they were wrapped in flowing robes. The Cave People were also similarly dressed. Pachunga thought they looked like the ancient barbarians who had swept across the Great Desert centuries before to conquer the tribes of the black man.

The entire procession of elephants, lions, Cave People, Cattle People and Kiritiris now marched North across the Great Grassland in search of battle. Muriel and Baree rode elephants, but Pachunga had chosen to walk with his warriors. He no longer wanted to be separated from them.

They sang chants and clapped their hands for the first part of the trip. This was when the sun was lower in the sky and it wasn't as hot. The music and the drums from the previous night's festival still played in their heads. Each warrior remembered the speeches given by each of the leaders. They were inspired and excited. For the first time since the armies had been called together, they felt completely optimistic about winning that day. Kjaz-Barbaroi and his Dark Creatures were going to be defeated—even if they had to chase them all the way back to the Land Where No One Dares to Live.

Kasuku rode with Baree and would make frequent scouting trips to find out where Kjaz-Barbaroi was sending his armies. Midway between the opposing camps were a series of low mounds that were considered hills by the Cattle People. They were called the Hills of Separation, because they marked the spot where Prince Mwailu had broken his pact with Olugbala and had joined forces with Kjaz-Barbaroi. They also served as a boundary line between the two groups of Cattle People. It was here, reasoned Kasuku, that the battle would take place.

He reported this to Baree. "We should go no further than the Hills," he counseled the Prince. "Once Kjaz-Barbaroi crosses that point, he will be in our territory, so we will have the right to defend it."

"That makes good sense," said Baree. "It is just as we discussed last night during the Council of War—if we do not meet them until we reach that point. Is there any sign of the enemy?"

"No, not yet," said Kasuku. "But they cannot be far."

"Okay, relay this information to Pachunga, Chief Mkumbo, Kalopa and Titi."

Kasuku flew away to deliver the message.

The morning passed on. The sun got higher and hotter. The clapping and singing stopped, for it took too much effort. Baree hoped that it didn't mean that their spirits were failing. Kasuku reported that the wildebeests they had seen the previous day were also moving North with them, just over the horizon to the East. They were too shy to march with the rest, but they were planning on entering into battle when the time came.

"They'll be the ace up our sleeve," said Muriel.

"Huh?" asked Baree. "What do you mean?" He soon regretted that he had asked that question. Muriel spent the next fifteen minutes trying to explain card games to him. He never did understand.

As time went on, the men, boys and animals began to wonder if there were going to be a battle that day after all. Kasuku still hadn't seen any sign of the enemy—it was as if they had vanished from the Great Grassland.

"We'll stop for water," said Baree. The word was passed around, and everyone came to a halt. Skins of water were shared. The Hills of Separation were now discernible through the hot, dusty air and they looked as empty and desolate as ever.

"What do you think?" Pachunga asked Baree.

"They're playing games with us. They're trying to test our patience. By putting the fighting later and later in the day, they are hoping to weaken our morale."

"Let's divide up into two flanks now that we are close to the Hills," suggested Pachunga. He squinted off into the distance. There were three hills in a row facing them. "Do you see that middle hill? I'll take my men, the elephants and the Tall Men around the right of it. You can take the lions, your warriors and the Cave People."

Chief Mkumbo joined them.

"What do you think, Chief Mkumbo?" asked Baree.

"That's fine by me and my men," he said. "We're new to this sort of thing. You're the ones with the experience." The Chief looked startling in the robes he wore. The cloth covered with red and brown stripes flapped in the wind that had been blowing all morning.

Kalopa and Mamosa agreed. "If one flank runs into difficulty, then the other one will be able to close in from a different side," said Kalopa.

"It is a good plan," said Mamosa.

"But let's not separate too soon," said Kalopa. "We'll wait until we're almost to that hill that's in the middle."

"Let's go then," said Baree. "It is getting later and later."

They divided up into two companies, but kept abreast of each other as they marched. Baree led the left flank, and Pachunga, the right. Muriel estimated they had almost two hours of walking ahead of them before they would split up.

An hour later, Kasuku came back with some news. "On the far side of the hills is a group of jackals, cheetahs, hyenas and baboons."

"How many?" asked Baree.

"There are about fifty or sixty jackals, ten cheetahs, thirty hyenas and an equal number of baboons. Where they came from, I don't know. There was no sign of them on my last trip."

"Good work," said Baree. "The question now is whether or not we should split up. If we do, then we can close them off from both sides."

"Yes," said Pachunga. "But what if they come around one side of the hill? That would mean that one flank would have to bear the brunt of the fighting until the other one could come in and help."

"I think it's worth the risk," said Baree. "There are only a hundred and twenty or so of them. And they are small animals. Each flank should be able to fight them off without any problem."

"That is true. But why such a small group? Is Kjaz-Barbaroi so arrogant that he thinks that that is all that it will take to defeat us?"

Baree questioned Kasuku again. "Are you sure you didn't see anything more? That was it?"

Kasuku's feathers were ruffled. "No, I didn't. I would have told you if I had. There is nothing more there. I even flew beyond them to see if there were something more over the next row of hills."

"What is Kjaz-Barbaroi up to?" asked Pachunga. He didn't expect to get an answer from anyone.

Mamosa expressed his reservations. "It could be that they are there to distract us. If we engage them in battle, then Kjaz-Barbaroi could send in other troops before we had time to re-group."

"How wide is this pass between the two right hills?" asked Baree. "It has been some time since I've been there." He knew that it was taking up precious time to answer these questions, but the information he received would figure in his final decision.

"The part that is between them is only about a hundred meters. It is very narrow for an army our size. If we were to be attacked there, everyone would get all jammed up and there would be no room to fight."

"That settles it," said Baree. "We will have to split up. It will make us too vulnerable to try and get through one side only. May Olugbala protect us!"

* * * *

Kasuku's scouting mission had not gone unnoticed by the enemy animals on the other side of the hill. One of the cheetahs growled, "Good, they have seen us. Everybody now up to the top of the hill! We will attack as soon as they enter the pass."

With screeches, cries, roars, yelps, barks and yowls, they ran up the hill and stopped just below the crest out of sight. Once there, they remained very quiet and waited.

* * * *

A short time later, Pachunga and his right flank drew closer to the pass that led between the two hills on the right. Kasuku joined him with an important message. "The enemy has moved its position to the top of the hill. Are you sure you still want to go through the pass?"

"We don't know when they're going to attack. We will go through and try and draw them out. We're ready for them, so—"

It didn't matter what he said next. The enemy animals had grown impatient, and some of them began the charge before they were supposed to. The rest followed, though the cheetah knew that those who had attacked before he gave the command would be punished—if they survived. Their impatience was their undoing. Had they waited, they might have won. They ran down the hill, bounding and racing across the short stretch of grassland that was between them.

"Report this to Baree!" said Pachunga. The left flank was too far away to be of any immediate assistance, but Pachunga was hoping to push the attackers around to the other side of the hill.

Pachunga raised his arm and signaled his forces to spread out so they wouldn't get too bunched together. He realized that he had the advantage, but as a good general, he wanted to repel this first attack with as little injury to his men and animals as possible.

The cheetahs were the ones to arrive first. They attacked the center part of the Kiritiris. Their long teeth were bared, their eyes were narrowed and protected by folds of thick skin and their claws stood out from their paws. Their job was to rip and tear as much flesh as possible.

The Kiritiris fought well. There were only ten cheetahs, and it was not much of an attack. The elephants helped out where they could, picking up the cats' bodies with their trunks and hurling them to the ground.

The hyenas and baboons arrived, and the fighting became fiercer. Bit by bit, the allies of Olugbala pushed forward, pressing their assailants back around the hill. Muriel was in the midst of the fighting as much as the Kiritiris and elephants. She jabbed and poked the animal hides with a Cave People spear and blocked their assaults with a shield. Lituli and Titi were fighting well for their first experience in battle. Their size gave them an advantage. Although old, they found strength from Olugbala and fought like young warriors.

Maringa had just stabbed a hyena with a knife when a baboon jumped onto his back and dug its sharp teeth into his neck. Pachunga saw that his friend was in serious trouble, so with fierce determination, he fought his way over to him. Grabbing the baboon by the short hair on top of its head, Pachunga was able to yank the animal off Maringa. One swift slice of the knife and the baboon was dead.

The elephants continued their valiant job. Mamuko and Mambimbo trampled the baboons and jackals with their feet. They bellowed and trumpeted with each small win. Mamosa was the best fighter. His tusks were a menace to all animals, and he could toss as many as two hyenas at a time through the air. Because of their size and thick skin, the only animal that presented a threat to them was the cheetah. But most of these had already been killed or wounded by the Kiritiris.

The ground became moist, and the air was filled with the smell of bloody dust and sweat. Claws scraped against shields and skin. Teeth snapped at spears and legs. Spears stabbed and knives slashed. More and more of the enemy lay dead around them. The sounds of battle became quieter and quieter because there were fewer and fewer fighting. Maringa was out of commission with severe bites on his neck and legs. Lulo was wounded in the stomach and was losing blood. Muriel stood by him to protect him from any animal that wanted to finish him off.

They pushed the remaining animals further and further around toward the other side of the hill. When they finally reached the far side, Pachunga cheered his soldiers on for a final push. Several hundred meters away, Baree was leading a charge of lions and Cave and Cattle People toward the site of the battle. They raced as fast as they could to attack from behind.

When the animals' leader, the cheetah, saw the reinforcements coming from the rear, he roared once and the surviving members of his company stopped fighting immediately. They escaped while they still had the opportunity. They ran across a small, narrow valley that was between the first hill and the second, yipping, yapping and growling as they went.

They had been defeated.

Pachunga took a deep breath and let the air out slowly. They had won.

He stooped down and rubbed some dirt over the blade of his knife to clean it before he put it back in his sheath. He had not been wounded seriously, but realized that there were many who had been. The fighting was not over either. How long they would have to wait until the next confrontation, he did not know. He hoped that there would be enough time to take care of the wounded first.

The men and elephants cheered loudly as the last of the enemy animals raced up the far hill out of sight. Of the hundred and twenty in the original attack, there were only thirty or so who returned to Kjaz-Barbaroi.

"Well, we did it," said Pachunga weakly to Mamosa, who was standing nearby. The old elephant was still twitching and could not stand completely still because of the adrenaline that coursed through his immense body. Short, loud blasts of air came out of his trunk.

"Thanks be to Olugbala," was all he said.

Kasuku was the first member of the left flank to reach Pachunga. He did not have encouraging news.

"On the other side of the next hill," he said breathlessly, "there are Dark Creatures and Cattle People. Hundreds of them. I have never seen so many." He described how they were marching in row after row to the beating of the Drum dressed for battle with their long spears and shields. Their faces were painted for war. He stopped to catch his breath. "And that is not the worst of it. There are Dark Creatures, too—more than I've ever seen in one place."

"I don't want to hear more," said Pachunga. The thrill of winning was brief, indeed. There had been hope, and now there appeared to be none. There were too many of them. "Give instructions to Kalopa to take care of the wounded as fast as possible. We need everyone."

Kasuku flew away with his new orders.

Soon, Kalopa was there to use the healing effects of his tongue. Other lions discovered that they had this gift, too. Quickly, they set about the task of making the injured well.

The wildebeests also came charging across the Great Grassland behind them and were disappointed that they had arrived too late to help in the first battle. They expressed their willingness to fight when the next attack came.

Baree and Chief Mkumbo finally joined them. The short Chief's face was contorted as he gasped for breath. He hadn't been able to walk as quickly as Baree and had had to jog. The first thing he did before he spoke was to get a gourd of water from one of the elephants, which he gulped down noisily. He poured the rest of the water over his head. At any other time, his antics would have been funny.

"What do you think?" asked Baree.

"It doesn't look good," said Pachunga.

They stood in silence and thought. Each one remembered all the things they had learned over numerous rainy seasons and from Olugbala. They knew that he had prepared them for this moment.

They could now hear the Dark Creatures as they chanted in their hyena-monkey voices to the steady beat of the Drum. Then, to their horror and fear, the hills in front of them suddenly became filled with Dark Creatures and Cattle People. Kasuku was right. There were hundreds of them. Possibly thousands. And there were more behind the ones that they could see in front.

217

Kalopa and his lions continued their task tirelessly, ignoring the threat of a second charge. It did not take long for the wounded to get back on their feet and to prepare themselves for the next battle.

As Pachunga saw the enemy forces continue to increase in size, he became more and more frustrated. Was this why he had been dragged out of his Village and made to face peril after peril—only to die in the middle of the Hills of Separation? It would have been much better if he had been killed at the outset, instead of having to die at the hands of Kjaz-Barbaroi. It was not fair. And it was not fair to the people and animals that he and Baree were now leading to their deaths.

"This is not right!" he exclaimed. "This is not the way it was supposed to happen!" His frustration erupted, and he was confused and angry. Olugbala had specifically asked him to put together an army. He had been made younger—for what now seemed to have been a pointless act on Olugbala's part—and here he was now with a small and pitiful army that had won the first little skirmish more because of a tactical error on the part of the enemy than their own military brilliance. He was honest with himself about that. With the number of Dark Creatures and Cattle People gathered on the hills above him, staring mercilessly and cruelly down upon them–with Kjaz-Barbaroi right up there already claiming victory—he was certain of it—it was more than he could take. "Why are we here? Why?"

Muriel tried to calm Pachunga down. "Pachunga, don't you—"

Pachunga glared at her and cut her off. "Don't I what? Don't I know what is happening? Don't I know that this whole entire escapade has been pointless from the very beginning? Don't I know that—"

"Pachunga!"

Whose voice was that?

From behind the gathering of people closest to Pachunga came a voice that was reedy because of age, but strong because of the conviction behind it.

It was Titi.

"Pachunga!" he said again.

"What?" responded Pachunga abruptly and rudely.

Titi winced at the response, but persevered. "Please listen to me."

The way Titi spoke quieted Pachunga a little. The anger and frustration he was feeling did not go away, but he was in a more receptive mood than he had been.

"Just recently, if you recall, I lost a very close friend—a friend I had had my entire life—a friend I did everything with. His name was Kanoti, and he was the last Torchlighter of our tribe. When he refused to turn towards Olugbala and fled into the Great Temple, I went after him to persuade him that this was something that he should do—that he should pay attention to what Kasuku had been saying and turn from the statues and images and worship the real Olugbala. I could see in his eyes that he wanted to respond—that he wanted to be a follower of Olugbala in the proper way—but the Drum started to beat strongly in him and in his crazed state he jumped to his death in the Cave of Perpetual Sorrow."

"What has this got to do with what is happening now?" asked Pachunga. "Just look at that army above us."

"It has everything to do with what is happening now," said Titi patiently. "As the Torchlighter—as the one leading our tribe—Kanoti thought that the burden of leadership fell squarely on his shoulders. Yes, he was the leader, but the trust that he put in the statues and images did him no good. His pride caused him to reject Olugbala at the moment when he was needed most—at the moment when Olugbala would have been most helpful to Kanoti and would have saved his life. Olugbala is the real leader. And you know that. Does your trust in Olugbala go far enough to believe that he has everything under control?

"Kanoti's pride killed him. Is your pride getting in the way of what needs to happen? Do you want to make the same mistake? Do you feel that only *you* can make things right here? By getting angry with Olugbala you are really saying that he is not capable of saving us or helping us. Don't you see that his purposes go far beyond this little group gathered here? Don't you really believe that Olugbala would not have brought us to this point if he didn't have something in mind?"

The angry look on Pachunga's face softened. At one point, he had wondered what use the elderly Tall Men would be in the fight against Kjaz-Barbaroi. What Titi had just said put everything in the right perspective. Once again, he was getting in the way of what needed to happen. Was he the last one in the group to understand?

Olugbala would not have had him bring the army together just to have them perish in the middle of battle and give the victory to Kjaz-Barbaroi. There must be something else—something more—that he had in mind. Now was the time for Olugbala to appear. Now was the time that he was needed.

"Thank you, Titi," said Pachunga sincerely, but simply. "I needed to hear that—as usual."

The number of Cattle People and Dark Creatures increased more and more on top of the hills that overlooked Pachunga and his small army. The good news was that they were not attacking. At the moment, Kjaz-Barbaroi seemed to be content just to show the size of his force.

Baree gazed up at the enemy. Fleeing at this point was impossible. They would not get away fast enough. And to fight them straight on would not be a battle. It would be a slaughter. It was doubtful that any of them would be permitted to live. Kjaz-Barbaroi would want to make sure that they were all dead. He saw Mwailu standing proudly next to Kjaz-Barbaroi and Ngaba. Why had he gone bad? Why had he forgotten the teachings of Olugbala from his youth? The thought of serving Kjaz-Barbaroi was repugnant to Baree. He could not imagine doing it for *any* reason. But Mwailu had always been personally ambitious. He was not content to rule just the Cattle People—he had to have more. And Kjaz-Barbaroi had promised him more. If only Mwailu were smart enough to realize what that "more" was costing him and the rest of the Cattle People.

Suddenly, the Dark Creatures and Cattle People began to descend the hills on either side of them. They marched slowly and purposefully to the beat of the Drum. There was no need to hurry. There was no need to break into a charge. From their vantage point, they knew that the battle was already won.

What did Olugbala have in mind?

Muriel became more and more numb from disbelief and fear. Where was Olugbala? Was he, in fact, letting them all down? The beating of the Drum was getting to her, and she remembered what Kjaz-Barbaroi had spoken to her when she was running away from the Land Where No One Dares to Live: "One day, Muriel Sniggins, you will come to me. You will hear my Drum..."

Was that prediction going to come true? There did not appear to be any hope that they could still win the battle now, and Muriel became afraid that she would forsake Olugbala and go to Kjaz-Barbaroi. Then she realized that Olugbala was capable of doing anything. Or was he? Already she was forgetting what Titi had just said. And besides, what does he really know? The Drum continued to beat. Why were the skies so silent? They were no longer blue with optimism, but cold with a gloomy grey cast.

"We need Olugbala," said Pachunga. "We need him now."

Hearing Pachunga mention Olugbala's name aloud brought Muriel back to her senses. The Drum stopped. "Olugbala," said Muriel, "Come, please! Please!"

Then the conversation that she had had with him while Kalopa had been licking her bullet wound came back to her. She remembered what he had said. She remembered also that she would never go over to Kjaz-Barbaroi. He was only trying to deceive her.

Everything, she knew, would work out for the best when Olugbala arrived.

And he was going to come.

He had told her so.

The Drum

The solitary figure walked around the hill and slowly approached the assembled group of humans, lions, elephants, and wildebeests. His head was slightly bent, and he walked with heavy but steady purpose. The lions recognized him first. One by one, they lowered themselves to the ground as he drew closer. The elephants followed, led by Mamosa. They first dropped to their forelegs and then to their haunches. The wildebeests, normally a noisy lot, were quiet and still in his presence. In one simple movement, they fell to the ground as well.

Cattle People, following Prince Baree's lead, lowered their heads and stood in silence as he came nearer. Kiritiris and Cave People also bowed. The Tall Men stiffly went down on one knee. For most of the assembled group, this was the first time that they had seen him in person. A lifelong desire was fulfilled.

Titi was close to tears in reverent awe and love. Muriel wanted to run up and give him a hug, but that would not have been appropriate then. The moment was too solemn.

He passed through the outer part of his creatures and stopped in the center near Baree, Pachunga, Kalopa, and Mamosa.

Kasuku lowered his head and extended one wing as he perched on Baree's shoulder.

For several long moments, the man allowed them to revere him. Then with a small motion of his hand, he signaled them to rise.

Olugbala had come to help them all—just as Muriel knew he would.

* * * *

Near the top of the hill, Kjaz-Barbaroi studied the arrival of Olugbala. He raised the Drumstick he held in his hand as a signal for his army to come to a halt. When they stopped, they all fixed their eyes on Olugbala. Some were scared and wanted to run away and hide. Others were angry and wanted to be the ones who had the privilege of killing him.

Kjaz-Barbaroi had known that Olugbala was going to turn up at some point—and he wondered why he hadn't done it sooner. Of course, Kjaz-Barbaroi was very pleased that Olugbala had waited so long. It had enabled him to get his armies together and to weaken the morale of the opposing forces. Even so, he was genuinely concerned. Kjaz-Barbaroi did not have a winning record in his personal encounters with Olugbala. Olugbala had ruined his previous efforts for the domination and control of all peoples and animals. But at those times, Olugbala had had stronger armies that were greater in number than the Dark Creatures and other creatures who served him. Now, Kjaz-Barbaroi's armies outnumbered Olugbala's by almost five to one—not including the wildebeests, which did not count because Kjaz-Barbaroi considered them to be almost worthless in battle. His armies were fiercer and more committed to him than any other army he had commanded. His power was also the strongest that it had ever been. As it had grown, he had become thirstier and thirstier for more. "I want MORE," he had said to himself over and over again. "I want more people and more animals and more lands under my rule. I want MORE!"

Kjaz-Barbaroi watched the animals and humans bow to Olugbala. He laughed. "Soon they will be bowing to me—then I will kill them very slowly," he said to Ngaba. "At least those who are still alive when my armies are finished with them."

"Yes, yes, yes!" said Ngaba gleefully. "As you permit, Your Perfection."

* * * *

Now that Olugbala was with them, Pachunga felt that it was all going to work out. How were they going to fight the battle? Olugbala would be in charge, of course, and Pachunga trusted him to provide them with abilities and powers that they otherwise would not have had. That was the only way that they would be able to defeat Kjaz-Barbaroi. Maybe they would make an attack right towards the center, and if all went well, they would kill Kjaz-Barbaroi and the rest of his army would surrender.

"Olugbala," he said. "How do you want to command us?"

Olugbala's face became very solemn. "There is only one way that we can defeat Kjaz-Barbaroi."

The group moved closer to him to hear better what he had to say. Kalopa and Mamosa also moved closer.

"He needs the willing sacrifice of one person. If one person gives up his life and dies, then the rest of you will be spared."

"What?" asked Pachunga. "I don't understand."

Baree stepped forward. "I'll do it, Olugbala. I have already been given more years than I was supposed to have. My time here is finished."

"No," said Olugbala. "Your time is not finished. And you cannot be the one."

Pachunga had to ask the question: "Am I the one?"

"No," said Olugbala simply. "It cannot be you, either."

Titi came forward. He towered over Olugbala, but instead of just standing there, he dropped to his knees. Lowering his head, he said humbly, "I can do it. My life is nearing its end here. Chief Pachunga and Prince Baree are young again and could have many years left to serve their people."

Olugbala smiled. "No, old one. You are not the one, either."

"Then who is it?" asked Muriel. She knew what Olugbala was going to say and she was afraid to hear it.

"I am the one," Olugbala said gently.

"What! You can't be!" said Pachunga. "How can it be you?"

"My life has to be given in exchange for yours." He smiled wryly. "It's a trade."

"That's not right!" said Baree fiercely. "Surely it has to be one of us. You are far too important. You are far too valuable."

Kalopa growled softly, expressing his displeasure, and Mamosa just looked worried and alarmed. This was not what they had anticipated.

Kasuku flew off of Baree's shoulder and started to fly in a tight circle over their heads. He was very agitated and could not believe what he was hearing. This was impossible.

"And what would we do if we don't have you anymore?" demanded Pachunga. "Kjaz-Barbaroi would just kill the rest of us."

"We need you," said Muriel.

"This is why I am here. This is why I came. I have to do it." He paused and looked at all the people and animals gathered around him. "This is for you—all of you. The only way that you can be safe and protected is if I die."

*   *   *   *

Kjaz-Barbaroi continued to stare at the scene below him. There was a long discussion between Baree, Kasuku, Pachunga, and Olugbala. The two boys appeared to be *arguing* with Olugbala. He smiled to himself. There was obviously trouble in their ranks. That was a good sign: armies that argued with each other usually did not win.

"What a weak leader he is," said Kjaz-Barbaroi aloud. "If any of my soldiers argued with me like that—why, I'd squeeze their little heads between my fingers until they went *pop!*"

"Yes," said Prince Mwailu. "That is the only way to handle subordinates." He spoke with an air of superiority that annoyed Kjaz-Barbaroi. If Mwailu continued in the way that he was, he would learn what it was like to have *his* head go *pop!*

"He's not severe enough," Kjaz-Barbaroi went on. "No wonder they have such a small army. There is no discipline. There is no fear."

The red haired girl then spoke to Olugbala. The little simp appeared to be crying. What was happening in front of Kjaz-Barbaroi was not making any sense. He couldn't figure out what was going on. For once, he couldn't hear the conversations of his enemies. That skill had been with him ever since Pachunga had entered the Great Grassland. It had grown stronger as he and the rest got closer to the camp and to the Drum.

Olugbala gave the girl a hug. Then he embraced Baree, Pachunga, Chief Mkumbo, and Titi for a long time each. He also put his arms around Kalopa's neck—as best he could—then gently grabbed a handful of mane and gave it an affectionate tug. Mamosa lowered himself to the ground again so that Olugbala could pat and stroke the side of his face by his trunk. He touched Kasuku's head. For the rest, Olugbala raised his hand as if he were blessing them.

"It is as if he is saying good-bye to them all," thought Kjaz-Barbaroi. But why would he do that? He had only just arrived to lead them into battle. Something very different from what he had been expecting was going on. What was it?

"Your Eminence," said Ngaba. "What is going on?" He was just as much in the dark as Kjaz-Barbaroi.

"Fool!" shouted Kjaz-Barbaroi. "Don't you know? Just wait and see what happens. Olugbala is playing right into my hands!" Kjaz-Barbaroi would never admit that he did not know something.

"Yes, yes! Oh, yes!" said Ngaba quickly. "Er, Your Most Wonderful Sublime Being!"

Olugbala turned around and left his army behind and walked toward the armies of Kjaz-Barbaroi. He looked like a man approaching the gallows or a firing squad. The only difference was that he was walking alone and his face was full of purpose. He knew what he was doing and he was doing it willingly.

"It looks as though he wants to have a parley," said Prince Mwailu.

"Yes," said Kjaz-Barbaroi. "He wants to make a deal with us." He turned to Ngaba. "You and Mwailu go down there and see what he wants."

"Y-You w-w-want m-me to g-g-go d-down there?" asked Ngaba. He was terrified of Olugbala. It had been very unpleasant for him to look at him—even from a safe distance.

Kjaz-Barbaroi hated it when anyone questioned his commands. He also decided that he hated Ngaba—not that he had ever had any love for him to begin with. He had only put up with him previously because he had been useful. Now he was no longer useful. He put his large paw around the front of Ngaba's forehead and squeezed. "What are you supposed to do when I give a command?" he asked through clenched teeth. Most of his question was only yips and yowls, but Ngaba understood very well what he was asking.

"To obey without question," said Ngaba. He could barely speak and was whining like a small dog. The pain was very great.

"Did you do that just now?" Kjaz-Barbaroi asked matter-of-factly.

"No, Your Worshipful!"

"What is the penalty for questioning my orders?"

226

Ngaba almost fainted. "D-Death."

"Are you prepared to die?"

"Your—Your—"

"Answer me, maggot!"

Ngaba's only chance for living—which was slim—was to answer positively. "Y-Yes."

"Then die."

His head went *pop!* Ngaba screamed once and went limp.

Kjaz-Barbaroi held Ngaba up effortlessly with one hand and flung him down the hill. Without even thinking about what he had just done, he said to another Dark Creature, "Nyaga, you are now my aide-de-camp. May you assist me more faithfully than your predecessor. You will accompany Prince Mwailu to the meeting with Olugbala."

"Yes, yes! O Most Supreme One!" He was just as afraid of Olugbala as Ngaba had been, though he knew what would happen to him if he showed any reluctance.

Prince Mwailu was most apprehensive about meeting Olugbala. He had once been allied with him. That alliance had not served him well, he had thought, so he had changed sides. It was as simple as that: a political maneuver and nothing more. However, now that he was actually looking at Olugbala, he became concerned.

The two pawns of Kjaz-Barbaroi walked down the hill and stopped a safe distance from the man who stood quietly and peacefully in front of them.

Olugbala spoke first. "Mwailu," he said. "You once knew me. Now you claim not to. You have rejected me." There was sadness in his voice.

Mwailu kept his mouth shut.

"I know what you are thinking. You claim that it is because I was never there with you. I was there, only you were more interested in your own gain than in doing my will. If you had taken the time to listen to me, you would have known that I had been there with you all along."

Mwailu wished that he were someplace else. The truth was hard to take.

"Come back to me," invited Olugbala gently.

Still, Mwailu was silent. He couldn't go back. He was a prince, and he had his honor to think about.

Olugbala gave him a penetrating look. "Send Kjaz-Barbaroi here."

This was not what they were expecting.

"Wh-What d-d-d y-you h-have to d-do with us?" stammered Nyaga.

"Send him here!" It was a command. Mwailu and Nyaga felt such a compelling urge to do Olugbala's bidding that they turned and ran up the hill as fast as they could.

"He—He wants you," said Mwailu.

Kjaz-Barbaroi glared at the two useless oafs in front of him. "Get out of my sight!" he hissed, "before I do away with you both!"

The two got out of his sight very quickly.

Kjaz-Barbaroi stood at the top of the hill and stared at the lone figure at the bottom. Olugbala stared back. Kjaz-Barbaroi thought that he should have Olugbala come to him—not the other way around. Yet Olugbala made him walk down the hill before he even knew what he was doing. Kjaz-Barbaroi was afraid, though he didn't show it on his face. He also could not stop himself from putting one foot in front of the other. He was being forced to recognize who had the greater power. In spite of his fears, the evil leader managed to keep his head high, giving the impression to his troops that he was in control of everything. He took longer steps and strode down the hill in the same manner that a leader of nations and kingdoms would meet another leader of kingdoms and nations, stopping two meters in front of Olugbala. The two of them continued to stare at each other for several minutes. Not a single person or animal moved on either side. They could all sense that the direction of history was going to change as a result of this meeting.

Finally, Kjaz-Barbaroi lowered his eyes. He felt more afraid and confused. What was it that Olugbala wanted him to do?

Olugbala spoke first. "The time has come that was established at the beginning of the age. I am to give myself up to you. You, in turn, are to promise not to harm my people and creatures ever again. It is my life for their lives. Do you understand?"

Kjaz-Barbaroi understood. It was more than he could have hoped for. Here was Olugbala willingly giving himself up in exchange for the safe passage of his creatures.

"You know that this means you *must* die," said Kjaz-Barbaroi.

"Yes. Such is the task that has been appointed for me."

An evil grin gradually spread across the face of Kjaz-Barbaroi. He couldn't help it. With Olugbala out of the way, there would be no stopping him in his quest to take over everything and to be ruler of all. A body could not live without its head. Of course, he would promise not to do anything to Pachunga and the rest of his criminal gang. But who would stop him from capturing them once Olugbala was out of the way? The prospects and possibilities of what lay in the future felt overwhelming. He thought that he would burst with joy.

Kjaz-Barbaroi noticed for the first time the ebony pendant that was hanging from Olugbala's neck along with necklaces that he wore. "What is that?" he demanded. For some reason, he was drawn to it.

"It was given to me by my Father when I became a man."

He growled. "You won't need that where you are going," said Kjaz-Barbaroi. He reached for the pendant and tried to yank it off Olugbala's neck. Olugbala grimaced in pain as the cord, woven from the strong fibers of the bark of the baobab tree, held. Frustrated, Kjaz-Barbaroi pulled down on the cord, forcing Olugbala to bow his head towards the Dark Creature. This time he was successful by lifting the pendant over his head.

"Victory is mine!" he said softly to himself, clutching the pendant. Then he lifted it up in his paw and shouted triumphantly: "Victory is mine!"

There was an exultant cheer from the Cattle People and the Dark Creatures.

"Victory is mine!"

And the Cattle People and the Dark Creatures cheered again even more loudly.

Nearby, Pachunga and the others remained in shock. They could not believe that Olugbala was allowing himself to be treated that way.

Pachunga reached for his knife and took a step towards Olugbala and Kjaz-Barbaroi.

"No!" said Titi, grabbing Pachunga's free arm and holding him tightly. "That is not what Olugbala wants!" Titi gripped Pachunga firmly until the Chief stopped struggling and the fight left him.

"It can't be," said Pachunga. "It just can't be." There was no more strength in his body. He was defeated. They had lost.

Kjaz-Barbaroi looked momentarily in Pachunga's direction as if to say, "I will deal with you later." Without turning his head, he bellowed, "Guards!"

Several of the Imperial Guards came running down the hill.

"Bind him and take him away!" Kjaz-Barbaroi wanted everyone to see the power that he now held over Olugbala. He was giddy with excitement. This was so much more than he had ever expected.

When the Dark Creatures arrived, one of them grabbed the necklaces that remained around Olugbala's neck. He gave them a violent jerk, breaking them and scattering the pieces all over the ground.

Before Olugbala's hands could be tied, another one stripped the bracelets off his arms and wrists and tossed them away. A large rope was put around his neck. The Dark Creatures sang praises to the greatness of Kjaz-Barbaroi and ridiculed Olugbala as he was led up the hill. They poked at him with their spears, spat on him, and dragged him across the rough terrain. At times, he tripped and almost fell, but the ropes that bound him kept him from hitting the ground. The guards painfully yanked him up into a standing position each time and forced him to keep walking.

Kjaz-Barbaroi's entire army turned around in one movement and began to march to the North again in time with the Drum. Their evil chants filled the air.

Mwailu timidly approached Kjaz-Barbaroi. "Don't you think we should keep half the troops here to fight against Pachunga? If they get away, it would take many risings of the full moon to round them all up."

"You have a point," said Kjaz-Barbaroi. He was in too good a mood to let Mwailu bother him. "But as long as Olugbala is alive, we have to stick to the agreement I made. He will be dead by tonight. After that, we can do what we want to Pachunga and the other outlaws. They won't last long."

"As you will, Your Excellency." A wicked smile came over the lips of Mwailu. "Just let me have Baree. He cannot be allowed to live." What Mwailu did not say was that Baree's existence was because Olugbala had brought him back to life and therefore was a threat to his plans for total control of the Cattle People.

"He is all yours."

* * * *

Muriel, Pachunga, Baree, and Kasuku watched numbly as Olugbala and the enemy armies disappeared from sight over the top of the hill. This was the biggest test of their trust in Olugbala that they had had to face thus far. They had to trust that he knew what he was doing. He could have refused and retreated to the safety of his Mountain, but that did not seem to be an option for him.

And now that Olugbala had actually gone and was under the control of Kjaz-Barbaroi, they all became afraid. They felt that at any moment, the enemy armies would come swooping down the hill and set upon them.

"We must go back to the Well and wait it out," said Mamosa. "That is the only safe place to be. We cannot stay here. We are too vulnerable."

"You are going to abandon Olugbala?" asked Muriel.

"We must do what he told us to do. I think that waiting for him in the camp is much better than waiting for him here."

"I agree," said Baree. "We cannot do anything for him now."

"Well, I'm not going with you," said Muriel. "I'm going to see where they are taking him."

Pachunga had the same thoughts, though not as strong. Muriel could not go alone to Kjaz-Barbaroi's camp—or wherever it was that they were taking Olugbala. Somebody had to be a witness. He made his decision and called Maringa. "Muriel and I are going to follow Olugbala and see where they take him. Don't worry. We'll be careful. You are in charge of the warriors until I return. If I—If I don't return, then you are to be the next Chief. And don't give me an argument this time. You made a pledge to me."

Maringa studied Pachunga's face for several seconds. He decided that he would not be able to change Pachunga's mind. He knew about Kjaz-Barbaroi's camp and what went on there, and wished that his Chief were not going.

"Let me go instead," he pleaded.

"No, this is for Muriel and me to do."

Kalopa thought that this was all foolishness, but he was not in a frame of mind to discuss it with Muriel and Pachunga. He was feeling a strong urge to get himself and his lions away from the Hills of

Separation. He had to think of their safety. Let Pachunga and Muriel do what they wanted.

"Are you sure about this?" asked Kasuku.

"Yes," said Pachunga. "I am sure."

"I couldn't do anything else," said Muriel.

"Then go with Olugbala."

"Farewell, Pachunga," said Baree. "We'll be looking for you at the Well when this is all over."

"See you then," said the Chief.

The boy and girl left the group and walked North toward the hill in front of them. They did not know what lay ahead, but they knew that they were doing the right thing.

The other animals and humans all turned South and began the long march to the camp at the Well of the Wildebeests. There they would wait until Olugbala appeared to them again.

* * * *

Pachunga and Muriel huddled together inside an empty hut that was in the middle of Kjaz-Barbaroi's camp. They had no trouble getting there. No guards were around the perimeter, for all the Dark Creatures and Prince Mwailu's Cattle People were clustered about the giant Drum that was in the center of the camp. The scene was well-lit by the floodlights which towered above the Drum on steel stands. Fires also burned around the camp giving off dark, sooty smoke. Torches were abundant. They seemed to want as much light for the spectacle as they could get.

Kjaz-Barbaroi, his lieutenants, and Prince Mwailu all stood on a platform that was above the Drum at one end. A second, narrower platform had been built around the Drum. It was a meter lower than the Drum's head. Pressed side by side, four hundred and twenty Dark Creatures and Cattle People held drumsticks.

The most awful thing that Muriel and Pachunga saw was not the Drum itself—nor was it Kjaz-Barbaroi and the hundreds of Dark Creatures and Cattle People. It was Olugbala. He was tied down on his back in the center of the Drum. His body was bruised and bleeding from the whippings and lashings of the Dark Creatures. Blood oozed from wounds in his sides where the Cattle People had stabbed him with their spears. He had been given just enough pain to torment him and to torture him—but not enough to kill him.

It was obvious to Pachunga and Muriel what was going to happen to him now. The Dark Creatures, Cattle People, and Kjaz-Barbaroi were going to beat and beat on the Drum until Olugbala died.

"The Drum!" cried Kjaz-Barbaroi suddenly, lifting his Drumstick high in the air. It was the one decorated with diamonds from the Kiritiri mines that he carried with him at all times.

"The Drum!" screamed everyone back to him. Those with drumsticks also held them high in the air as a salute to their leader.

"This is a great moment in the history of the world–in the history of *my* world," said Kjaz-Barbaroi. "This is the moment that we all have been waiting for rainy season after rainy season. Look at the man who is now in the middle of the Drum. Where is the power that he claims to have? If he is so strong, why doesn't he break his bonds and destroy us all? Where is that strength? He considers himself to be their leader. He considers himself to be the Chief of chiefs and the Son of the Father the Creator. He has been called a King by some. And look at him now. Look at this poor wretch. He has finally admitted by his surrender that I—yes, I, Kjaz-Barbaroi—am greater than he—that he is no match for me. By his surrender, he acknowledged that I have more power and that I shall be the ruler of the world.

"Behold him! Behold him, I say! Look on the face of the one who is responsible for all the agony and suffering in this world! See the one who has been a treacherous foe and adversary! Let him pay for the crimes he has committed! The time has come for the new ruler to rule—the true ruler. Let us do away with this scum! The time is now!"

"Behold the Drum!" he shouted.

"The Drum!" responded everyone else.

"Behold the man!"

Kjaz-Barbaroi's speech was so rousing that many of the Dark Creatures had to be held back from running across the top of the Drum and killing Olugbala right then and there. Their mouths foamed and they could not speak in clear words, but yipped and hooted and yelped and howled. Even the Cattle People started making the same noise.

Kjaz-Barbaroi placed the diamond studded Drumstick on the edge of the Drum. There was a hushed silence. No one moved.

Then, in a deliberate, methodical way, he started to tap slowly on the surface of the tightly drawn cattle skins. Around him, Dark Creatures and Cattle People, who were not on the platform, chanted and danced to his solo beating. While keeping the same tempo, he beat the Drum harder so that it made a louder noise.

Those dancing seemed to jerk in agony with every beat. It was certain that Olugbala was feeling tremendous pain—and the drumming had only just started.

The rest holding drumsticks now joined in. They kept in time with their master. Olugbala's body started to shake and jerk. He could not move from where he was because of the tight cords that held him firmly fixed on the cattle skins. It was doubtful that he would have moved anyway. He knew what he had to do.

The drumming started to pick up speed. The dancers moved faster and faster in their wild movements. They imitated the jerking movements of Olugbala. They screamed and yelled in pleasure. The wails and cries grew louder. They enjoyed every moment of Olugbala's pain and agony. They believed that they would finally be free once Olugbala died.

Yet Olugbala did not cry out in pain. He kept his mouth firmly shut.

Boom! Boom! Boom! Boom! Boom! Boom! Boom! Boom! Boom! Boom!

Pachunga and Muriel could see the torment on Olugbala's face. Blood started to trickle from his ears. Muriel knew that his eardrums had burst from the noise.

The Drum beat faster and faster.

Boom! Boom! Boom!

How long could Olugbala endure it?

Boom! Boom! Boom!

Pachunga wanted to turn his head away. But he could not. He had to watch. There had to be witnesses to what was happening to Olugbala. He saw that tears were flowing unchecked down Muriel's face. He felt wetness on his own cheeks. He hadn't been aware that he was crying, too.

Boom! Boom! Boom! Boom! Boom! Boom! Boom!

Kjaz-Barbaroi's eyes were bright with sadistic pleasure. He beat his Drumstick faster and faster on the Drum's head. There was no stopping him now. Soon, all the sticks were hitting the Drum so quickly that they were only a blur of motion.

Boom! Boom! Boom! Boom! Boom! Boom! Boom! Boom! Boom! Boom! Boom! Boom!

The sound of the Drum crossed the Great Grassland and reached the ears of the people, elephants, and lions arriving at the Well of the Wildebeests. The children and their mothers who had remained there during the battle hid in their huts and cried. It reached the High Falls and penetrated the caves there. It went up the Great River and reached the Village of the Cave Peoples.

Humans and animals alike stopped what they were doing and listened. It penetrated the mine. The workers set down their picks and shovels. What was going on? Some cheered and others were sad, although they didn't why. They only knew that the beating of the Drum meant that something momentous was happening.

Boom! Boom! Boom! Boom! Boom! Boom! Boom! Boom! Boom! Boom! Boom!

Pachunga and Muriel were unaware of it at first, because they were partially protected by the wall of the hut they were hiding in. At the moment the Drum was beaten, a wind from the East began to blow. It started off as a gentle breeze. But as the drumming increased in intensity, so did the wind. The fronds and grass on top of the huts rustled. The walls started to shake and quiver. The robes and clothes of the Dark Creatures and Cattle People flapped. Dust from the ground blew in circles around the camp. But still, the Drum continued to beat. Still, the Dark Creatures and Cattle People continued on in their frenzy. They ignored the storm blowing around them.

BOOM!BOOM!BOOM!BOOM!BOOM!BOOM!BOOM!BOOM! BOOM!BOOM!

A long, piercing cry left the lips of Olugbala. It was louder than the booming of the Drum. It was the first sound that he had uttered since he had been taken into captivity. With that, he closed his eyes and died. The drumming stopped immediately.

A howl of satisfaction came from Kjaz-Barbaroi. He held the Drumstick over his head and waved it victoriously. The ebony pendant appeared in his hand and with a sneer he threw it contemptuously at

Olugbala. The necklace bounced once on the surface of the Drum and then landed on his still chest.

"The Drum!" he cried. "The Drum!"

"The Drum!" screamed everyone else in a crazed rage.

"Hail to the new ruler of the age!" shouted Prince Mwailu.

"Hail, O Blessed One, Hail!"

Their shouts and cries could hardly be heard over the roar of the wind. But they didn't pay any attention to it. They were too delirious in their joy. They embraced each other. They had won. Olugbala had lost. It was over. It was finished. Kjaz-Barbaroi was now the unchallenged ruler of all creatures.

But it was not over yet.

The wind turned into a full blast. It blew branches out of trees and knocked down huts in its fury and anger. The platform around the Drum shook dangerously. Dark Creatures and Cattle People hurled themselves to the ground in their fear as part of the platform finally collapsed with a slow sigh and cracking of wood. Screams of pleasure turned into cries of pain. Some clung to the side of the high Drum before they fell into the wreckage. The Drum itself shook and trembled. Those who were on the ground tried to grasp anything they could to keep from being blown away. But there was nothing secure. Everything around them was getting blown apart. The floodlights on their towers toppled over. Sparks flew and it became darker.

"Save us! Save us!" wailed the Dark Creatures and Cattle People.

Kjaz-Barbaroi ignored them. He was thinking of how he could save himself.

Now it was the Drum's turn. It shuddered and shook. The cattle skins that were sewn together unraveled and blew away. The wooden frame supporting the Drum finally crashed to the ground, burying the body of Olugbala in its ruin.

The platform with Kjaz-Barbaroi and Prince Mwailu fell with the Drum. The Prince would never have the opportunity to take out his revenge on Prince Baree. As he fell, he was impaled by the spear of one of his own warriors. Kjaz-Barbaroi disappeared into a mass of splintered wood.

From beneath the pile of remains a paw slowly emerged. Pachunga could see it quite clearly. Blood dripped from the fingers. Then it dropped and was still.

Was it the paw of Kjaz-Barbaroi?

"Come!" said Pachunga into Muriel's ear. "We have to get out of here!"

"But what about Olugbala's body?"

"That doesn't matter. It's not serving him now."

Just at that moment, the hut where they had been hiding lost its roof. The walls fell around them, but flew away before they could strike them. Pachunga grabbed Muriel's hand and they ran with the wind behind them to the western edge of the camp. They were suddenly picked up off their feet and thrown into the brush and grass. Dazed and bruised, they stayed close to the ground with the wind blowing over them and continued to watch the destruction of Kjaz-Barbaroi's camp.

A fire started in the pile of broken sticks and poles that had once been the Drum and platform. It must have been ignited by a torch or one of the bonfires. The flames grew larger and larger, feeding on the dry wood. Everything near the pile began to burn as well. Flaming pieces of wood were picked up and blown away by the wind. But the wind was losing its intensity now. Its anger was gone.

But the fire continued to burn until there was nothing left but smoldering ash.

* * * *

When the light of the morning sun lit the entire scene, nothing was left standing. Already, vultures were circling above the camp. They would take care of the Dark Creatures and Cattle People who had perished. Nothing moved. The camp was dead. It was really over now.

Dazed, though still able to walk, Pachunga and Muriel headed South toward the Well of the Wildebeests. What the future for them would be, they did not know. All they knew was that they had to report what had happened and to wait for Olugbala to come back to them.

But how could he now?

The Return

I t was all that they could do to get back to the Well of the Wildebeests. The sun had been as hot as ever all day, and they did not have any water to drink during their long journey. There were no baobab trees around that held any water worth knowing about. When they tried to dig into the dried-up stream beds, there was only damp mud. But their thirst was not such that they were willing to try and suck the water out of it. They would make it.

When they finally reached the Well at sunset, they could not speak because their throats were too dry and their lips too swollen and burned from the sun. Kiritiri warriors assisted their Chief and Muriel to a hut where they were given water. The women of the Cattle People washed their dried, burned faces.

After a rest, they were able to come out and tell the group what had happened. No one knew what to say. While they held on to the hope that Olugbala was going to return, they still felt cut off and isolated from him. They could not feel his presence in the way that they each had felt it during other absences.

Baree finally spoke. "What do you think happened to Kjaz-Barbaroi and all the Dark Creatures? Do you think they are all dead, or do you think the wind just blew some of them away?"

"I don't know," said Pachunga. "There were a lot of dead ones early in the morning we saw when the sun came up. Kjaz-Barbaroi could be dead or seriously injured. But then there was the fire. I don't see how anyone could have survived that if he were trapped in it."

"I don't think we are going to have to worry about him for a long, long time," said Muriel. "The Drum has been destroyed. I don't think it will ever be built again."

"Let's hope not," said Titi.

The night passed and another day came. Each person went through the motions of looking busy, but it was obvious that nobody was doing anything other than wait. When would Olugbala come? Many doubted already that he was ever going to come at all.

"Didn't Pachunga say that he died on the Drum?" asked one.

"I don't think anyone can come back from the dead," said another.

"But remember that Prince Baree and Kasuku were brought back from the dead."

"Yes, but that was Olugbala himself who did it. Can he bring himself back?"

"I don't know," said yet another.

And so the conversations went through most of the morning.

Muriel—just before lunch—heard some of the whisperings and mutterings, and tried to be optimistic. She was just going over to the hut that Chief Mkumbo stayed in, when she heard a voice inside her head say, "Come."

She knew who it was who was speaking to her. But even so, she wondered if she had just imagined it. Perhaps in her desire to have Olugbala come back, her mind was fooling her. She decided to test the voice. "Come where?" she asked. "Where should I go?" If anyone had been near to hear her, they would have thought she was talking to the air.

"Come," said the voice again.

She looked across the camp to Pachunga. He had a bewildered look on his face. He must have received the same message.

"What do you think?" she asked when she got close enough to him to talk with him.

"I think we'd better do what the voice—I mean, Olugbala—is telling us to do."

"But go where?"

"I think he means this way," said Pachunga.

Muriel followed Pachunga to the edge of the camp. When they reached the barren, open savannah, they started to walk in an easterly direction for several minutes. There was no sign of Olugbala in front of them.

"Are you sure this is the right way?" asked Muriel.

"Yes," said Pachunga. "Look! There he is!"

Sitting under an acacia tree was Olugbala. The branches above him were covered with brilliant yellow flowers. Around him, the flowers normally associated with the rainy season bloomed in the lush, green grass. There were pink, white, purple and red ones. This was odd, but then, Olugbala usually did something unusual whenever he was present. It was as if he had brought his Mountain with him.

Everything was always better somehow. What mattered more than the flowers blooming was the fact that Olugbala was there. He had come back!

"Olugbala!" cried Muriel. She ran up to him, and he stood up to greet her. "You're here! You're here!" Tears of joy streamed down her face. How different were those tears from the ones she had shed two nights before in the camp of Kjaz-Barbaroi.

"Yes, dear one. I am here." The voice was gentle.

"And you have your pendant back again!" she said.

"Kjaz-Barbaroi gave it back to me, remember?" He smiled.

"I guess he did," admitted Muriel.

Pachunga stood some distance away. "Is it really you?"

"Of course," said Olugbala. "Greet me properly, instead of standing there open-mouthed. You knew I was going to return."

Pachunga embraced him. His doubts and misgivings were replaced by his master's warmth and assurance. Olugbala was just as solid and real as he had been before the Drum.

"We have to tell the others that we've seen you!" exclaimed Muriel.

"Are you coming to the camp with us?" asked Pachunga.

"All in good time," said Olugbala.

"But why is it that you only asked us to see you?" asked Muriel. It was strange that only they were called.

"I didn't just call you two. I called everyone, and you were the only ones who heard my voice."

"Why was that?" asked Pachunga.

"They have shut themselves off from me. They really don't think that I have come back."

"Then they won't believe us if we tell them that we saw you," said Muriel.

"What are we going to do?" asked Pachunga.

"Go back and tell them that they are to gather by the main cooking fire. I will join you there."

"You promise?" asked Pachunga. That was not the right thing to say.

Olugbala's face stiffened into a rebuke. "My word is my word," he said.

"I'm sorry," said Pachunga. "I know that. It's just—"

"Go back and do what I told you to do," said Olugbala.

Pachunga and Muriel raced back to the camp and called to the first group of people and animals they came across in the camp.

"Listen to this!" said Pachunga.

"He's here!" shouted Muriel. "He's here! Olugbala's back!"

"What?" asked Baree. "Where did you see him?"

"He called us to him at a place just East of here," said Pachunga. "It was under an acacia tree. All the flowers were blooming around him."

"Are you sure?" asked Titi. "You both are still pretty tired from that long walk you had yesterday. Perhaps you only imagined that—"

"Titi," said Muriel insistently, "I—*We*—saw him. We talked with him. He talked with us and embraced us."

"Why didn't he call us?" asked Kalopa. "Why did he just call you two?"

"He said that he called all of us," said Pachunga carefully, "though we were the only ones to hear him."

"When was that?" asked Kasuku.

"Not long ago."

"So that is what I heard," said Mamosa. "I thought I heard someone say, 'Come,' but I thought I had just imagined it."

"I guess we'd better go and see if he's still there," suggested Baree. He was not hopeful, but he felt that Muriel and Pachunga should be humored along. They had been through a lot. Still, they both claimed to have seen him...

"No, we can't do that," said Pachunga. "He said he would meet us at the cooking fire."

"Oh, he did, did he?" asked Kasuku. "This is all very unusual."

"What hasn't been unusual about these past few days?" asked Muriel. "Believe us. We saw him. Do what he wants us to do."

"All right," said Kalopa. "But I'm not expecting anything."

"What's the matter with all of you?" demanded Pachunga. His tone was cross. He hadn't been expected to be treated this way. He could not accept their attitude. "You used to trust Olugbala all the time—even at times when I didn't. He has fed you and sustained all of you from the time you first met him. He has taught you every good thing that you know. Why are you turning your backs on him now? Some of you he has even entertained and hosted on his Mountain."

No one answered.

"We said we'd go!" snapped Baree. He wished he hadn't spoken so strongly. He saw Pachunga's hurt face. "I'm sorry, Pachunga. I guess I'm mad at myself for not having heard his voice like you and Muriel."

"It's okay," said Pachunga. "Let's get everybody together."

The Prince pulled out his whistle and blew it. Kalopa roared, Mamosa trumpeted, and Titi and Chief Mkumbo sent runners to get their warriors together. Pachunga told Maringa to gather all the Kiritiris at the central cooking fire.

When they arrived, Olugbala wasn't there. They waited. And they waited some more. The sun passed its zenith and dropped toward the western horizon. Murmurings and grumblings from certain warriors and animals started to get louder and more pronounced. Muriel and Pachunga still clung to their belief that Olugbala was going to come as he had said he would.

Baree tried to be sympathetic. "Are you sure he said the center of the camp and not where you met him?"

"Yes, we're sure," said Pachunga.

"It wasn't supposed to be at one of the other cooking fires?" asked Chief Mkumbo.

"No, he said the central one," said Muriel. "Isn't this the central cooking fire?" she asked Kasuku.

"Yes," he said. "We had the Council of War here the other evening."

More time passed. Some were thinking of drifting off and doing something more important than sitting around waiting for someone who really wasn't going to come. But they respected Pachunga so much that they knew that as long as he was there waiting, they would wait with him.

And then Olugbala was there. No one saw him come. It was almost as if he had been there all along and was waiting for somebody to notice him. Pachunga saw him first, then Baree.

"Olugbala!" shouted Baree. "You did come back after all!"

"Yes, I am back," he said. "And I am here to stay."

* * * *

Olugbala did stay with them. He restored Pachunga to his rightful place on the High Seat of the Kiritiri peoples. Baree was given responsibility for governing all the Great Grassland, and Mamosa and Kalopa stayed there with him with all their elephants and lions. Kasuku kept by Baree's side, never to leave him again.

Chief Mkumbo was given the entire domain under the caves and eventually died and went to Olugbala's Mountain. When that happened, his people called him "Chief Mkumbo the Strong"—a title that would have made him feel self-conscious, but proud at the same time.

When Titi and the Tall Men were offered some land from Baree, they accepted it. "We don't have much time left," said Titi. "Soon we will be going to the Mountain."

And Muriel—well, she had some other adventures, which are too numerous to recount here.

Lightning Source UK Ltd.
Milton Keynes UK
19 April 2010

153011UK00002B/94/P